The Hyperion Library of World Literature

CLASSICS OF RUSSIAN LITERATURE

THE
CREATED LEGEND
BY FEODOR SOLOGUB

**AUTHORIZED
TRANSLATION FROM
THE RUSSIAN BY
JOHN COURNOS**

HYPERION PRESS, INC.
Westport, Connecticut

Published in 1916 by Martin Secker, London
Hyperion reprint edition 1977
Library of Congress Catalog Number 76-23899
ISBN 0-88355-518-2 (paper ed.)
Printed in the United States of America

Library of Congress Cataloging in Publication Data

Teternikov, Fedor Kuz'mich, 1863-1927.
    The created legend.

    *(Classics of Russian literature) (The Hyperion
library of world literature)*
    Translation of Tvorimaia legenda.
    *Reprint of the 1916 ed. published by M. Secker,
London.*
    I. Title.
[PZ3.T292Cr10]   [PG3470.T4]   891.7'3'3   76-23899
ISBN 0-88355-518-2

INTRODUCTION

> " For there is nothing either good or
> bad but thinking makes it so."
> SHAKESPEARE
> " To the impure all things are im-
> pure." NIETZSCHE

In " *The Little Demon* " *Sologub has shown us how
the evil within us peering out through our imagination makes all the world seem evil to us. In* " *The
Created Legend,*" *feeling perhaps the need of reacting
from his morose creation Peredonov, the author has
set himself the task of showing the reverse of the
picture : how the imagination, no longer warped, but
sensitized with beauty, is capable of creating a world
of its own, legendary yet none the less real for the
legend.*

*The Russian title of the book is more descriptive
of the author's intentions than an English translation
will permit it to be.* " *Tvorimaya Legenda* " *actually
means* " *The legend in the course of creation.*" *The
legend that Sologub has in mind is the active, eternally
changing process of life, orderly and structural in
spite of the external confusion. The author makes
an effort to bring order out of apparent chaos by
stripping life of its complex modern detail and re-
ducing it to a few significant symbols, as in a rather
more subtle* " *morality play.*" *The modern novel
is perhaps over-psychologized ; eternal truths and
eternal passions are perhaps too often lost sight of
under the mass of unnecessary naturalistic detail.*

In this novel life passes by the author as a kind of

dream, a dream within that nightmare Reality, a legend within that amorphousness called Life. And the nightmare and the dream, like a sensitive individual's ideas of the world as it is and as it ought to be, alternate here like moods. The author has expressed this changeableness of mood curiously by alternating a crudely realistic, deliberately naïve, sometimes journalese style with an extremely decorative, lyrical manner—this taxing the translator to the utmost in view of the urgency to translate the mood as well as the ideas.

As a background we have " the abortive revolution of 1905." This novel is an emotional statement of those " nightmarish " days. Against this rather hazy, tempestuous background we have the sharply outlined portrait of an individual, a poet, containing a world within himself, a more radiant and orderly world than the one which his eyes look upon outwardly. It is this " inner vision " which permits him to see the legend in the outer chaos, and we read in this book of his efforts to disentangle the thread of this legend by the establishment of a kind of Hellenic Utopia.

It is not alone the poet who is capable of creating his legend, but any one who refuses to be subject to the whims of fate and to serve the goddess of chance and chaos, "the prodigal scatterer of episodes " (Aisa). The tragic thing about this philosophy, as one Russian critic points out, is that even the definite settling of the question does not assure one complete consolation, for, like Ivan Karamazov in Dostoyevsky's " Brothers Karamazov," one may say : " I do not accept God, I do not accept the world created by Him, God's world ; I simply return Him the ticket most respectfully." Still it is with some

6

such definite decision that he enters the kingdom of Ananke, the goddess of Necessity. Readers of " The Little Demon " have seen a practical illustration of the two forces in Peredonov and Liudmilla. Peredonov was petty and pitiful, " a little demon "— nevertheless he too " strove towards the truth in common with all conscious life, and this striving tormented him. He himself did not understand that he, like all men, was striving towards the truth, and that was why he had that confused unrest. He could not find his truth, and he became entangled, and was perishing." Liudmilla, however, had saved herself from the pettiness and provinciality of this " unclean, impotent earth " by creating a new world for herself. She, at any rate, had her beautiful legend, knew her truth.

Elisaveta, of " The Created Legend," also belongs to the Kingdom of Ananke. She finds her salvation in " the dream of liberation," the dream dreamt by all good Russians and made an active creative legend by the efforts to realize it in life. Being an antithesis to the analytical novel, this novel treats of sex, not as a psychology but as a philosophy ; nuances are avoided, the feminine figure becomes a symbol, drawn, not photographically but broadly, in fluent, even exaggerated Botticellian outlines. I might go even further and say that as a symbol of Russian revolution the figure of Elisaveta is perhaps meant to stand out with the statuesque boldness of the Victory of Samothrace. The feminine figure, nude or thinly draped, has been used as symbol for ideas in the plastic arts ever since art was born ; our puritans have never been faced with the problem of what some of the mythological divinities in stone would do if they should suddenly

7

come to life, become human. Yet it is a problem of this sort that Sologub has attempted to solve—the problem of the gods in exile. As for Elisaveta, Sologub goes indeed the length of describing her previous existence in the second of the series of novels that go under the general head of " The Created Legend " ; she was then the Queen Ortruda of some beautiful isles in the Mediterranean, and she is fated to carry her queenliness into her later life.

" The Little Demon " is Sologub's " Inferno," " The Created Legend " his " Paradiso." And just as the problem there was the abuse of bodily beauty, so it is here the idealism of bodily beauty. It is natural that the over-draping of our bodies, the supposed symbol of our modesty, but in reality an evidence of our lust, should form part of his thesis. But M. Anatole France has already pointed out brilliantly in " Penguin Island " how immodesty originated in the invention of clothes.

The conclusion is quite clear : it is beauty that can save the world, it is our eyes and our imaginations behind our eyes that can remodel the world into " a chaste dream." Like Don Quixote, whom Sologub loves, we must see Dulcinea in our Aldonza, and our persistent thought of her as Dulcinea may make her Dulcinea in actuality.

Such are the thoughts behind this strange book, in which fantasy and reality rub unfriendly shoulders. But it would be robbing the reader of his prerogative to explain the various symbols the author employs ; for this is in the full sense a Symbolist novel, and, like a piece of music or a picture in patterns, its charm to him who will like it will lie in individual interpretation. I cannot, however, resist the desire

8

to speak of my own personal preference for Chapter *XIII*, in which the death of certain musty Russian institutions is brilliantly symbolized by the author in the passage of the risen dead on St. John's Eve.

In the " quiet children " the author has resurrected, as it were, the child heroes in which his stories abound, and given them an existence on a new plane, " beyond good and evil." It is only children, beings chaste and impressionable, who are capable of transformation—or shall we say transfiguration ?—and if they happen to be in this case more paradisian than earthly it is because truth expressed in symbols must of necessity appear fantastic and exaggerated. It is, for the same reason, that we find the worthlessness of Matov expressed in his being turned by Trirodov into a paper-weight. Then there is the Sun, the Flaming Dragon, the infuriator of men's passions, powerless, however, to affect the " quiet children," who, freed of all passion—" the beast in man "—may have their white feet covered with the light dust of the earth, but never scorched by the evil heat.

The various references to the art and ideas of the poet Trirodov and to the poet's tardy recognition are certain to be recognized as autobiographical.

I must add that in the original this first of " Created Legend " novels is called " Drops of Blood," a phrase which recurs several times in the course of the narrative in connexion with the problem of cruelty in life.

JOHN COURNOS

February 1916

CHAPTER I

I TAKE a piece of life, coarse and poor, and create from it a delightful legend—because I am a poet. Whether it linger in the darkness; whether it be dim, commonplace, or raging with a furious fire—life is before you; I, a poet, will erect the legend I have created about the enchanting and the beautiful.

Chance caught in the entangling net of circumstance brings about every beginning. Yet it is better to begin with what is splendid in earthly experience, or at any rate with what is beautiful and pleasing. Splendid are the body, the youth, and the gaiety in man; splendid are the water, the light, and the summer in nature.

It was a bright, hot midday in summer, and the heavy glances of the flaming Dragon fell on the River Skorodyen. The water, the light, and the summer beamed and were glad; they beamed because of the sunlight that filled the immense space, they were glad because of the wind that blew from some far land, because of the many birds, because of the two nude maidens.

Two sisters, Elisaveta and Elena, were bathing in the River Skorodyen. And the sun and the water were gay, because the two maidens were beautiful and were naked. And the two girls felt also gay and cool, and they wanted to scamper and to laugh, to chatter and to jest. They were talking about a man who had aroused their curiosity.

They were the daughters of a rich proprietor. The place where they bathed adjoined the spacious old garden of their estate. Perhaps they enjoyed their bathing because they felt themselves the mistresses of these fast-flowing waters and of the sand-shoals under their agile feet. And they swam about and laughed in this river with the assurance and freedom of princesses born to rule. Few know the boundaries of their kingdom—but fortunate are they who know what they possess and exercise their sway.

They swam up and down and across the river, and tried to outswim and outdive one another. Their bodies, immersed in the water, would have presented an entrancing sight to any one who might have looked down upon them from the bench in the garden on the high bank and watched the exquisite play of their muscles under their thin elastic skin. Pink tones lost themselves in the skin-yellow pearl of their bodies. But pink triumphed in their faces, and in those parts of the body most often exposed.

The river-bank opposite rose in a slope. There were bushes here ; behind them for a great distance stretched fields of rye, while just over the edge, where the earth and the sky met, were visible the far huts of the suburban village. Peasant boys passed by on the bank. They did not look at the bathing women. But a schoolboy, who had come a long way from the other end of the town, sat on his heels behind the bushes. He called himself an ass because he had not brought his camera. But he consoled himself with the thought :

" To-morrow I'll surely bring it."

The schoolboy quickly looked at his watch in order to make a note of the time the girls went out bathing. He knew them, and often came to their house to see his friend, their relative. Elena, the younger, now appealed most to him ; she was plump, cheerful, white, rosy, her hands and feet were small. He did not like the hands and feet of the elder sister, Elisaveta—they seemed to him to be too large and too red. Her face also was red, very sunburnt, and she was altogether quite large.

" Oh well," he reflected, " she is certainly well formed, you can't deny her that."

About a year had now passed since the retired *privat-docent* Giorgiy Sergeyevitch Trirodov, a doctor of chemistry, had settled in the town of Skorodozh.* From the very first he had caused much talk in the town, mostly unsympathetic. It was quite natural that the two rose-yellow, black-haired girls in the water should also talk of him. They splashed about gaily, and as they raised jewel-like spray with their feet they kept up a conversation.

" How puzzling it all is ! " said Elena, the younger sister. " No one knows where his income comes from, what he does in his house, and why he has this colony of children. There are all sorts of strange rumours about him. It's certainly a mystery."

Elena's words reminded Elisaveta of an article she had read lately in a philosophic periodical

* Also the scene of Sologub's " Little Demon."

published at Moscow. Elisaveta had a good memory. She recalled a phrase :

" In our world reason will never dominate, and the mysterious will always maintain its place."

She tried to recall more, but suddenly realizing that it would not interest Elena, she gave a sigh and grew silent. Elena gave her a tender, appealing look and said :

" When it is so bright you want everything to be as clear as it is around us now."

" Is everything really clear now ? " exclaimed Elisaveta. " The sun blinds your eyes, the water flashes and dazzles, and in this ragingly bright world we do not even know whether there isn't some one a couple of paces away peeping at us."

At this moment the sisters were standing breast-high in the water, near the overgrown bank. The schoolboy who sat on his heels behind the bush heard Elisaveta's words. He grew cold in his confusion, and began to crawl on all-fours between the bushes, away from the river. He got in among the rye, then perched himself on the rail-fence and pretended to rest, as though he were not even aware of the closeness of the river. But no one had noticed him, as if he were non-existent.

The schoolboy sat there a little while, then went home with a vague feeling of disenchantment, injury, and irritation. There was something especially humiliating to him in the thought that to the two girl bathers he was merely a possibility speculated upon but actually non-existent.

Everything in this world has an end. There was an end also to the sisters' bathing. They made their way silently together out of the pleasant, cool, deep water towards the dry ground, heaven's terrestrial footstool, and out into the air, where they met the hot kisses of the slowly, cumbrously rising Dragon. They stood a while on the bank, yielding themselves to the Dragon's kisses, then entered the protected bath-house where they had left their clothes.

Elisaveta's clothes were very simple. They consisted of a greenish yellow, not over-long tunic-dress without sleeves, and a plain straw hat. Elisaveta nearly always wore yellow dresses. She loved yellow, she loved buttercups and gold, and though she sometimes said that she wore yellow in order to soften her ruddy complexion, she really loved it simply, sincerely, and for its own sake. Yellow delighted Elisaveta. There was something remote and unpremeditated in this, as if it were a thing remembered from another, previous life.

Elisaveta's heavy black braid of hair was coiled tightly and attractively around her head, and as it was lifted quite high at the back, her neck showed—sunburnt and gracefully erect. Elisaveta's face had a keen, almost exaggerated, expression of the mastery of will and intellect over the emotions. The long and peculiarly straight parting of her lips was very exquisite. Her blue eyes were cheerful—even when her lips did not smile. Their glance was thoughtful and gentle. The bright ruddiness and strong tan of the face seemed strangely alien to it.

While waiting for Elena to finish dressing Elisaveta walked slowly on the sandy bank and looked into the monotonous distances. The fine warm grains of sand gently warmed her bare feet, which had grown cold in the water.

Elena dressed slowly. She enjoyed dressing; everything that she put on seemed an adornment to her. She delighted in the rosy reflections of her skin, in her pretty light dress of a pinkish white material, in her broad sash of pink silk fastened behind with a buckle of mother-of-pearl, in her straw hat trimmed with bright pink ribbons on top and yellow-pink velvet on its underbrim.

At last Elena was dressed. The sisters climbed the sloping bank and went where their curiosity drew them. They loved to take long walks. They had already passed several times the house and grounds of Giorgiy Trirodov, whom they had not yet seen once. To-day they wished to go that way again and to try and see what was to be seen.

The sisters walked two versts through the wood. They spoke quietly of various things, and felt a little agitated. Curiosity often agitates people.

The sinuous road with two wagon-ruts revealed picturesque views at every turn. The path finally chosen by the sisters led to a hollow. Its sides, overgrown with bushes and weeds, looked wildly beautiful. From its depth came the sweet, warm odour of clover, and down below its white bosom grass was visible. A small narrow bridge, propped up from below with thin slender stakes, hung over the hollow. On the other side of the bridge a low hedge stretched right and left, and in this hedge, quite facing the bridge, a small gate was visible.

The sisters crossed the bridge, holding on to its

16

slender hand-rail of birch. They tried the gate—
it was closed. They looked at one another.
Elisaveta, growing red with vexation, said :

" We'll have to go back again."

" Every one says that you can't get into the
place," said Elena, " that you've got to get over
the hedge, and that even that is impossible for
some reason or other. It's very strange. I
wonder what they can be up to ? "

Suddenly there was a slight rustle in the bushes
by the hedge. The branches parted. A pale boy
ran up to them. He looked quickly at the sisters
with his clear, intensely calm, almost dead eyes.
There was something strange in the shape of his
pale lips, thought Elisaveta. A motionless, sorrow-
ful expression lurked in the corners of his mouth.
He opened the gate ; he seemed to say something,
but so quietly that the sisters could not catch his
words. Or was it the sound of the light breeze
in the wavering foliage ?

The boy hid himself behind the bushes so quickly
that it was hard to believe that he had been there
at all ; the sisters had no time to be astonished
or to thank him. It was as if the gate had opened
by itself, or had been pushed open by one of the
sisters by chance.

They stood there undecided. An incomprehensible unrest took possession of them for an
instant and as quickly went from them. Curiosity
again dominated them. The sisters entered.

" How did he open it ? " asked Elena.

Elisaveta, without a word, went quickly forward.
She was so elated at getting in that she had almost
forgotten the pale boy. Only somewhere, within

the domain of vague consciousness, there gleamed dimly a strange white face.

The wood was quite like the one by which they had come to the gate, quite as pensive and as tall and as isolated from the sky,' and as absorbed in its own mysteries. But here it seemed to have been conquered by human activity. Not far away voices, cries, laughter resounded. Here and there were evidences of left-off games. The narrow footpaths often led to wider paths of sand. The sisters quickly followed the winding path in the direction from which the children's voices sounded loudest. · Afterwards all this jumble of sound seemed to collapse, and it renewed itself in loud, sweet singing.

At last there appeared before them a small glade —oval in shape. Tall firs edged this open space as evenly as graceful columns in a magnificent *salle*. The blue of the sky above it seemed especially bright, pure and dominant. The glade was full of children of various ages. They were sitting and reclining all around in ones, twos, and threes. In the middle some thirty boys and girls were singing and dancing ; their dance followed strictly the rhythm of the tune and interpreted the words of the song with beautiful fidelity. They were directed by a tall, graceful girl who had a strong, sonorous voice, braids of magnificent golden hair, and grey, cheerful eyes.

All of them, the children as well as their instructresses—of whom three or four were to be seen— were dressed quite simply ,and alike. Their simple, light attire seemed beautiful. It was pleasant to look at them, perhaps because their dress revealed the active parts of their body, the arms and the legs. Dress here was made to protect, and not to conceal ; to clothe, and not to muffle.

The blue and red of the hats and of the dresses gave emphasis to the vivid tones of the faces and of the arms and legs. There was a spirit of gaiety here, a sense of holiday splendour in these naturally adorned bodies, boldly revealed under clear azure skies.

Some of the children from among those who did not sing approached the sisters and looked at them in a friendly manner, smiling trustfully.

" You may sit down if you like," said a boy with very blue eyes ; " here is a bench."

" Thank you, my dear," said Elisaveta.

The sisters sat down. The children wished to talk to them. One little girl said :

" I've just seen a little squirrel. It was sitting on a pine. Then I gave a shout—you should have seen it run ! "

The others also began to talk and to ask questions. The singers ended their song and scattered in all directions to play. The golden-haired instructress went up to the sisters and asked :

" Have you come from town ? Are you pleased with what you have seen here ? "

" Yes, it's splendid here," said Elisaveta. " Our place adjoins this. We are the Rameyevs. I am Elisaveta. And this is my sister Elena."

The golden-haired girl suddenly blushed as if she felt ashamed that the wealthy young women were looking at her naked shoulders and at her legs naked to the knee. But seeing that they too were barefoot and wore short skirts, she quickly recovered and smiled at them.

" My name is Nadezhda Vestchezerova," she said.

She looked attentively at the sisters. Elisaveta thought that she had heard the name somewhere in town—perhaps a tale in connexion with it, she could not remember exactly what. For some reason she did not mention this to Nadezhda. Perhaps it was a tragic history.

This fear of talking about the past occasionally came upon Elisaveta. Who knows what sorrow is hid behind a bright smile, and from what darkness has sprung the blossoming which gives sudden joy to a glance, elusively beautiful and born of unhappy worldly experience ?

" Did you find your way in easily ? " asked the golden-haired Nadezhda with a friendly but subtle smile. " It's usually not a simple matter," she explained.

Elisaveta replied :

" A white boy opened the gate for us. He ran off so quickly that we had not even the time to thank him."

Nadezhda suddenly ceased smiling.

" Oh yes—he isn't one of us," she said falteringly. " They live over there with Trirodov. There are several of them. Wouldn't you like to have lunch with us ? " she asked, cutting short her previous remarks.

Elisaveta suspected that Nadezhda wanted to change the subject.

" We live here all day long, we eat here, we learn here, and we play here—do everything here," said Nadezhda. " People have built cities to escape the wild beast, but they themselves have become like wild beasts, like savages."

A bitter note crept into her voice—was it the echo of her past life or was it a thing foreign to her and grafted upon her sensitive nature ? She continued :

" We have come from the town into the woods. From the wild beast, from the savages of the town. The beast must be killed. The wolf and the fox and the hawk—all those who prey upon others— they must be killed."

Elisaveta asked :

" How is one to kill a beast who has grown iron and steel nails, and who has built his lair in the town ? It is he who does the killing, and there's no end in sight to his ferocity."

Nadezhda knitted her eyebrows, pressed her hands, and stubbornly repeated :

" We shall kill him, we shall kill him."

CHAPTER II

THE sisters stayed to lunch.

They remained over an hour chattering cheerfully with the children and their instructresses. The children were sweet and confiding. The instructresses, no less simple and charming, seemed cheerful, care-free, and restful. Yet they were always busy, and nothing escaped them. Besides many of the children did certain things without being urged, this being evidently a part of a system, of which the sisters had as yet barely an inkling.

Instruction was mixed up with play. One of the instructresses invited the sisters to listen to what she called her lesson. The sisters listened with enjoyment to an interesting discourse concerning the objects the children had observed that day in the wood. There were other instructresses who had just returned from the depths of the wood— some children were going into the wood, others were coming out, quite different ones.

The instructress to whom the sisters were listening ended her discourse and suddenly scampered off somewhere. Through the dark foliage of the trees could be seen the glimmer of red caps and of sunburnt arms and legs. The sisters were again left alone. No one paid especial attention to them any longer ; evidently there was no one they either embarrassed or hindered.

" It's time to go," said Elena.

Elisaveta made a move.

" Yes, let's go," she agreed. " It's very interesting and delightful here, but we can't stay for ever."

The departure of the sisters had been noticed. A few of the children ran up to them. The children cried gaily :

" We will show you the way, or you'll get lost."

When the sisters paused at the gate, Elisaveta thought that some one was looking at her, out of a hiding-place, with a gaze of astonishment. In perplexity, strange and distressing, she looked around her. Behind the hedge in the bushes a small boy and a small girl were hiding. They were like the others she had seen here, except that they were very white, as though the kisses of the stern Dragon floating in the hot sky had left no traces upon their tender skin. Both the little boy and the little girl were staring with a motionless but attentive gaze. Their chaste look seemed to penetrate into the very depth of one's soul ; this rather disconcerted Elisaveta. She whispered to Elena :

" Look, what strange beings ! "

Elena looked in the direction of Elisaveta's glance and said indifferently :

" Monsters ! "

Elisaveta was astonished at her sister's observation—the faces of these hiding children seemed to her like the faces of praying angels.

By this time the children who had escorted the sisters ran back, jostling each other and laughing. Only one boy remained with them. He opened the gate and waited for the sisters to go out so

23

that he could shut it again. Elisaveta quietly asked him :

" Who are these ? "

With a light movement of her head she indicated the bushes, where the boy and the girl were hiding. The cheerful urchin looked in the direction of her glance, then at her, and said :

" There's no one there."

And actually no one was now visible in the bushes. Elisaveta persisted :

" But I did see a boy and a girl there. Both were quite white, not at all brown like the rest of you. They stood ever so quietly and looked."

The cheery, dark-eyed lad looked attentively at Elisaveta, frowned slightly, lowered his eyes, reflected, then again eyed the sisters attentively and sadly, and said :

" In the main building, where Giorgiy Sergeye-vitch lives, there are more of these quiet children. They are never with us. They are quiet ones. They do not play. They have been ill. It's likely they haven't improved yet. I don't know. They are kept separately."

The boy said this slowly and thoughtfully, as if he were astonished because there, in the house of the master, were other children, quiet ones, who did not join in their play. Suddenly he shook his head lustily, banishing, as it were, unaccustomed thoughts, then took off his cap and exclaimed cheerily and with some tenderness :

" A happy journey, darlings ! Follow this foot-path."

He made an obeisance and ran off. The sisters were quite alone now. They went on in the direc-
24

tion given them by the boy. A quiet vale opened up before them, and in the distance a white wall was visible, which concealed Trirodov's house. They continued their way towards the house. In front of them, keeping close to the bushes, walked a boy in a white dress ; he appeared to be showing them the way.

It was very quiet. High above them, protecting himself from the human eye by dark purple shields, the flaming Dragon rested. His look from behind the deceptive, vacillant shields was hot and evil ; he poured out his dazzling light, tormented men with it, yet wished them to rejoice in his presence and to compose hymns to him. He wished to rule, and it seemed as though he were motionless, as though he would never decide to retire. But his livid weariness already began to incline him westwards. Still his passion grew, and his kisses were scorching, and his infuriated gaze with its livid purple dimmed the glances of the two girls.

The girls' glances were seeking—seeking Trirodov's house.

Trirodov's house stood about a verst and a half from the edge of the town, not at the end where the dirty and smoky factory buildings squatted, but quite at the other end, along the River Skorodyen, above the town of Skorodozh. This house and the estate attached to it occupied a considerable space, surrounded by a stone wall. One side of the place faced the river, the other the town, the rest adjoined the fields and woods. The house stood in the middle of an old garden. From behind the tall white stone wall the tops of the trees were to be seen, while between them, quite high, two turrets of the house, one somewhat higher than the other, were visible. The sisters felt as if some one in the high turret were looking down upon them.

There were ominous rumours concerning the house even in the days when it belonged to the previous tenant Matov, a kinsman of the Rameyev sisters. It was said that the house was inhabited by ghosts, and by phantoms who had left their graves. There was a footpath close to the house which led across the northern part of the estate, through a wood, to the Krutitsk cemetery. In the town they called this the footpath of Navii,* and they were afraid to walk upon it even by day. Many legends grew up around it. The local *intelligentsia* tried vainly to disprove them. The whole property was sometimes called Navii's playground. There were some who said that they had seen with their own eyes this enigmatic inscription on the gates : " Three went in, two came out." This inscription was, of course, no longer there. Now only lightly cut-out figures were to be seen, one under the other : ' 3 ' on top, ' 2 ' lower, and ' 1 ' at the bottom.

All the evil rumours and warnings did not prevent Giorgiy Sergeyevitch Trirodov from buying the house. He made changes in it, and then settled here after his comparatively brief educational career had been rudely cut short.

It took a long time to rebuild and transform the house. The high walls prevented any one from seeing what was being done there. This aroused

* Footpath of the dead.

the curiosity of the townsfolk and caused all sorts of malicious gossip. The working men did not belong to the place, but were brought from a distance. Dark and short and rather gruff-looking, they did not understand the local speech, and seldom showed themselves in the streets.

" They are wicked and dark " was said about them in the town. " They carry knives about with them, and dig underground passages in Navii's playground. He himself is clean-shaven like a German, and he's imported these foreign earth-diggers."

" I like that red-haired instructress, Nadezhda Vestchezerova," said Elena.

She looked searchingly at her sister.

" Yes, she's very sincere," answered Elisaveta. " A fine girl."

" They are all charming," said Elena with greater assurance.

" Yes," observed Elisaveta, with indecision in her voice. " But there is that other—the one that ran away from us—there's something I don't like about her. Perhaps it's a slight veneer of hypocrisy."

" Why do you say so ? " asked Elena.

" I simply feel it. She smiles too pleasantly, too lovingly. She seems in every way phlegmatic, yet she tries to appear animated. Her words come rather easily sometimes, and she exaggerates."

It was quiet in the garden behind the stone wall. This was Kirsha's free hour. But he could not play; though he tried to.

27

Little Kirsha, Trirodov's son, whose mother had died not long before, was dark and thin. He had a very mobile face and restless dark eyes. He was dressed like the boys in the wood. He was quite restless to-day. He felt sad without knowing why. He felt as if some invisible being were drawing him on, calling to him in an inaudible whisper, demanding something—what ? And who was it approaching their house ? Why ? Friend or foe ? It was a stranger—yet curiously intimate.

At that moment, when the sisters were taking leave of the children in the wood, Kirsha felt especially perturbed. In the far corner of the garden he saw a boy in white dress ; he ran up to him. They spoke long and quietly. Then Kirsha ran to his father.

Giorgiy Sergeyevitch Trirodov was all alone at home. He was lying on the sofa, reading a book by Wilde.

Trirodov was forty years old. He was slender and erect. His short-trimmed hair and clean-shaven face made him look very young. Only on closer scrutiny it was possible to detect the many grey hairs, the wrinkles on the forehead around the eyes. His face was pale. His broad forehead seemed very large—it was partly due to a narrow chin, lean cheeks, and baldness.

The room where Trirodov was reading—his study—was large, bright, and simple, with a white, unpainted floor as smooth as a mirror. The walls were lined with open bookcases. In the wall opposite the windows, between the bookcases, a narrow space was left, large enough for a man to stand in. It gave the impression of a door being there, hidden by hangings. In the middle of the room stood a very large table, upon which lay books, papers, and several strange objects—hexahedral prisms of an unfamiliar substance, heavy and solid in appearance, dark red in colour, with purple, blue, grey, and black spots, and with veins running across it.

Kirsha knocked on the door and entered—quiet, small, troubled. Trirodov looked at him anxiously. Kirsha said :

" There are two young women in the wood. Such an inquisitive pair. They have been looking over our colony. Now they'd like to come here to take a look round."

Trirodov let the pale green ribbon with a lightly stamped pattern fall upon the page he was reading and laid the book on the small table at his side. He then took Kirsha by the hand, drew him close, and looked attentively at him, with a slight stir in his eyes ; then said quietly :

" You've been asking questions of those quiet boys again."

Kirsha grew red, but stood erect and calm. Trirodov continued to reproach him :

" How often have I told you that this is wicked. It is bad for you and for them."

" It's all the same to them," said Kirsha quietly.

" How do you know ? " asked Trirodov.

Kirsha shrugged his shoulders and said obstinately :

" Why are they here ? What are they to us ? "

Trirodov turned away, then rose abruptly, went to the window, and looked gloomily into the garden. Clearly something was agitating his consciousness, something that needed deciding. Kirsha quietly walked up to him, stepping softly upon the white, warm floor with his sunburnt graceful feet, high in instep, and with long, beautiful, well-formed toes. He touched his father on the shoulder, quietly rested his sunburnt hand there, and said :

" You know, daddy, that I seldom do this, only when I must. I felt very much troubled to-day. I knew that something would happen."

" What will happen ? " asked his father.

" I have a feeling," said Kirsha with a pleading voice, " that you must let them in to us—these inquisitive girls."

Trirodov looked very attentively at his son and smiled. Kirsha said gravely :

" The elder one is very charming. In some way she is like mother. But the other is also nice."

" What brings them here ? " again asked Trirodov. " They might have waited until their elders brought them here."

Kirsha smiled, sighed lightly, and said thoughtfully, shrugging his small shoulders :

" All women are curious. What's to be done with them ? "

Smiling now joyously, now gravely, Trirodov asked :

" And will mother not come to us ? "

" Oh, if she only came, if only for one little minute ! " exclaimed Kirsha.

" What are we to do with these girls ? " asked Trirodov.

" Invite them in, show them the house," replied Kirsha.

30

"And the quiet children?" quietly asked Trirodov.

"The quiet children also like the elder one," answered Kirsha.

"And who are they, these girls?" asked Trirodov.

"They are our neighbours, the Rameyevs," said Kirsha.

Trirodov smiled again and said:

"Yes, one can understand why they are so curious."

He frowned, went to the table, put his hand on one of the dark, heavy prisms and picked it up cautiously, and again carefully put it back in its place, saying at the same time to Kirsha:

"Go, then, and meet them and bring them here."

Kirsha, growing animated, asked:

"By the door or through the grotto?"

"Yes, bring them through the dark passage, underground."

Kirsha went out. Trirodov was left alone. He opened the drawer of his writing-table, took out a strangely shaped flagon of green glass filled with a dark fluid, and looked in the direction of the secret door. At that instant it opened quietly and easily. A pale, quiet boy entered and looked at Trirodov with his dispassionate and innocent, but understanding eyes.

Trirodov went up to him. A reproach was ripe on his tongue but he could not say it. Pity and tenderness clung to his lips. Silently he gave the strange-shaped flagon to the boy. The boy went out quietly.

CHAPTER III

THE sisters entered a thicket. The path's many turnings made them giddy. Suddenly the turrets of the old house vanished from sight. Everything around them assumed an unfamiliar look.

" We seem to have lost our way," said Elena cheerfully.

" Never fear, we'll find our way out," replied Elisaveta. ' " We are bound to get somewhere."

At that instant there came towards them from among the bushes the small, sunburnt, handsome Kirsha. His dark, closely grown eyebrows and black wavy hair, unspoiled by headgear, gave him the wild look of a wood-sprite.

" Dear boy, where do you come from ? " asked Elisaveta.

Kirsha eyed the sisters with an attentive, direct, and innocent gaze. He said :

" I am Kirsha Trirodov. Follow this path, and you'll find yourselves where you want to go. I'll go ahead of you."

He turned and walked on. The sisters followed him upon the narrow path between the tall trees. Here and there flowers were visible — small, white, odorous flowers. They emitted a strange, pungent smell. It made the sisters feel both gay and languid. Kirsha walked silently before them.

At the end of the road loomed a mound, over-grown by tangled, ugly grass. At the foot of the mound was a rusty door which looked as if it were meant to hide some treasure.

Kirsha felt in his pocket, took out a key, and opened the door. It creaked unpleasantly and breathed out cold, dampness, and fear. A long dark passage became discernible. Kirsha pressed a spot near the door. The dark passage became lit up as though by electric light, but the lights themselves were not visible.

The sisters entered the grotto. The light poured from everywhere. But the sources of light remained a mystery. The walls themselves seemed to radiate. The light fell evenly, and neither bright reflections nor shadowy places were to be seen.

The sisters went on. Now they were alone. The door closed behind them with a grating sound. Kirsha ran on ahead. The sisters no longer saw him. The corridor was sinuous. It was difficult to walk fast for some unknown reason. A kind of weight seemed to fetter their limbs. The passage inclined slightly downwards. They walked on like this a long time. It grew hotter and damper the farther they advanced. There was an aroma—strange, sad, and exotic. The fragrance increased, became more and more languorous. It made the head dizzy and the heart ready to faint with a sweetness not free from pain.

It seemed an incredibly long way. Their legs now moved more slowly. The stone floor was cruelly hard.

"It's almost impossible to walk," whispered Elisaveta.

Those few moments seemed like ages in that

dank, sultry underground. There seemed to be no end to the narrow winding passage; the two sisters felt as though they were doomed to walk on and on, for ever and ever, without reaching any place.

The light gradually grew dimmer, a thin mist rose before their eyes. Still they walked on along the cruel, endless way.

Suddenly their journey was done. Before them was an open door, a shaft of white, exultant light came pouring in—freedom's own ecstasy.

The door opened into an immense greenhouse. Strange, muscular, monstrously green plants grew here. The air was very humid, very oppressive. The glass walls intersected by iron bars let through much light. The light was painfully, pitilessly dazzling, so that everything appeared in a whirl before their eyes.

Elena glanced at her dress. It struck her as being grey, worn out. But the bright light diverted her glances elsewhere and made her forget herself. The blue-green glass sky of the greenhouse flung down sparks and heat. The cruel Dragon rejoiced at the earthly respirations confined in this prison of glass. He furiously kissed his beloved poisonous grasses.

"It is even more terrible here than in the passage," said Elisaveta. "Let's leave this place quickly."

"No, it is pleasant here," said Elena with a happy smile. She was enjoying the pink and purple flowers which bloomed in a round basin.

But Elisaveta walked rapidly towards the door

leading to the garden. Elena overtook her, and grumbled :

"Why are you running? Here is a bench; let's rest here."

Trirodov met them in the garden just outside the greenhouse. His manner of addressing them was simple and direct.

"I believe," he began, "that you are interested in this house and its owner. Well, if you like I'll show you a part of my kingdom."

Elena blushed. Elisaveta calmly bowed and said :

"Yes, we are an inquisitive pair. This house once belonged to a relative, but it was left abandoned. It is said that many changes have been made."

"Yes, many changes have been made," said Trirodov quietly, "but the greater part remains as it was."

"Every one was astonished," continued Elisaveta, "when you decided to settle here. The reputation of the house did not hinder you."

Trirodov led the sisters through the house and the garden. The conversation ran on smoothly. The sisters' embarrassment was soon gone. They felt quite natural with Trirodov. His calm, friendly voice put them wholly at ease. They continued to walk and to observe. But they felt conscious that another life, intimate yet remote, hovered round them all the while. Sounds of music came to them at intervals; sometimes it was the doleful tones of a violin, sometimes the quiet plaint of a flute; again it was the reed-like voice of some unseen singer which sang a tender and restful song.

Upon one small lawn, in the shade of old trees, whose foliage protected them from the hot glare of the Dragon, making it pleasantly cool and pleasantly dark there, a number of small boys and girls, dressed in white, had formed a ring and were dancing. As the sisters approached them the children dispersed. They scampered off so quietly that they barely made a sound even when they brushed against the twigs; they vanished as though they had not been there.

The sisters listened to Trirodov as they walked, pausing often to admire the beauties of the garden —its trees, lawns, ponds, islands, its quietly murmuring fountains, its picturesque arbours, its profusely gay flower-beds. They felt a keen elation at having penetrated this mysterious house —they were as happy as schoolgirls at the thought of having infringed the commonly accepted rules of good society in coming here.

As they entered one room of the house Elena exclaimed :

" What a strange room ! "

" A magic room," said Trirodov with a smile.

It was indeed a strange room—everything in it had an odd shape : the ceiling sloped, the floor was concave, the corners were round, upon the walls were incomprehensible pictures and unfamiliar hieroglyphics. In one corner was a dark, flat object in a carved frame of black wood.

" It's a mirror in which it is interesting to take a look at oneself," said Trirodov. " Only you have to stand in that triangle close to the wall, near the corner."

The sisters went there and glanced in the mirror :

two old wrinkled faces were reflected in it. Elena cried out in fright. Elisaveta, growing pale, turned towards her sister and smiled.

"Don't be afraid," she said, "it's a trick of some sort."

Elena looked at her and cried out in horror:

"You have become quite old—grey-haired! How awful!"

She ran from the mirror, crying out in her fright:

"What is it? What is it?"

Elisaveta followed her. She did not understand what had happened; she was agitated, and tried to hide her confusion. Trirodov looked at them in a self-possessed manner. He opened a cupboard, inset in the wall.

"Be calm," he said to Elena. "I'll give you some water in a moment."

He gave her a glass containing a fluid as colourless as water. Elena quickly drank the sour-sweet water, and suddenly felt cheerful. Elisaveta also drank it. Elena threw herself towards the mirror.

"I'm young again," she exclaimed in a high voice.

Then she ran forward, embraced Elisaveta, and said cheerfully:

"And you too, Elisaveta, have grown young."

An impetuous joy seized both sisters. They caught each other by the hands and began to dance and to twirl round the room. Then they suddenly felt ashamed. They stopped, and did not know which way to look; they laughed in their confusion. Elisaveta said:

"What a stupid pair we are! You think us ridiculous, don't you?"

Trirodov smiled in a friendly fashion :

" That is the nature of this place," he observed.
" Terror and joy live here together."

The sisters were shown many interesting things
in the house—objects of art and of worship ; things
which told of distant lands and of hoary anti-
quity ; engravings of a strange and disturbing
character ; variegated stones, turquoise, pearls ;
ugly, amorphous, and grotesque idols ; representa-
tions of the god-child—there were many of these,
but only one face profoundly stirred Elisaveta. . . .

Elena enjoyed the objects that resembled toys.
There were many things there that one could play
with, and thus indulge in a jumble of magic reflections of time and space.

The sisters had seen so much that it seemed as
if an age had passed, but actually they had spent
only two hours here. It is impossible to measure
time. One hour is an age, another is an instant ;
but humanity makes no distinction, levels the
hours down to an average.

" What, only two hours ! " exclaimed Elena.
" How long we've spent here. It's time to go
home for dinner."

" Do you mind being a little late ? " asked
Trirodov.

" How can we ? " said Elena.

Elisaveta explained :

" The hour of dinner is strictly kept in our
house."

" I'll have a cart ready for you."

The sisters thanked him. But they must start
at once. They both suddenly felt sad and tired.

They bade their host good-bye and left him. The boy in white went before them in the garden and showed them the way.

No sooner had they again entered the underground passage than they saw a soft couch, and a fatigue so poignant suddenly overcame them that they could not advance another step.

" Let's sit down," said Elena.

" Yes," replied Elisaveta, " I too am tired. How strange ! What a weariness ! "

The sisters sat down. Elisaveta said quietly :

" The light that falls upon us here from an unknown source is not a living light, and it is terrifying—but the stern face of the monster, burning yet not consuming itself, is even more terrifying."

" The lovely sun," said Elena.

" It will become extinguished," said Elisaveta, " extinguished—this unrighteous luminary, and in the depth of subterranean passages, freed from the scorching Dragon and from cold that kills, men will erect a new life full of wisdom."

Elena whispered :

" When the earth grows cold, men will die."

" The earth will not die," answered Elisaveta no less quietly.

The sisters fell into a sleep. They did not sleep long, and when both awakened quite suddenly, everything that had just happened seemed like a dream. They made haste.

" We must hurry home," said Elena in an anxious voice.

They ran quickly. The door of the underground passage was open. Just outside the door, in the road, stood a cart. Kirsha sat in it and held the reins. The sisters seated themselves. Elisaveta took the reins. Kirsha spoke a word now and then. They said little on the way, in odd, disjointed words.

Arrived at their destination, they got out of the cart. They were in a half-somnolent state. Kirsha was off before they realized that they had not thanked him. When they looked for him they could only see a cloud of dust and hear the clatter of hoofs and the rattle of wheels on the cobblestones.

CHAPTER IV

THE sisters had barely time to change for dinner. They entered the dining-room somewhat weary and distraught. They were awaited there by their father Rameyev, the two Matovs—the student Piotr Dmitrievitch and the schoolboy Misha, sons of Rameyev's lately deceased cousin to whom Trirodov's estate had previously belonged.

The sisters spoke little at the table, and they said nothing of their day's adventure. Yet before this they used to be frank and loved to chat, to tell the things that had happened to them.

Piotr Matov, a tall, spare, pale youth with sparkling eyes, who looked like a man about to enter a prophetic school, seemed worried and irritated. His nervousness reflected itself, in embarrassed smiles and awkward movements, in Misha. The latter was a well-nourished, rosy-cheeked lad, with a quick, merry eye, but betraying his intense impressionableness. His smiling mouth trembled slightly around the corners, apparently without cause.

The old Rameyev, who was more robust than tall, and had the tranquil manners of a well-trained, well-balanced individual, did not betray his impatience at his daughters' tardy appearance, but took his place at the partially extended table, which seemed small in the middle of the immense dining-room of dark, embellished oak. Miss Harrison, unembarrassed, began to ladle out the soup;

41

she was a plump, calm, slightly grey-haired woman, the personification of a successful household.

Rameyev noticed that his daughters were tired. A vague alarm stirred within him. But he quickly extinguished this tiny spark of displeasure, smiled tenderly at his daughters, and said very quietly, as if cautiously hinting at something :

" You have walked a little too far, my dears."

There was a short but awkward silence ; then, in order to soften the hidden significance of his words and to ease his daughters' embarrassment, he added :

" I see you don't ride horseback as much as you used to."

After this he turned to the eldest of the brothers :

" Well, Petya, have you brought any news from town ? "

The sisters felt uneasy. They tried to take part in the conversation.

This was in those days when the red demon of murder was prowling in our native land, and his terrible deeds brought discord and hate into the bosom of peaceful families. The young people in this house, as elsewhere, often talked and wrangled about what had happened and what was yet to be. For all their wrangling, they could not reach any agreement. Friendship from childhood and good breeding mitigated to some extent this antagonism of ideas. But more than once their discussions ended in bitter words.

Piotr, in reply to Rameyev, began to tell about working-men's disturbances and projected strikes. Irritation was evident in his voice. He was one of those who was intensely troubled by problems

42

of a religious-philosophical character. He thought that the mystical existence of human unities might be achieved only under the brilliant and alluring sway of Cæsars and Popes. He imagined that he loved freedom—Christian freedom—yet all the turbulent movements of newly awakened life aroused only hate in his heart.

"There's terrible news," said Piotr; "a general strike is talked of. It is reported that all the factories will shut down to-morrow."

Misha burst into an unexpected laugh; it was loud, merry, and childlike; and there was almost rapture in his remark:

"But you ought to see the sort of face the Headmaster makes on all such occasions."

His voice was tender and sonorous, and it rang so softly and sweetly that he might have been telling about the blessed and the innocent, about the chaste play on the threshold of paradisian abodes. The words "strike" and "obstruction" came from his lips like the names of rare, sweet morsels. He grew cheerful and had a sudden desire to make things lively in schoolboy fashion. He began to sing loudly:

"Awake, rise up . . ."

But he became confused, stopped sadly, grew quiet, and blushed. The sisters laughed. Piotr had a surly look. Rameyev smiled benignly. Miss Harrison, pretending not to have noticed the discordant incident, calmly pressed the button of the electric bell attached on a cord to the hanging light to bring on the next course.

The dinner proceeded slowly in the usual order. The discussion grew hotter, and went helter-skelter from subject to subject. Such is said to be the Russian manner in argument. Perhaps it is the universal manner of people when discussing something that touches them deeply.

Piotr exclaimed hotly :

" Why is the autocracy of the proletariat better than the one already in force ? And what wild, barbarous watchwords they have ! ' Who is not with us, he is against us ! ' ' Who is master, let him get down from his place ; it's our banquet.' "

" It's yet too early to speak of our banquet," said Elena in a restrained voice.

" Do you know where we are drifting ? " continued Piotr. " There will be a reign of terror, and a shaking up such as Russia has not yet experienced. The point at issue is not that there is talking or doing here or there by certain gentry who imagine that they are making history. The real issue is in the clash of two classes, two interests, two cultures, two conceptions of the world, two moral systems. Who is it that wishes to seize the crown of lordship ? It is the *Kham*,* it is he who threatens to devour our culture."

Elisaveta said reproachfully :

" What a word—*Kham* ! "

Piotr smiled in a nervous and aggrieved manner, and asked :

* This word, which is the Russian equivalent for *Ham* of the Bible, describes a man in a state of serfdom. Since the abolition of serfdom in Russia, it has come to define the plebeian ; and is a sort of personification of the rabble. The satirist Stchedrin has defined *Kham* as " one who eats with a knife and takes milk with his after-dinner coffee." Merezhkovsky has written a book on Gorky under the title of " The Future Kham." —*Translator*.

44

"You don't like it?"

"I don't like it," said Elisaveta calmly.

With her habitual subjection to the thoughts and moods of her elder sister, Elena said :

"It is a rude word. I feel a reminiscence of a once helpless serfdom in it."

"Nevertheless this word is now sufficiently literary," said Piotr, with a vague smile. "And why shouldn't one use it? It's not the word that matters. We have seen countless instances with our own eyes of the progress of the spiritual *bossiak* * who is savagely indifferent to everything, who is hopelessly wild, malicious, and drunken for generations to come. He will crush everything—science, art, everything! A good characteristic specimen of a *kham* is your Stchemilov, with whom, Elisaveta, you sympathize so strongly. He's a familiar young fellow, a handsome flunkey."

Piotr fixed his eyes on Elisaveta. She replied calmly :

"I think you very unjust to him. He is a good man."

Every one was glad when dinner was ended. It was a provoking conversation. Even the imperturbable Miss Harrison rose from her place rather sooner than usual. Rameyev went to his own room to get his hour's nap. The young people went into the garden. Misha and Elena ran downhill to the river. They had a keen desire to run one after the other and to laugh.

* *Bossiak* literally means "a barefooted one," but may be more freely translated a "tramp." This type has come very much into vogue since Gorky has put him into his stories.— *Translator*.

45

" Elisaveta ! " called out Piotr.

His voice trembled nervously. Elisaveta paused. She now stood within the deep shadow of an old linden. She looked questioningly at Piotr, her graceful bare arms folded on her breast ; suddenly her heart beat faster. What a power of bewitchment was in those most lovable arms—oh, why did not some sudden impulse of passion throw them upon his shoulders !

" May I speak a few words to you, Elisaveta ? " asked Piotr.

Elisaveta flushed a little, lowered her head, and said quietly :

" Let's sit down somewhere."

She walked along the path towards the small summer-house which looked down the slope. Piotr followed her silently. In silence also they ascended the steep passage. Elisaveta seated herself and rested her arms upon the low rail of the open summer-house. The undulating distances lay before her in one broad panoramic sweep—a view intimate from childhood, and which never failed to awaken the same delightful emotion. She was looking no longer at the separate objects—Nature poured herself out like music before her, in an inexhaustible play of colour and of soothing sound. Piotr stood before her and looked at her handsome face. The setting Dragon caressed Elisaveta's face with its warm light ; the skin thus suffused exulted in its radiance and bloom.

They were silent. Both felt a painful awkwardness. Piotr was nervously breaking twigs from a birch near by. . Elisaveta began :

" What is it you wish to tell me ? "

46

A cold remoteness, almost enmity, sounded in her deeply agitated voice. She felt her own harshness, to soften which she smiled gently and timidly.

" What's there to say," began Piotr quietly and irresolutely, " but one and the same thing. Elisaveta, I love you ! "

Elisaveta flushed. Her eyes gave a sudden flare, then grew dull. She rose from her seat and spoke in an agitated manner :

" Piotr, why do you again torment yourself and me needlessly ? We have been so intimate from childhood—yet it seems that we must part ! Our ways are different, we think differently, and believe differently."

Piotr listened to her with an expression of intense impatience and vexation. Elisaveta wished to continue, but he interrupted :

" Ah, but what's the good of saying that ? Elisaveta, do, I beg you, forget our differences. They are so petty ! Or let us admit that they are significant. What I wish to say is that politics and all that separates us is only a light scum, a momentary froth on the broad surface of our life. In love there is revelation, there is eternal truth. He who does not love, he who does not strive towards union with a beloved, he is dead."

" I love the people, I love freedom," said Elisaveta quietly. " My love is revolt."

Piotr, ignoring her words, went on :

" You know that I love you. I have loved you a long time. My whole soul is absorbed as with light with my love for you. I am jealous—and I'm not ashamed to tell you I am jealous of your favour to any one ; I am even jealous of this bloused workman, whose accomplice you would be if he had had the sufficient boldness and the brain to be a conspirator ; I am jealous of the half-truths which have captivated you and screen your love of me."

Again Elisaveta spoke quietly :

" You reproach me for what is dear to me, for my better part, you wish that I should become different. You do not love me, you are tempted by the beautiful Beast—my young body with its smiles and its caresses. . . ."

And again ignoring what she said, Piotr asserted passionately :

" Elisaveta, dearest, love me ! You surely do not love any one else ! Isn't that so ? You do not love any one ? You have had no time to fall in love, to fetter your soul to any one else's. You are as free as man's first bride, you are as superb as his last wife. You have grown ripe for love—for my love—you too are thirsty for kisses and embraces, even as I. O Elisaveta, love me, love me ! "

" How can I ? " said Elisaveta.

" Elisaveta, if you'd only will it ! " exclaimed Piotr. " One must wish to love. If you only understood how I love you, you would love me also. My love should fire in you a responsive love."

" My friend, you do not love anything that is mine," answered Elisaveta. " You do not love me. I don't believe you—forgive me—I don't understand your love."

Piotr frowned gloomily and said gruffly :

" You have been fascinated by that false, empty

word freedom. You have never thought over its true meaning."

" I've had little time to think over anything," observed Elisaveta calmly, " but the feeling of freedom is the thing nearest to me. I cannot express it in words—I only know that we are fettered on this earth by iron bonds of necessity and of circumstance, but the nature of my soul is freedom ; its fire is consuming the chains of my material dependence. I know that we human beings will always be frail, poor, lonely ; but a time will surely come when we shall pass through the purifying flame of a great conflagration ; then a new earth and a new heaven shall open up to us ; through union we shall attain our final freedom. I know I am saying all this badly, incoherently— I cannot say clearly what I feel—but let us, please, say no more."

Elisaveta strode out of the summer-house. Piotr slowly followed her. His face was sad and his eyes shone feverishly, but he could not utter a word—inertia gripped his mind. Quite suddenly he roused himself, raised his head, smiled, overtook Elisaveta.

" You love me, Elisaveta," he said with joyous assurance. " You love me, though you won't admit it. You are not speaking the truth when you say that you don't understand my love. You do know my love, you do believe in it—tell me, is it possible to love so strongly and not be loved in return ? "

Elisaveta stopped. Her eyes lit up with a strange joy.

" I tell you once more," she said with calm

resolution, " it is not me you love—you love the First Bride.   I am going where I must."

Piotr stood there and looked after her—helpless, pale, dejected.   Between the bushes a sun-yellow dress fluttered against the now dull sky of a setting sun.

CHAPTER V

PIOTR and Elisaveta descended towards the boat landing. Two rowing-boats seemed to rock on the water, though there was no breeze and the water was smooth like a mirror. A little farther, behind the bushes, the canvas roof of the bath-house stood revealed. Elena, Misha, and Miss Harrison were already there. They were sitting on a bench halfway down the slope, where the path to the landing was broken. The view from here, showing the bend of the river, was very restful. The water was growing darker, heavier, gradually assuming a leadlike dullness.

Misha and Elena, flushed with running, could not suppress their smiles. The Englishwoman looked calmly at the river, and nothing shocked her in the evening landscape and in the peaceful water. But now two persons came who brought with them their poignant unrest, their uneasiness, their confusion—and again an endless wrangle began.

They left this bench, from which one could look into such a great distance and see nothing but calm and peace everywhere. They descended below to the very bank. Even at this close range the water was still and smooth, and the agitated words of the restless people did not cause the broad sheet to stir. Misha picked up thin, flat stones and threw them underhand into the distance so that, touching the water, they skipped repeatedly on the surface. He did this habitually whenever

51

the wrangling distressed him. His hands trembled, the little stones ricochetted badly sometimes; this annoyed him, but he tried to hide his annoyance and to look cheerful.

Elisaveta said :

" Misha, let's see who can throw the better. Let's try for pennies."

They began to play. Misha was losing.

At the turn of the river, from the direction of the town, a rowing-boat appeared. Piotr looked searchingly into the distance, and said in a vexed voice :

" Mr. Stchemilov, our intelligent workman, the Social Democrat of the Russia Party, is again about to honour us."

Elisaveta smiled. She asked with gentle reproof :

" Why do you dislike him so ? "

" No, you tell me," exclaimed Piotr, " why this party calls itself the Russia Party, and not the Russian Party ? Why this high tone ? "

Elisaveta answered with her usual calm :

" It is called the Russia and not the Russian Party because it includes not only the Russian, but also the Lithuanian, the Armenian, the Jew, and men of other races who happen to be citizens of Russia. It seems to me this is quite comprehensible."

" No, I do not understand," said Piotr obstinately. " I see in it only unnecessary pretence."

In the meantime the boat drew nearer. Two men were sitting in it. Aleksei Makarovitch Stchemilov, a young working man, a locksmith by trade, sat at the oars. He was thin and of medium height ; there was a suggestion of irony in the shape of his lips. Elisaveta had known Stchemilov

52

since the past autumn, when she became acquainted with other labouring men and party workmen.

The boat touched the landing, and Stchemilov sprang out gracefully. Piotr remarked derisively as he bowed with exaggerated politeness :

" My homage to the proletariat of all lands."

Stchemilov answered quietly :

" My most humble respects to the gentleman student."

He exchanged greetings with all ; then, turning with special deference towards Elisaveta, said :

" I've rowed back your property. It was almost taken from me. Our suburbanites have their own conceptions of the divine rights of ownership."

Piotr boiled over with vexation—the very sight of this young blouse-wearer irritated him beyond bounds ; he thought Stchemilov's manners and speech arrogant. Piotr said sharply :

" As far as I understand your notion of things, it is not rights that are holy, but brute force."

Stchemilov whistled and said :

" That is the origin of all ownership. You simply took a thing—and that's all there was to it. ' Blessed are the strong ' is a little adage among those who have conquered violently."

And how did you get hold of this ? " asked Piotr with derision.

" Crumbs of wisdom fall from the tables of the rich even to us," answered Stchemilov in a no less contemptuous tone ; " we nourish ourselves on these small trifles."

The other young man, clearly a workman also, remained in the boat. He looked rather timid, lean, and taciturn, and had gleaming eyes.

He sat holding on to the ropes of the rudder, and was looking cautiously towards the bank. Stchemilov looked at him with amused tenderness and called to him :

" Come here, Kiril, don't be afraid ; there are kindly people here — quite disposed to us, in fact."

Piotr grumbled angrily under his breath. Misha smiled. He was eager to see the new-comer, though he hated violent discussions. Kiril got out of the boat awkwardly, and no less awkwardly stood up on the sand, his face averted ; he smiled to hide his uneasiness. Piotr's irritation grew.

" Please be seated," he said, trying to assume a pleasant tone.

" I've done a lot of sitting," answered Kiril in an artificial bass voice.

He continued to smile, but sat down on the edge of the bench, so that he nearly fell over ; his arms shot up into the air, and one of his hands brushed against Elisaveta. He felt vexed with himself, and he flushed. As he moved away from the edge he remarked :

" I've sat two months in administrative order." *

Every one understood these strange words. Piotr asked :

" For what ? "

Kiril seemed embarrassed. He answered with a morose uneasiness :

" It's all a very simple affair with us—you do the slightest thing, and they try at once the most murderous measures."

* This phrase signifies punishment inflicted by the authorities without a trial.

At this moment Stchemilov said very quietly to Elisaveta :

"Not a bad chap. He wants to become acquainted with you, comrade."

Elisaveta silently inclined her head, smiled amiably at Kiril, and pressed his hand. His face brightened.

Rameyev came up to them. He greeted his visitors pleasantly but coldly, giving an impression of studied correctness. The conversation continued somewhat awkwardly. Elisaveta's blue eyes looked gently and pensively at the irritated Piotr and at his deliberately inimical adversary Stchemilov.

Piotr asked :

"Mr. Stchemilov, would you care to explain to me this talk of an autocracy by the proletariat ? You admit the need of an autocracy, but only wish to shift it to another centre ? In what way is this an improvement ? "

Stchemilov answered quite simply :

"You masters and possessors do not wish to give us anything—neither a fraction of an ounce of power nor of possessions ; what's left for us to do ? "

"What's your immediate object ? " put in Rameyev.

"Immediate or ultimate—what's that ! " answered Stchemilov. "We have only one object : the public ownership of the machinery of production."

"What of the land ? " cried out Piotr rather shrilly.

"Yes, the land too we consider as machinery of production," answered Stchemilov.

"You imagine that there is an infinite amount of land in Russia?" asked Piotr with bitter irony.

"Not an infinite amount, but certainly enough to go round—and plenty for every one," was Stchemilov's calm reply.

"Ten—or, say, a hundred—acres per soul? Is that what you mean?" continued Piotr in loud derision. "You've got that idea into the heads of the muzhiks, and now they're in revolt."

Stchemilov again whistled, and said with contemptuous calm:

"Fiddlesticks! The muzhik is not as stupid as all that. And in any case, let me ask you what hindered the opposing side from hammering the right ideas into the muzhik's mind?"

Piotr got up angrily and strode away without saying another word. Rameyev looked quietly after him and said to Stchemilov:

"Piotr loves culture, or, more properly speaking, civilization, too well to appreciate freedom. You insist too strongly on your class interests, and therefore freedom is no such great lure to you. But we Russian constitutionalists are carrying on the struggle for freedom almost alone."

Stchemilov listened to him and made an effort to suppress an ironic smile.

"It's true," he said, "we won't join hands with you. You wish to fly about in the free air, while we are still ravenously hungry and want to eat."

Rameyev said after a brief silence:

"I am appalled at this savagery. Murders every day, every day."

"What's there to do?" asked Stchemilov, persisting in his ironic tone. "I suppose you'd
56

like to have freedom for domestic use, the sort you could fold up and put in your pocket."

Rameyev, making no effort to disguise his desire of closing the conversation, rose, smiling, and stretched out his hand to Stchemilov.

" I must 'go now."

Misha was about to follow him, but changed his mind and ran towards the river. He found his fishing-rod near the bath-house and entered the water up to his knees. He had long ago accustomed himself to go to the river when agitated by sadness or joy or when he had to think about something very seriously. He was a shy and self-sufficient boy and loved to be alone with his thoughts and his dreams. The coolness of the water running fast about his legs comforted him and banished evil moods. As he stood here, with his naked legs in the water, he became gentle and calm.

Elena soon came there also. She stood silently on the bank and looked at the water. For some reason she felt sad and wanted to cry.

The water glided past her tranquilly, almost noiselessly. Its surface was smooth—and thus it ran on.

Elisaveta looked at Stchemilov with mild displeasure.

" Why are you so sharp, Aleksei ? " she asked.

" You don't like it, comrade ? " he asked in return.

" No, I don't like it," said Elisaveta in simple, unmistakable tones.

Stchemilov did not reply at once. He grew thoughtful, then said :

" The abyss that separates us from your cousin is too broad. And even between us and your father. It is hard to come together with them. Their chief concern, as you very well know, is to construct a pyramid out of people ; ours to scatter this pyramid in an even stratum over the earth. That's how it is, Elizaveta."

Elisaveta showed her annoyance and corrected him :

" *Elisaveta*. How many times have I told you ? "

Stchemilov smiled.

" A lordly caprice, comrade Elisaveta. Well, as you like, though it is a trifle hard to pronounce. Now we would say *Lizaveta*."

Kiril complained of his failures, of the police, of the detectives, of the patriots. His complaints were pitiful and depressing. He had been arrested and had lost his job. It was easy to see that he had suffered. The gleam of hunger trembled in his eyes.

" The police treated me most horribly," complained Kiril, " and then there's my family . . ."

After an awkward silence he continued :

" Not a single thing escapes them at our factory, you get humiliated at every step. They actually search you."

Again he lapsed into silence. Again he complained :

" They force their way into your soul. You can't hold private conversations. . . . They stop at nothing."

He told of hunger, he told of a sick old woman.

All this was very touching, but it had lost its freshness by constant repetition—the pity of it had become, as it were, stamped out. Kiril, indeed, was a common type, whose state of mind made him valuable as material to be used up at an opportune moment in the interests of a political cause.

Stchemilov was saying :

"The Black Hundred are organizing. Zherbenev is very busy at this—he's one of your genuine Russians."

"Kerbakh is with him—another patriot for you," observed Kiril.

"The most dangerous man in our town, this Zherbenev. Vermin of the most foul kind," said Stchemilov contemptuously.

"I am going to kill him," said Kiril hotly.

To this Elisaveta said :

"In order to kill a man you need to believe that one man is essentially better or worse than another, that he is distinct from the other not accidentally or socially, but in the mystic sense. That is to say, murder only confirms inequality."

"By the way, Elisaveta," remarked Stchemilov, "we have come to talk business with you."

"Tell me what it is," answered Elisaveta calmly.

"We are expecting some comrades from Rouban within the next few days. They are coming to talk things over," said Stchemilov ; "but of course you know all that."

"Yes, I know," said Elisaveta.

"We want to use the occasion," went on Stchemilov, "to organize a mass meeting not far from here for our town factory folk. So here, at last, is your chance to appear as an orator."

"How can I be of any use?" asked Elisaveta.

"You have the gift of expression, Elisaveta," said Stchemilov. "You have a good voice, an easy flow of language, and you have a way of putting the case simply and clearly. It would be a sin for you not to speak."

"We will bring down the Cadets * a peg or two," said Kiril in his bass voice.

"You'll forgive Kiril, comrade Elisaveta," said Stchemilov. "I don't think he knows that your father is a Cadet. Besides, he's a rather simple, frank fellow."

Kiril grew red.

"I know so little," said Elisaveta timidly. "What shall I talk about, and how?"

"You know enough," said the other confidently; "more than myself and Kiril put together. You do things remarkably well. Everything you say is so clear and accurate."

"What shall I talk about?"

"You can draw a picture of the general condition of working men," answered Stchemilov, "and how capital is forging a hammer against itself and compelling labour to organize."

Elisaveta grew red and silently inclined her head.

"Then it's all settled, comrade?" asked Stchemilov.

Elisaveta burst into a laugh.

"Yes, settled," she exclaimed cheerfully.

It was good to hear this gravely and simply pronounced word "comrade."

* The name by which the members of the Constitutional Democratic Party are known. It is a development of the initials "C. D."

60

CHAPTER VI

THE sweet, quiet night came, and brought her enchantments. The weary din of day lost itself in oblivion. The clear, tranquil, anæmic moon encircled herself with her own radiance, basked in her own light. She looked at the earth and did not dissipate the mist—it was as if she had taken to herself all the brightness and translucence of the sun's last afterglow. A calm poured itself out upon the earth and upon the water, and embraced every tree, every bush, every blade of grass.

A soothing mood took possession of Elisaveta. It struck her as strange that they should have quarrelled and stood facing one another like enemies. Why shouldn't she love him? Why not give herself up to him, submit to the will of another, make it her will? Why all this noisy discussion, these fine, yet remote words about a struggle, about ideals?

Every one in the house, she thought, was tired— was it with the heat? With wrangling? With a secret sorrow inducing sleep, soothingness? The sisters went to their rooms somewhat earlier than usual. Fatigue and a languorous sadness oppressed them. The sisters' bedrooms were next to each other, one entering the other by a wide, always open door. They could hear one another. The even breathing of her sleeping sister gave a poignant reality to the terrible world of night and slumber.

Elisaveta and Elena did not converse long that night. They parted early. Elisaveta undressed herself, lit a candle, and began to admire herself in the cold, dead, indifferent mirror. Pearl-like were the moon's reflections on the lines of her graceful body. Palpitating were her white girlish breasts, crowned by two rubies. The living, passionate form stood flaming and throbbing, strangely white in the tranquil rays of the moon. The gradual curves of the body and legs were precise and delicate. The skin stretched across the knees hinted at the elastic energy that it covered. And equally elastic and energetic were the curves of the calves and the feet.

Elisaveta's body flamed all over, as though a fire had penetrated the whole sweet, sensitive flesh; and oh, how she wished to press, to cling, to embrace! If he would only come! Only by day he spoke to her his dead-sounding words of love, kindled by the kisses of the accursed Dragon. Oh, if he would only come by night to the secretly flaming great Fire of the blossoming Flesh!

Did he love her? Was his a final and a single-souled love conquering by the eternal spirit of the divine Aphrodite? Where love is there daring should be also. Is love, then, gentle, meek, obedient? Is it not a flame, decreed to take what is its own without waiting?

Her eager, impatient fancies seethed. If he only had come he would have been a young god. But he was only a human being who bowed down before his idol; he was a small slave of a small demon. He did not come, he had not dared, he had not guessed : a dark grief came over Elisaveta from the secret seething of her passion.

As she looked at her wonderful image in the mirror, Elisaveta thought :

" Perhaps he is praying. The weak and the haughty—why do they pray ? They should be taught to be joyous, to remake their religion and be the first in the new sect."

Elisaveta could not sleep. Desire tormented her ; she did not know what she wanted—was it to go ?—to wait ? She walked out on the balcony. The nocturnal coolness caressed her naked body. She stood there long ; the contact of her naked feet with the warm, moist boards was pleasant. She looked into the pale light of the mist-wrapt garden dreaming there under the moon. She recalled at this moment the details of the day's walk, and all that they had seen in Trirodov's house ; she recalled it all so clearly, with almost the vividness of a hallucination. Then a drowsiness crept up, seized her. And Elisaveta could not recall later how she found herself in her bed. It was almost as if an invisible being had carried her, tucked her in, and rocked her to sleep.

It was a restless, tormenting sleep. She saw horrible visions, nightmares. They were remarkably clear and real.

She was in a very dusty room. The air in it was stifling, it oppressed her breast. The walls were covered with bookcases filled with books. The tables were also covered with books—all new, slender, with bright covers. The title-pages were for some reason ponderous, terrible to look at. A tall, gaunt, long-haired student entered ; his hair was very straight, his face morose and grey, he wore spectacles. He whispered :

" Hide them."

And he placed on the table a bundle of books and pamphlets. Some one behind Elisaveta stretched out a hand, took the books, and thrust them under the table. Then came a woman student, strangely resembling the man student yet quite different ; she was short, thick, red-cheeked, short-haired, cheerful, and wore pince-nez. She also brought a bundle of books, and said quietly :

" Hide them."

Elisaveta hid the books in the bookcase and was afraid of something.

Then came more students, working men, young women, schoolboys, military men, officials, and clerks ; each, placing a packet of books on the table, whispered :

" Hide them."

Each one slipped away. And Elisaveta went to work to hide the books. She put them in the table drawer, in the cupboard, under the sofas, behind the doors, and in the fireplace. But the pile of books on the table grew and grew ; more and more persistent became the whisper :

" Hide them."

There was no hiding-place left, and yet the books were still being brought in—there was no end to them. Everywhere books—they were pressing on her breast. . . .

Elisaveta awakened. Some one's face was bending over her. The bedcover slipped from her handsome body. Elena was whispering something. Elisaveta asked her in a drowsy voice :

" Did I wake you ? "

" You cried out so," said Elena.

" I've had such a stupid dream," whispered Elisaveta.

She went to sleep again, and again the same hoard of books. There were so many books that even the window-sills were piled up with them, and a dim and dusty gleam of light barely penetrated. An ominous silence tormented her. Behind the counter at her side stood a student and two boys, strangely erect ; they were pale, and seemed to wait for something. All at once the door opened noiselessly. Many men entered, making a loud noise with their boots—first a police official, then another, then a detective in gold-rimmed spectacles, a house-porter, another house-porter, a muzhik, a policeman, another muzhik, another house-porter. More and more came ; they filled the room, and still they came—huge, moody, silent fellows. Elisaveta felt it stifling ; she awoke.

Again she dropped into sleep, again she was tormented by horrible visions oppressing the breast.

She dreamt that the house was being searched.

" An illegal book ! " exclaimed a detective, looking ominously at her as he put a book on the table.

The pile of the illegal books on the table began to grow. They were examined and shaken. A police official sat down to make out a list. The pen ran on, but there was not enough paper.

" More paper ! " cried the official.

Page was filled after page. The official mocked at her, threatened her with a revolver.

Once more she awoke, once more she fell asleep. And still another dream.

A small, frail schoolmaster with a squeaky voice came. Then another, a third, and still others—an endless flock of peaceful men with wails of revolt.

And yet another dream.

The city square was bathed in the bright sunlight. A muzhik appeared and shouted at the top of his voice :

" Hey there ! Stand up for your gov'r-ment, and for holy Russia ! "

Another muzhik came in answer to his shout, then a third and a fourth. Slowly and steadily the crowd grew, the turmoil increased. A muzhik in a white apron wearing a conspicuous emblem * made his way through the crowd and, screwing up his mouth, cried like a madman :

" For Rush-ya, I say, fel-lows, kill 'em ! "

He threw himself on Elisaveta and began to strangle her.

She awoke.

Again there was a dark, terrible dream. Nothing as yet was to be seen, it was hard to tell what was happening. But fear filled the intense darkness. Dark figures seemed to throng in it. The darkness cleared a little, the atmosphere became ominously grey. A narrow courtyard slowly outlined itself, flanked by high walls with windows closely intersected by bars. Her heart whispered· audibly :

* Reference to the identity of the Black Hundred.

"A prison. A prison courtyard."

Out of a narrow door prisoners were being conducted into the still dark courtyard on a cold early morning in winter. They walked in single file—a soldier, a prisoner, a soldier, a prisoner, a soldier—there seemed to be no end to it; there was a steady shuffling of feet across the courtyard. A small gate opened in the wall with a creaking sound. All walked through it. And beyond the wall Elisaveta already caught a glimpse of a flat, endless field of snow, and of a whole row of gallows that stretched into the invisible distance. They were approaching these nearer and nearer—to meet their fate.

She could not remember how it happened, but she also walked with them. A soldier strode in front of her and in front of the soldier was a boy. Though the boy had his back to her she recognized him—it was Misha. Terror paralysed her tongue— when she tried to cry out she could not find her voice. Terror fettered her feet—when she tried to run she remained rooted to the spot. Terror gripped her arms—when she tried to lift them they hung helplessly at her sides.

People were being hanged at the nearest gallows and the prisoners had to walk past the hanged ones to the gallows beyond. Misha was being hanged, but he broke loose. He was hanged again, and again he broke loose. This happened an endless number of times, and each time he broke loose.

She could see a furious face and the grey bristles of trimmed moustaches. She could hear the malignant cry:

"We must finish him off!"

A shot was fired ; there was a low, dull discharge : the boy fell and began to toss on the ground. Another shot—the boy kept on tossing. The shots came faster—but the boy was still alive.

Elisaveta awoke ; this time she did not go to sleep again. Her heart beat half with pain, half with joy, because it was but a dream—but a dream ! Her heart was bright with exultant joy.

The golden arrows of the yet quiet and gentle Dragon fell softly with sidelong glances. Evidently it was still early. In the distance Elisaveta could hear the sound of a horn and the lowing of cows. The bedroom walls were tinged with rose light. The early light stole in through the windows and messaged an altogether new, better day. A refreshing breeze blew in through the open window, the twitter of birds also entered, the air resounded with early morning joy.

Elisaveta was soon aware that Elena was also awake.

CHAPTER VII

Both sisters had slept badly that night. Elisaveta was worn out by nightmares, while Elena woke several times and went to her. Both felt the sweet after-dizziness of sleep suddenly cut short by the Dragon's sickles. Their memories pursued one another in a confused, vivid flock. They began to recall the circumstances of yesterday's visit. A secret agitation, akin to shame, stole over them. Little by little they conquered this feeling during the day. Alone again, they discussed what they had seen at Trirodov's. A strange forgetfulness came upon them. The details of the visit grew more vague the more they tried to recall them. They found themselves in constant disagreement, and corrected one another. It might have been a dream. Now it seemed one, now the other. Was it reality or a dream? Where is the border-line? Whether life be a sweet or a bitter dream, it passes by like a swift vision!

Three days passed by. Again the day was quiet and clear, again the high Dragon smiled his malignant, excessively bright smile. He counted, as he rose, his livid seconds, his flaming minutes; and he let fall upon the earth, with a scarcely perceptible echo, his lead-heavy but transparent hours. It was three o'clock in the afternoon; they had just finished luncheon. The Rameyevs and the Matovs were at home. Again Elisaveta wrangled with Piotr and, as before, the discussion was long, heated and discordant—every one left the table flustered and depressed ; the hopeless confusion of it all deeply affected even the usually composed Miss Harrison.

The sisters were left by themselves. They went out on the lower balcony and pretended to read. They appeared to be waiting for something. This waiting made their hearts beat fast under their heaving breasts.

Elisaveta, letting the book fall upon her knees, was the first to break the heavy silence.

" I think he is coming to-day."

The breeze blew at that moment, there was a rustle in the foliage and a little bird suddenly began to chirp away somewhere—and it seemed as if the depressed garden were glad because of these lively, resonant, quickly uttered words.

" Who ? " asked Elena.

The insincerity of her question made her flush quite suddenly. She knew very well whom Elisaveta meant. The latter glanced at her and said :

" Trirodov, of course. It is strange that we should be waiting for him."

" I think he promised to come," said Elena indecisively.

" Yes," answered Elisaveta, " I think he said something at that strange mirror."

" It was earlier," observed Elena.

" Yes, I am mixing it all up," said Elisaveta. " I don't understand how I could forget so quickly."

" I too am tangling things up badly," confessed

Elena, astonished at herself. "I feel very tired, I don't know why."

The soft noise of wheels over a sandy road grew closer and closer. At last a light trap, drawn by a horse in English harness, could be seen turning into the alley of birches and stopping before the house. The sisters rose nervously. Their faces wore their habitually pleasant smiles and their hands did not tremble.

Trirodov gave the reins to Kirsha, who drove away.

The meeting proved an embarrassing one. The sisters' agitation was evident in their polite, empty phrases. They entered the drawing-room. Presently Rameyev, accompanied by the Matov brothers, came in to welcome the guest. There was the usual exchange of compliments, of meaningless phrases—as everywhere, as always.

Piotr was uneasy and hostile. He spoke abruptly and with evident unwillingness. Misha looked on with curiosity. He liked Trirodov—he had already heard something about him which assured pleasant relations between them.

The conversation developed rapidly and politely. Not a word was said about the sisters' visit to Trirodov.

"We've heard a great deal about you," began Rameyev, "I'm glad to know you."

Trirodov smiled, and his smile seemed slightly derisive. Elisaveta remarked:

"I suppose you think our being glad to see you merely a polite phrase."

There was sharpness in her voice. Elisaveta, realizing this, suddenly flushed. Rameyev looked at her in astonishment.

"No, I don't think that," put in Trirodov. "There's real pleasure in meeting."

"That's the usual thing to say in polite society," said Piotr quietly.

Trirodov glanced at him with a smile and turned to Rameyev.

"I say it in all sincerity, I am glad to have made your acquaintance. I live very much alone and so am all the more glad of the fortunate circumstance that has brought me here on a matter of business."

"Business?" asked Rameyev in astonishment.

"I can put the matter in a few words," said Trirodov. "I wish to extend my estate."

There was a tinge of sadness in Rameyev's answer :

"You have bought the better part of the Prosianiya Meadows."

Trirodov said :

"It's not quite large enough. I should like to acquire the rest of it—for my colony."

"I shouldn't like to let the rest go," remarked Rameyev. "It belongs to Piotr and Misha."

"As far as it concerns me," put in Piotr, "I'd sell my share with the greatest pleasure before those 'comrade' fellows take it from me for nothing."

Misha was silent, but it was evident that the thought of selling his native soil was distasteful to him. He seemed on the point of bursting into tears.

"In my opinion," observed Rameyev, "the land needn't be sold. I shouldn't advise it. I wouldn't think of selling Misha's share until he came of

72

age—and I shouldn't advise you to sell yours either, Piotr."

Misha, gladdened, glanced gratefully at Rameyev, who continued :

" I can direct you to another plot of land which happens to be on sale. I hope it will suit your needs."

Trirodov thanked him.

His educational institution now became the topic of conversation.

" Your school, of course, brings you into contact with the Headmaster of the National Schools. How do you manage to get along with him ? " asked Rameyev.

Trirodov smiled contemptuously.

" Not at all," he said.

" A clumsy person, this fellow with his feminine voice," went on Rameyev. " He's an ambitious, cold-blooded man. He's likely to do you an injury."

" I'm used to it," answered Trirodov calmly. " We are all used to it."

" They might close your school," suggested Piotr in a tone of sharp derision.

" And again they might not," asserted Trirodov.

" But if they should ? " persisted Piotr.

" Let us hope for the best," said Rameyev.

Elisaveta looked affectionately at her father. But Trirodov said quietly in his own defence :

" The school might be closed, but it is hard to prevent any one from living on the soil and running a farm. If the school should cease being a mere school and become an educational farm, it would succeed in replacing the large farms as they are now run by their proprietors."

"But that is Utopia," said Piotr in some irritation.

"Very well, then, we'll establish Utopia," said Trirodov, unruffled.

"But as a beginning you hope to destroy what exists?" asked Piotr.

"Why?" exclaimed Trirodov, astonished.

Strangely agitated, Piotr said:

"The comrades' proposed division of land, if carried into force, would lead to a crushing of culture and science."

"I don't understand this alarm for science and culture," replied Trirodov. "Both one and the other are sufficiently strong to stand up for themselves."

"Nevertheless," argued Piotr," "monuments of civilization are being demolished by this *Kham* * who is trying to replace us."

"It is not our monuments of civilization alone that are being destroyed," retorted Trirodov patiently. "This is very sad, of course, and proper measures should be taken. But the sufferings of the people are so great. . . . The value of human life is, after all, greater than the value of such monuments."

In this peculiarly Russian manner the conversation quickly passed on to general themes. Trirodov, who took a large share in it, spoke with a calm assurance. They listened to him with deep attention.

Of his five auditors only Piotr was not captivated.

* See note on page 44.

He was tormented by a feeling of hostility to Trirodov. He glanced at Trirodov with suspicion and hate. He was exasperated by Trirodov's confident tone and facile speech. Piotr's remarks addressed to the visitor were often caustic, even coarse. Rameyev looked vexed at Piotr now and then, but Trirodov appeared not to notice his sallies, and was simple, tranquil, and courteous. In the end Piotr was compelled to restrain himself and abandon his sharp manner. Then he grew silent altogether. After Trirodov's departure Piotr left the room. It was evident that he did not wish to join in any discussion about the visitor.

CHAPTER VIII

THE day was hot, sultry, windless—helplessly prostrate before the arrowed glances of the infuriated Dragon. A number of city folk sought coolness on the float, as the buffet at the steamboat-landing was called in Skorodozh. It was less oppressive under the canvas roof of the float, where at intervals gusts of breeze came from the river.

Piotr and Misha were in town to do some shopping. They stopped on the float to get a glass of lemonade. A steamboat had just come in below them. It began to unload the passengers and wares it brought from neighbouring manufacturing towns. It was the boat's last stopping-point, the river higher up being too shallow. For a while there was much bustle and noise on the float. The little tables were soon occupied by towns-folk and new arrivals, chiefly officials and land-lords. They drank wine and talked loudly, though peacefully ; they shouted in the provincial manner, and it was easy to hear that many of the conversations touched more or less on political themes.

Two men who sat at one table were in evident agreement, yet spoke in tones of anger. They were the retired District Attorney Kerbakh and the retired Colonel Zherbenev, both large land-proprietors and patriots—members of the Union of Russian People.* Their speech was loud and

* The Black Hundred.

vehement, and interpolated with such strange words and phrases as " treachery," " sedition," " hang them," " wipe them out," " give it to them."

Nikolai Ilyitch Kerbakh was a small, thin, puny-looking man. The long, drooping moustache on his otherwise clean-shaven face seemed to be there merely to add to its already savage appearance. He rocked in his chair as he lazily stretched himself. His large coat hung about his shoulders like a bag, his highly coloured waistcoat was unbuttoned, his string necktie hung loose, half undone. Altogether he had the look of a man who would not let such small trifles stand in the way of his comfort. Near him, fidgeting restlessly in his chair, was his son, a slobbering, black-toothed youngster of eight, with a flagging, carmine-red under-lip.

Andrey Lavrentyevitch Zherbenev, a tall, lank man with an important air, sat motionless and erect as though he were nailed to his chair, and surveyed those round him with a stern glance. His white linen coat, with all its buttons fastened, sat on him as on a bronze idol.

" In everything, I say, the parents are to blame," continued Kerbakh in the same savage voice as before. " It is necessary to instil the right ideas from very childhood. Now look at my children . . ."

And he shouted at his son with unnecessary loudness, though the two sat almost nudging each other :

" Sergey ! "

" Yeth ? " lisped the slobbering boy.

" Stand up before me and answer."

The youngster slipped off his chair, stretched

himself smartly to his full height in front of his father, and lisped again :

" Yeth, father ? "

And he surveyed those sitting at the other tables with a quick, sly look.

" What should be done with the enemies of the Tsar and the Fatherland ? " asked Kerbakh.

" They should be destroyed ! " answered the boy alertly.

" And afterwards ? " continued his father.

The boy quickly repeated the words he had studied :

" And afterwards the foul corpses of the vile enemies of the Fatherland should be thrown on the dunghill."

Kerbakh and Zherbenev laughed gleefully.

" That describes them—foul carrion, that's what they are ! " said Zherbenev in a hoarse voice.

A new-comer at the next table, a stranger apparently to those present, was giving an order for a bottle of beer. Of middle age and medium height, he was stout, or rather flabby ; he had small glittering eyes ; and his dress had seen much wear. Kerbakh and Zherbenev gave him an occasional passing glance, not of a very friendly nature. As though they took it for granted that the stranger held antagonistic views, they increased the vehemence of their speeches and spoke more and more furiously of agitators and of Little Mother Russia, and mentioned, by the way, a number of local undesirables, Trirodov among them.

The new-comer scrutinized the two speakers for a long time. It was evident that the name of Trirodov, often repeated in Kerbakh's remarks, aroused an intense interest, even agitation, in the stranger. His fixed scrutiny of his two neighbours at last attracted their attention and they exchanged annoyed glances.

Then the stranger ventured to join in their conversation.

" I beg your pardon," he said, " unless I am mistaken, you were speaking of Mr. Trirodov—am I right ? "

" My dear sir, you . . ." began Kerbakh.

The new-comer immediately jumped to his feet and began to apologize profusely.

" May I impose upon your good nature to forgive my impertinent curiosity. I am Ostrov, the actor —tragedian. You may have heard of me ? "

" For the first time," said Kerbakh surlily.

" I've never heard the name," said Zherbenev.

The stranger smiled pleasantly, as if he had been commended, and continued to speak without showing the slightest embarrassment :

" Well—er—I've played in many cities. I'm just passing through here. I'm on my way to attend to some personal business in the Rouban Government. And you just happened to mention a name very familiar to me."

Kerbakh and Zherbenev exchanged glances. Malignant thoughts about Trirodov again took possession of their minds. Ostrov continued :

" I had no suspicion that Trirodov lived here. He is a very old and intimate acquaintance of mine. I might say we are friends."

" So-o," said Zherbenev severely, glancing at Ostrov with disapproval.

Something in Ostrov's voice and manner aroused

their antagonism. His glance was certainly impudent. Indeed his words and his whole demeanour were provokingly arrogant. But it was impossible to be rude with him. His words were proper enough in themselves.

"We haven't met for some years," Ostrov went on. "How does he manage to get on?"

"Mr. Trirodov is to all appearances a rich man," said Kerbakh unwillingly.

"A rich man? That's agreeable news. In fact, this wealth of Mr. Trirodov's is of comparatively recent origin. I'm quite sure of that. Of recent origin, I assure you," repeated Ostrov, giving a sly wink.

"And not of the cleanest?" asked Kerbakh.

He winked at Zherbenev. The latter made a grimace and chuckled. Ostrov looked cautiously at Kerbakh.

"Why do you assume so?" he asked. "No-o, I shouldn't say that. Quite clean. Indeed, I can assure you of its clean origin," he repeated with peculiar emphasis.

Misha looked with curiosity at the speakers. He wished to hear something about Trirodov. But Piotr quickly paid his bill and rose to go. Kerbakh tried to hold him.

"Here's a friend of your friend Trirodov," he said.

"I haven't yet had time to become a friend of Trirodov's," Piotr answered sharply, "and I don't intend to. As for his friends, nearly every one has his more or less strange acquaintance."

And he quickly left with Misha. Ostrov glanced after him with a smile and said:

" A grave young man."

" Mr. Trirodov has bought some land belonging
to him and his brother," explained Kerbakh.

Piotr Matov's hostility to Trirodov evidently
had its roots in the chance circumstance that
Trirodov had bought the house and part of the
estate, the Prosianiya Meadows, which formerly
belonged to the paternal Matov.

Many in the town of Skorodozh remembered very
well Dmitry Alexandrovitch Matov, the father of
Piotr and Mikhail Matov. He had been a member
of the local District Council for a single term, and
was not chosen again. He could not hide his
connexions and his affairs, and lost his reputation,
though the scandal was hushed up. This happened
when times were still quiet. During his term of
office he paid visits to the governor more often
than necessary.

About the same time, in response to some one's
complaint, the President of the District Council
had been dispatched " in administrative order "
to the Olonetsk Government. There were dark
rumours about Matov. At the next election a
few votes were given in his favour, but not enough.
He ceased to have any connexion with the District
Council.

Matov's money affairs were in a bad state. He
led a heedless life, dissipated, and roamed from
place to place. Bold, headstrong, unrestrained,
he lived only for his own pleasure. More than once
he squandered all—to the last farthing. But
invariably he found sudden means again, no one
knew how, and again he would lead a dissipated,

gay, profligate life. His estate was mortgaged and re-mortgaged. His relations with the peasants began to be unbearable. Their own difficulties and his temper led to constant disputes. A reign of spite began : the cattle were driven into the corn, some of the buildings were set afire, some of the peasants were gaoled.

The Prosianiya Meadows more than once passed from a period of lavish prosperity to a state of complete and hopeless poverty. This was because Matov was lucky enough to fall heir to several inheritances. Not only did people say that luck was on his side, but they also hinted at forged wills, strangled aunts, and poisoned children. Dark adventures of some sort enriched and ruined Matov by turns. It was all like some dubious, fantastic game of chance. . . .

During the lean days the ingeniously constructed buildings on his estate were in a state of disrepair, the live stock showed decrease, the wheat was got rid of quickly and cheaply, the wood was sold for a trifling sum for lumber, the labourers were not paid for the work they had done. On the other hand, during prosperous days, following the death of some relative, things used to pick up in a marvellous way. Companies of carpenters, masons, roofers, and painters would make their appearance. The owner's fancies were swiftly and energetically carried out. Money was spent lavishly, without reckoning the cost.

Dmitry Alexandrovitch Matov was already forty years old, and many dark, mad misdeeds weighed on his shoulders, when, quite unexpectedly to all and possibly to himself, he married a young girl with excellent means and a dark past. There was a report that she had been the mistress of a dignitary, who had begun to grow weary of her. She managed, none the less, to keep up her connexions and to collect capital. She would have been very beautiful but for a strange stain—as from fire — on her left cheek, which disfigured her. This spot was very conspicuous and completely marred the beauty of her face.

Very shortly a fierce hatred arose between husband and wife, no one knew why. The gossips said he was disappointed in his expectations, while she had found out about his mistresses and revels and had got wind of the dark rumours about his inheritances. The quarrels grew more frequent. Quite often he left his home, and always suddenly. Once he took all valuables with him and decamped, leaving with his wife only his mortgaged estate, his debts, and their two sons. A short time afterwards all sorts of reports came in about him. Some had seen him in Odessa, others in Manchuria. Later even rumours ceased.

Then came the unexpected news of his death in a remote southern town. Its cause remained unknown. Even his body had not been found. It was only certain that he had been lured into an empty, uninhabited house—there all trace of him was lost.

Matov's widow soon died from a sudden, sharp illness. Her sons remained in the house of Rameyev. He became their guardian.

"He's an agitator and a conspirator," said Zherbenev sharply.

Ostrov smiled.

"All the same, I must stand up for my friend. Pardon me if I ask the question: are these calumnies against my friend actuated by patriotic reasons? Of course, from the most honourable impulses!"

"I do not take up my time with calumnies," said Zherbenev dryly.

"Oh, I beg your pardon. But I'll not intrude upon you any longer. I'm very grateful for the pleasant conversation and for the interesting information."

Ostrov left them. Kerbakh and Zherbenev quietly discussed him.

"What a strange-looking man! Quite a beast!"

"Yes, what a character! I shouldn't like to meet him alone in the woods."

"Our poet and doctor of chemistry has fine friends, I must say!"

CHAPTER IX

ELISAVETA and Elena were walking again on a path close to the road that connected the Prosianiya Meadows and the Rameyev estate. The sisters were glad that it was so still and deserted around them and that the turmoil of life seemed so remote from them. Life with all its bustling movement seemed indeed distant, and it was a joy to dismiss all its conditions and proprieties from their minds and to walk with bare feet upon the soft ground, the sand, the clay, and the grass; it filled their hearts with a simple, childlike, and chaste delight.

Both were dressed alike, in short frocks; there was a sash raised rather high at the waist, two other bands crossed each other at the breast, the sleeves were cut quite short at the shoulders.

They walked on farther, and their eyes contemplated gaily and affectionately the half-hidden depths of the valleys, the woods, and the thickets. A simple-hearted devotion to this lovable nature possessed them—it was a sweet and tender devotion. It struck a deep note in Elisaveta, who was in a mood of expectancy. If only she could have met some one deserving of her love whom she might place at the crossings of all earthly and heavenly roads, and to whom she might do obeisance!

This tender devotion aroused young virginal intoxication in Elena also. She felt herself in love—not with any one in particular, but with everything: as the air loves in the springtime, kissing all in its gladness; as a stream's currents love when they brush caressingly past boys' and girls' pink knees—such were the currents of the stream that suddenly became visible, winding its way among the green in the direction of the River Skorodyen, into which it emptied itself.

The bridge was some way off, and so the sisters waded the stream. There was the delicious coolness of the water round their knees. They remained standing on the bank and admired the porcupines of sand, studded sparsely with tall blades of grass as with spines; also the round pebbles made smooth by the water. Their cooled legs felt for some time afterwards the sensation of the water's loving caresses.

Just as the running water falls in love with all beauty that is immersed in it, so Elena fell in love with all that her vision evoked for her.

Most of all her love was directed towards Piotr. His love for Elisaveta wounded her with a sweet pain.

The sisters descended into the hollow near Trirodov's colony, ascended it again to the other side, walked along the already familiar path, and opened the gate—this time it yielded without effort. They entered. Soon they saw a lake before them. The children and their instructresses were bathing. There was a spirit of buoyancy in the brown nakedness disporting itself in the buoyant waters—buoyant were the splashes, the laughter, and the outcries!

The children and the instructresses walked out of the water upon the dry ground and ran naked upon the sand. Their legs, bare and sunburnt, seemed white in the green grass, like young birch-saplings growing out of the earth.

They suddenly caught sight of the sisters, formed a ring of beautiful wet bodies around them, and twirled in a circle at a fast, furious pace. The discarded clothes that lay there close by seemed unnecessary to the sisters at that moment. What, after all, was more beautiful and lovely than the nude, eternal body ?

The sisters learnt afterwards that they more often walked about naked here than in their clothes.

The radiantly sad Nadezhda said to them :

" To lull the beast to sleep and to awaken the human being—that is the reason of our naked-ness."

The dark, black-haired Maria said with ecstasy :

" We have bared our feet in order to come in closer contact with the earth ; we have become simple and happy, like people in the first garden. We have discarded our clothes in order to come closer to the elements. Caressed by these, clothed by the fire of the sun's rays, we have discovered the human being in us. This being is not the uncouth beast thirsting for blood, or the townsman counting his profits—it is the human being, clean in body and alive with love."

So natural, indispensable, and inevitable seemed the nakedness of these young, beautiful bodies that it appeared rather stupid to put on one's clothes afterwards. The sisters joined in with the naked dancers, and went into the water and lay on the grass under the trees. It was pleasant to feel the beauty, the grace, and the agility of their bodies among these other twirling, beautiful, strong bodies.

Elisaveta's observant glance detected two types among the girl instructresses. There were the rapturous ones and the dissembling ones.

The rapturous ones gave themselves up with a bacchic joy to a life lived in the embrace of chaste nature : they fervently carried out all the rites of the colony, joyously divested themselves of all fear and shame, made great efforts and self-denials ; and they laughed and they flamed, overcome by a passionate thirst of noble actions and of love—a thirst which not all the waters of this poor earth can quench. Among this number were the sad Nadezhda and the ecstatic Maria.

The others, the dissembling ones, were those who had sold their time and had parted with all their habits, inclinations, and proprieties for money. They pretended that they loved children, simple life, and bodily beauty. They did not find it hard to dissemble, for the others served them as excellent models.

This time the sisters were shown the buildings of the colony, or at least as much of them as they could see in an hour, and all sorts of things made by the children—books and pictures—things that belonged to this or that child. They were shown the fruit-orchard and the garden-beds, above which the bees buzzed ; and the air was fresh with the honeyed aroma of flowers half lost in the tender softness of profuse grasses.

But the sisters soon left.

They had intended to go home, but somehow they lost their way among the paths and found themselves in sight of Trirodov's house. Elisaveta espied the high turrets rising above the white wall and recalled Trirodov's neither young nor handsome face : she became suffused with a sweet passion, as with a rich wine—but it was an emotion not free from pain.

Before they realized it they were quite close to the white wall, near the ponderous closed gates. The small gate was open. A quiet, white boy was looking at the sisters through the crevice with an inviting glance. The sisters exchanged irresolute glances.

"Shall we go in, Vetochka * ? " asked Elena.

"Yes, let's go in," said Elisaveta.

The sisters entered and found themselves in the garden. They found old Elikonida at the entrance. She was sitting on the bench near the small gate and was mumbling something slowly and indistinctly. Evidently no one was there to listen to her. Perhaps the old woman was talking to herself.

Old Elikonida was first engaged to nurse Kirsha ; now she carried out the duties of a housekeeper. She had always been austere and never wasted a word in speaking with people. The sisters tried to draw her into conversation ; they wanted to ask her things, about the ways of the house, the habits of Trirodov—they were such inquisitive girls ! Elena asked many questions, although Elisaveta tried to restrain her ; but they found out nothing. The old woman looked past the sisters and mumbled in answer to all questions :

"I know what I know. I have seen what I have seen."

* Betty.

The quiet children approached them. They stood motionless and inanimate in the shade of the old trees, and looked at the sisters with a fixed, expressionless stare. The sisters felt uncomfortable and made haste to depart. They could hear behind them the austere mumbling of Elikonida:

" I've seen what I've seen."

And the quiet children laughed their quiet, quiet laughter, which was truly like the sudden rustle of autumn leaves all aflutter in the air.

The sisters walked home silently. They found the right path and walked without blundering. The evening darkness was coming on. They made haste. The warm, damp earth clung to their feet and seemed to hinder their movements.

They were not far from their own house when they suddenly came upon Ostrov in the woods. He seemed to be on the look-out for something as he walked. When he saw the sisters he turned aside and stood behind the trees ; then he strode forward quickly and faced them with an unexpected suddenness that made Elena shudder and Elisaveta frown. Ostrov bowed to them with derisive politeness and said :

" May I ask you something, fair ladies ? "

Elisaveta surveyed him calmly and said without haste :

" What is it ? "

Elena was silent with fear.

" Are you taking a walk ? " asked Ostrov.

" Yes," answered Elisaveta briefly.

" Mr. Trirodov's house is somewhere hereabouts, unless I'm mistaken," said Ostrov, half questioningly.

"Yes, you'll find it by following the direction from which we came," replied Elena.

She wanted to conquer her fear. Ostrov winked at her insolently and said:

"Thank you most humbly. And who may you be?"

"Perhaps it is not necessary that you should know," replied Elisaveta with a half-question.

Ostrov burst into laughter and said with unpleasant familiarity:

"It may not be necessary, but it would be interesting."

The sisters walked on rapidly, but he did not desist. They thought him repulsive. There was something alarming in his obtrusiveness.

"You evidently live hereabouts, fair ladies," continued Ostrov; "I will therefore venture to ask you what you know about Mr. Trirodov, who interests me immensely."

Elena laughed, perhaps somewhat dissemblingly, in order to hide her agitation and fear.

"Perhaps we don't live hereabouts," she said.

Ostrov whistled.

"Very likely, isn't it, that you've come all the way from Moscow with your bare little feet," he shouted angrily.

"We cannot tell you anything that can interest you," said Elena coldly. "You had better apply to him personally. It would be more proper."

Ostrov again burst into a sarcastic laugh and exclaimed:

"I can't deny that that would be proper, my handsome barefoot one. But suppose he's very busy, eh ? How, then, would you advise me to get this interesting information I want ? "

The sisters were silent and walked on rapidly. Ostrov persisted :

" You are of his colony ? Unless I'm mistaken you are instructresses there. As far as one could judge from your light dresses and your contempt of footwear, I think I'm not mistaken, eh? Tell me, it's an amusing life there, isn't it ? "

" No," said Elisaveta, " we are not instructresses and we do not live there."

" What a pity ! " said Ostrov incredulously. " I might have told you something about Mr. Trirodov."

He looked at the sisters attentively. They were silent.

" I've got together all sorts of information here and elsewhere," he went on. " Curious things they tell about him, very curious indeed. And where did he get his money ? In general there are many suspicious circumstances about his life."

" Suspicious for whom ? " asked Elena. " And what affair is it of ours ? "

" What affair is it of yours, my charming maidens ? " repeated Ostrov after her. " I have a well-founded suspicion that you are acquainted with Mr. Trirodov, and I therefore hope that you'll tell me something about him."

" You had better not hope," said Elisaveta.

" And why not ? " observed Ostrov in a familiar tone. " He's an old acquaintance of mine. In years gone by we lived, drank, and roamed together. And quite suddenly I lost sight of him, and now quite as suddenly I've found him again. Naturally, I'm interested. As an old friend, you see ! "

" Now, look here," said Elisaveta, " we do not wish to converse with you. You had better go where you were going. We know nothing that would interest you and we have nothing to say to you."

" So that's it ! " said Ostrov, with an insolent smile. " And now, my beauty, I'd better tell you that you're expressing yourself a little carelessly. Suppose I whistled suddenly, eh ? "

" What for ? " asked Elisaveta, astonished.

" What for-r ? Well, some one may come out to my whistle."

" What then ? " asked Elisaveta.

After a short silence Ostrov resumed his threatening tone :

" You may be asked to give a few details about what Mr. Trirodov is doing behind his walls."

" Nonsense ! " said Elisaveta in vexation.

" In any case, I'm only joking," said Ostrov, suddenly changing his tone.

He was listening intently. Some one was coming towards them. The sisters recognized Piotr and walked quickly to meet him. From their haste and flustered manner Piotr understood that the man was distasteful to them. He eyed him fixedly and recalled where he had met him, whereupon he frowned and asked the sisters :

" Who is this ? "

" A very inquisitive person who somehow has got an idea that we have many interesting things to tell him about Trirodov," said Elisaveta with a smile.

Ostrov raised his hat and said:

" I've had the honour to see you on the float."

" Well, what of it ? " asked Piotr sharply.

" Well—er, I have the honour to remind you," said Ostrov with exaggerated politeness.

" What are you doing here ? " asked Piotr.

" I've had the pleasure of meeting these charming young ladies," Ostrov began to explain.

Piotr interrupted him sharply:

" And now you let the young ladies alone and go away from here."

" Why shouldn't I have turned to these young ladies with a polite question and an interesting tale ? " asked Ostrov.

Piotr, without replying, turned to the sisters:

" You little girls are ready to enter into conversation with every vagrant."

An expression of bitterness crept into Ostrov's face. Possibly this was only a game, but it was certainly well played. It made Piotr feel uncomfortable.

" A vagrant ? And what is a vagrant ? " asked Ostrov.

" What is a vagrant ? " repeated Piotr in confusion. " What a question ! "

" Well, sir, you have permitted yourself to use the word, and I'm rather interested to know in what sense you've used it in its application to me."

Piotr, annoyed at being disconcerted by the stranger's question, said sharply:

" A vagrant is one who roams about without shelter and without money and obtrudes upon others instead of attending to his own business."

94

"Thank you for the definition," said Ostrov with a bow. 'It is true that I have but little money and that I'm compelled to roam about— such is the nature of my profession."

"What is your profession?" asked Piotr.

Ostrov bowed with dignity and said:

"I'm an actor!"

"I doubt it," said Piotr once more sharply, "you look more like a detective."

"You are mistaken," said Ostrov in a flustered way.

Piotr turned away from him.

"Let us go home at once," he said to the sisters.

CHAPTER X

Iᴛ was growing dark. Ostrov was approaching Trirodov's gates. His face betrayed agitation. It was even more clear now than by daylight that life had used him hardly. He felt painfully timid in going to Trirodov, in whom he evidently had certain hopes. Before Ostrov could make up his mind to ring the bell at the gates he walked the entire length of the stone wall that surrounded Trirodov's house and garden and examined it attentively, without learning anything. Only the entire length of the tall wall was before his eyes.

It was already quite dark when Ostrov stopped at last at the main gate. The half-effaced figures and old heraldic emblems held his attention for a moment only. He had already taken hold of the brass bell-handle and paused cautiously, as if it were his habit to reconsider at the last moment ; he gave a sudden shiver. A clear, childish voice behind his back uttered quietly :

" Not here."

Ostrov looked on both sides timidly, half stealthily, bending his head low and letting it sink between his shoulders. Quite close by a pale, blue-eyed boy dressed in white was standing and eyeing him with intent scrutiny.

" They won't hear you here. Every one has left," he said.

" Where is one to ring ? " Ostrov asked harshly.

The boy pointed his finger to the left; it was a slow, graceful gesture.

"Ring at the small gate there."

He ran off so quickly and quietly it seemed as if he had not been there. Ostrov went in the direction indicated. He came to a high, narrow gate. A white electric bell-button shone in a round wooden recess. Ostrov rang and listened. He could hear somewhere the rapid shivering tones of a tiny bell. Ostrov waited. The door did not open. Ostrov rang once more. It was quiet behind the door.

"I wonder how long there's to wait?" he grumbled, then gave a shout: "Hey, you in there!"

A faint, muffled sound vibrated in the damp air, as if some one had tittered lightly. Ostrov caught hold of the brass handle of the gate. The gate opened towards him easily and without a sound. Ostrov looked round cautiously as he entered, and purposely left the gate open.

He found himself in a small court on either side of which was a low wall. The gate swung to behind him with a metallic click. Had he himself pulled it to rather quickly? He could not recall now. He walked forward about ten paces, when he came upon a wall twice as high as the side walls. It had a massive oak door; an electric bell-button shone very white on one side. Ostrov rang once more. The bell-button was very cold, almost icy, to the touch. A sensation of chill passed down his whole body.

A round window, like a dim, motionless, observing eye, was visible high above the door.

97

Ostrov could not say whether he waited there a long or a short time. He experienced a strange feeling of having become congealed and of having lost all sense of time. Whole days seemed to pass before him like a single minute. Rays of bright light fell on his face and disappeared. Ostrov thought that some one flashed this light on his face by means of a lantern from the window over the door—a light so intense that his eyes felt uncomfortable. He turned his face aside in vexation. He did not wish to be recognized before he entered. That was why he came in the dark of the evening.

But evidently he had been recognized. This door swung open as soundlessly as the first. He entered a short, dark corridor in the thick wall; then another court. No one was there. The door closed noiselessly behind him.

" How many courts are there in this devilish hole ? " growled Ostrov.

A narrow path paved with stone stretched before him. It was lit up by a lamp from a distance, the reflection of which was directed straight towards Ostrov, so that he could see only the smooth grey slabs of stone under his feet. It was altogether dark on either side of the path, and it was impossible to know whether a wall was there or trees. There was nothing for him to do but to walk straight on. Nevertheless he occasionally thrust his foot out to either side of him and felt there ; he was convinced that thickly planted, prickly bushes grew there. He thought there was another hedge beyond that.

" Tricks ! " he grumbled.

As he slowly moved forward he experienced a vague and growing fear. So as not to be caught off his guard, he put his left hand into the pocket of his dusty and greasy trousers and felt there the hard body of a revolver, which he then transferred to his right-hand pocket.

On the threshold of the house he was met by Trirodov. Trirodov's face expressed nothing except an apparent effort to suppress his feelings. There was no warmth or welcome in his voice :

" I did not expect to see you."

" I've come, all the same," said Ostrov. " Whether you like it or not, you've got to receive your dear guest."

There was contemptuous defiance in his voice. His eyes looked more insolent than ever. Trirodov frowned lightly and looked straight into Ostrov's eyes, which were compelled to turn aside.

" Come in," said Trirodov. " Why didn't you write and tell me that you wished to see me ? "

" How should I know that you were here ? " growled Ostrov surlily.

" Nevertheless, you found out," said Trirodov, with a vexed smile.

" Found out quite by accident on the float," replied Ostrov. " Heard you mentioned in conversation. I don't think you'll care to know what they said."

He gave an insinuating smile. Trirodov merely said :

" Come in. Follow me."

They ascended a narrow, very steep staircase with low, wide stairs ; there were frequent turnings in various directions round all sorts of odd corners, interrupted by long landings between the climbs; each landing revealed a tightly shut door. The light was clear and unwavering. A cold gaiety and malice, a half-hidden, motionless irony, were in the gleam of the incandescent wires bent inside the glass pears.

Some one walked behind with a light, cautious step. There were the clicking sounds of lights being extinguished; the passages they had just passed through were plunged in darkness.

At last they reached the top of the stairway. They walked through a long corridor and found themselves in a large gloomy room. There was a sideboard against one of the walls and a table in the middle; cut-glass dishes rested along shelves around the room. It was to all appearances a dining-room.

"It's quite the proper thing to do," grumbled Ostrov. "A meal would do me no harm."

The light was strangely distributed. Half of the room and half of the table were in the shadow. Two boys dressed in white waited at the table. Ostrov winked at them insolently.

But they looked on calmly and departed quite simply. Trirodov settled himself in the dark part of the room. Ostrov sat down at the table. Trirodov began:

"Well, what do you want of me?"

"Now that's a businesslike question," answered Ostrov, with a hoarse laugh, "very much a business question, not so much a gracious as a businesslike question. What do I want? In the first place, I am delighted to see you. There is a certain bond between us—our childhood and all the rest of it."

" I'm very glad," said Trirodov dryly.

" I doubt it," responded Ostrov impudently. " Then again, my dear chap, I've come for something else. In fact, you've guessed what I've come for. You've been a psychologist ever since I can remember."

" What is it you want ? " asked Trirodov.

" Can't you guess ? " said Ostrov, winking his eye.

" No," replied Trirodov dryly.

" In that case there's nothing left for me to do but to tell you straight : I need money."

He laughed hoarsely, unnaturally ; then, pouring out a glass of wine, mumbled as he gulped it down :

" Good wine."

" Every one needs money," answered Trirodov coldly. " Where do you intend to get it ? "

Ostrov turned in his chair. He chuckled nervously and said :

" I've come to you, as you see. You evidently have lots of money, and I have little. Comment is needless, as the newspapers would say."

" So that's it ! And suppose I refuse ? " asked Trirodov.

Ostrov whistled sharply and looked insolently at Trirodov.

" Well, old chap," he said rudely, " I don't count on your permitting yourself such a stupid mistake."

" Why not ? "

" Why not ? " repeated Ostrov after him. " I think the facts must be as clear to you as to me, if not more so—and there's nothing to be gained by the world getting wind of them."

"I owe you nothing," said Trirodov quietly. "I don't understand why I should give you money. You'd only spend it recklessly—squander it most likely."

"And do you spend it any more sensibly?" asked Ostrov with a malicious smile.

"If not more sensibly, at least with more reckoning," retorted Trirodov. "In any case, I'm prepared to help you. Only I may as well tell you that I have little spare cash and that even if I had it I'd not give you much."

Ostrov gave a short, abrupt laugh and said with decision:

"A little is of no use to me. I need a lot of money. But perhaps you'll not think it much."

"How much do you want?" asked Trirodov abruptly.

"Twenty thousand roubles," replied Ostrov, making a determined effort to brazen it out.

"I'll not give you so much," said Trirodov, "and I couldn't even if I wished to."

Ostrov drew nearer to Trirodov and whispered:

"I'll inform against you."

"What then?" asked Trirodov, untouched by the threat.

"It will be bad for you. It's a capital crime, as you know, my dear chap, and of a no mean order," said Ostrov in a menacing tone.

"Yours, my good fellow," said Trirodov in his usual calm voice.

"I'll manage to wriggle out of it somehow, but will see that you get your due," said Ostrov with a laugh.

"You're making a sad mistake if you think that

I have anything to fear," observed Trirodov, with a shrug of his shoulders.

Ostrov seemed to grow more insolent every minute. He whistled and said banteringly :

" Tell me now, if you please ! Didn't you kill him ? "

" I ? No, I didn't kill him," answered Trirodov.

" Who then ? " asked Ostrov in his derisive voice.

" He's alive," said Trirodov.

" Fiddlesticks ! " exclaimed Ostrov.

And he burst out into a loud, insolent, hoarse laugh, though he seemed panic-stricken at the same time. He asked :

" What of those little prisms which you've manufactured ? I've heard that even now they are lying on the table in your study."

" That's true," said Trirodov dryly.

" And I'm told that your present is not absolutely clean either," observed Ostrov.

" Yes ? " asked Trirodov derisively.

" Yes-s," continued Ostrov jeeringly. " The first business in your colony is conspiracy, the second corruption, the third cruelty."

Trirodov gave a stern frown and asked scornfully :

" You've had enough time to gather a bouquet of slanders."

" Yes-s, I've managed, as you see. Whether they are slanders is quite another matter. I can only say that they fit you somehow. Take, for instance, those perverse habits of yours ; need I recall them to you ? I could remind you, if I wished, of certain facts from your early life."

" You know you are talking nonsense," said Trirodov.

" It is reported," went on Ostrov, " that all this is being repeated in the quiet of your asylum."

" Even if it were all true," said Trirodov, " I do not see that you have anything to gain by it."

Trirodov's eyes had a tranquil look. He seemed remote. His voice had a calm, hollow sound. Ostrov exclaimed vehemently :

" Don't imagine for a moment that I have fallen into a trap. If I don't leave this place, I have prepared something that will send you to gaol."

" Nonsense," said Trirodov as quietly as before. " I'm not afraid. In the last resort I can emigrate."

" I suppose you'll put on the mantle of a political exile," laughed Ostrov. " It's useless ! Our police, they'll keep a sharp look-out for you, clever fellows that they are. Never fear, they'll get you. They'll get you anywhere. You may be sure of that."

" They'll not give me up where I'm going," said Trirodov. " It's a safe place, and you'll not be able to reach me there."

" What sort of place have you prepared for yourself ? " asked Ostrov, smiling malignantly. " Or is it a secret ? "

" It is the moon," was Trirodov's simple and tranquil answer.

Ostrov laughed boisterously. Trirodov added :

" Moreover, the moon has been created by me. She is before my window, ready to take me."

Ostrov jumped up in great rage from his place, stamped violently with his feet, and shouted :

" You are laughing at me ! It is useless. You

can't fool me with those stupid fairy-tales of yours. Tell those sweet little stories to the silly little girls of the provinces! I'm an old sparrow. You can't feed me on chaff."

Trirodov remained unruffled.

"You're fuming all for nothing. I'll help you with money on a condition."

"What sort of condition?" asked Ostrov with restrained anger.

"You'll have to go from here—very far—for always," answered Trirodov.

"I'll have to think that over," said Ostrov.

"I give you a week. Come to me exactly within a week, and you'll receive the money."

Ostrov suddenly felt an incomprehensible fear. He experienced the feeling of having passed into another's power. He felt oppressed. A stern smile marked Trirodov's face. He said quietly:

"You are of such little value that I could kill you without scruple—like a snake. But I am tired even of other people's murders."

"My value?" Ostrov muttered hoarsely and absurdly.

"What is your value?" went on Trirodov. "You are a hired murderer, a spy, a traitor."

Ostrov said in a meek voice:

"Nevertheless, I've not betrayed you so far."

"Because it wouldn't pay, that's why you've not betrayed me. Again, you dare not."

"What do you want me to do?" asked Ostrov humbly. "What is your condition? Where do you want me to go?"

CHAPTER XI

TRIRODOV left a pleasant impression on Rameyev. Rameyev made haste to return his visit : he went together with Piotr. Piotr did not wish to go to Trirodov's, but could not make up his mind to refuse. He kept frowning on the way, but once in Trirodov's house he tried to be courteous. This he did constrainedly.

Misha soon made friends with Kirsha and with some of the boys. An intimacy sprang up between the Rameyevs and Trirodov—that is, to the extent that Trirodov's unsociableness and love of a solitary life permitted him to become intimate.

It once happened that Trirodov took Kirsha with him to the Rameyevs and remained to dinner. Several other close acquaintances of the Rameyevs came to dinner. The older of the visitors were the Cadets, the younger were the Es-Deks * and the Es-Ers.†

At the beginning there was a long agitated discussion in connexion with the news brought by one of the younger guests, a public school instructor named Voronok, an Es-Er. The Chief of Police had been killed that day near his house. The culprits managed to escape.

Trirodov took almost no part in the conversation. Elisaveta looked at him with anxious eyes, and the yellow of her dress appeared like the colour

* Nickname for Social Democrats.
† Nickname for Social Revolutionaries.

of sadness. It had been remarked by all that Trirodov was thoughtful and gloomy; he seemed to be tormented by some secret agitation, which he made obvious efforts to control. At last the attention of all was turned upon him. This happened after he had answered one of the girls' questions.

Trirodov noticed that they were looking at him. He felt uneasy and vexed with himself. This vexation, however, helped him to control his agitation. He became more animated, threw off, as it were, some weight, and began to talk. The glance of Elisaveta's deep blue eyes grew joyous at this.

Piotr put in a remark just then, in his usual parochial, self-confident manner:

" If it were not for the wild changes in Peter's time, everything would have gone differently."

There was a tinge of derision in Trirodov's smile.

" A mistake, wasn't it ? " he observed. " But if you are going to look for mistakes in Russian history, why not start earlier ? "

" You mean at the beginning of creation ? " said Piotr.

" Precisely then. But without going so far back, let us pause at the Mongolian period," replied Trirodov. " The historical error was that Russia did not amalgamate with the Tartars."

" As if there were not enough Tartars in Russia now ! " said Piotr, provoked.

" That's precisely why there are many—because they didn't amalgamate," observed Trirodov. " They should have had the sense to establish a Russo-Mongolian empire."

"And become Mohammedans?" asked Dr. Svetilovitch, a very agreeable person but very confident of all that was obvious.

"Not at all!" answered Trirodov. "Wasn't Boris Godunov a Christian? That's not the point at issue. All the same, we and the Catholics of Western Europe have regarded each other as heretics; and our empire might have become a universal one. Even if they had counted us among the yellow race, it should be remembered that the yellow race might have been considered under the circumstances quite noble and the yellow skin a very elegant thing."

"You are developing a strange Mongolian paradox," said Piotr contemptuously.

"Even now," retorted Trirodov, "we are looked upon by the rest of Europe as almost Mongols, as a race mixed with Mongolian elements. You know the saying: 'Scratch a Russian and you will find a Tartar.'"

A discussion arose which continued until they left the table.

Piotr Matov was very much out of sorts during the entire dinner. He found almost nothing to say to his neighbour, a young girl, a dark-eyed, dark-haired beauty, an Es-Dek. And the handsome Es-Dek began to turn more and more towards the diner on the other side of her, the priest Zakrasin. He belonged to the Cadets, but was nearer to her in his convictions than the Octobrist * Matov.

Piotr was displeased because Elisaveta paid no

* A political party of moderate liberals which owes its name to the fact that on October 17, 1905, the Russian Constitution was established and the Duma organized.

attention to him and appeared to be absorbed in Trirodov and in what he was saying; and it vexed him because Elena also now and then let her softened gaze rest upon Trirodov. He felt he wanted to say provoking things to Trirodov.

"Yet he is a guest," reflected Piotr to himself, but at last he could hold out no longer; he felt that he must in one way or another shake Trirodov's self-assurance. Piotr walked up to him and, swaying before him on his long thin legs, remarked, without almost the slightest effort to conceal his animosity:

"Some days ago on the pier a stranger made inquiries about you. Kerbakh and Zherbenev were talking nonsense, and he sat down near them and seemed very interested in you."

"Rather flattering," said Trirodov unwillingly.

"I cannot say to what an extent it is flattering," said Piotr maliciously. "In my opinion there was little to recommend him. His appearance was rather suspicious—that of a ragamuffin, in fact. Though he insists he's an actor, I have my doubts. He says you are old friends. A most insolent fellow."

Trirodov smiled. Elisaveta remarked with some agitation:

"We met him some days ago not far from your house."

"It's quite a lonely place," observed Trirodov in an uncertain voice.

Piotr went on to describe him.

"Yes, that's the actor Ostrov," assented Trirodov.

Elisaveta, feeling a strange unrest, put in:

109

" He seemed to have gone around the neighbourhood looking about and asking questions. I
wonder what he can be up to."

" Evidently a spy," said the young Es-Dek
contemptuously.

Trirodov, without expressing the slightest astonishment, remarked :

" Do you think so ? It's possible. I really don't
know. I haven't seen him for five years now."

The young Es-Dek, thinking that Trirodov felt
offended at her reference to his acquaintance,
added affectedly :

" You know him well ; then please pardon me."

" I don't know his present condition," put in
Trirodov. " Everything is possible."

" It's impossible to be responsible for all chance
acquaintances ! " interpolated Rameyev.

Trirodov turned to Piotr :

" And what did he say about me ? "

But his voice did not express any especial
curiosity. Piotr replied with a sarcastic smile :

" He said very little, but asked a great deal.
He said that you knew him very well. In any
case, I soon left."

" Yes, I have known him a long time," was
Trirodov's calm answer. " Perhaps not too well,
yet I know him. I had some dealings with him."

" I think he paid you a visit yesterday ? "

" Yes," said Trirodov in reply to Elisaveta's
question, " he came to see me last evening, quite
late. I don't know why he chose such a late hour.
He asked assistance. His demands were large.
I will give him what I can. He's going away
from here."

110

All this was said in jerks, unwillingly. No one seemed to care to continue the subject further, but at this moment, quite unexpectedly to all, Kirsha entered into the conversation. He went up to his father and said in a quiet but audible voice :

" He purposely came late, while I slept, so that I shouldn't see him. But I remember him. When I was very little he used to show me dreadful tricks. I don't remember them now. I can only remember that I used to get frightened and that I cried."

All looked in astonishment at Kirsha, exchanged glances and smiled.

" You must have seen it in a dream, Kirsha,' said Trirodov quietly. Then, turning to the older people : " Boys of his age love fantastic tales. Even we love Utopia and read Wells. The very life which we are now creating is a joining, as it were, of real existence with fantastic and Utopian elements. Take, for example, this affair of . . ."

In this manner Trirodov interrupted the conversation about Ostrov and changed it to another subject that was agitating all circles at the time. He left very soon after that. The others also stayed but a short time.

There was an atmosphere of irritation and hostility after the guests had gone. Rameyev reproached Piotr.

" My dear Petya, you shouldn't have done that. It isn't hospitable. You were looking all the time at Trirodov as if you were getting ready to send him to all the devils."

Piotr replied with a controlled gruffness :

111

"Yes, precisely, to all the devils. You have guessed my feelings, uncle."

Rameyev eyed him incredulously and said:

"Why, my dear fellow?"

"Why?" repeated Piotr, giving free rein to his irritation. "What is he? A charlatan? A visionary? A magician? Is he in partnership with some unclean power? What do you think of it? Or is it the devil himself come in a human shape—a little grey, cloven-hoofed demon?"

"That's enough, Petya; what are you saying?" said Rameyev with annoyance.

Elisaveta smiled an incredulous smile, full of gentle irony; a golden, saddened smile, set off by the melancholy yellow rose in her black hair. And Elena's astonished eyes dilated widely.

"Think it over yourself, uncle," went on Piotr, "and look around you. He has bewitched our little girls completely!"

"Well, if he has," said Elena with a gay smile, "it's only just a little as far as I am concerned."

Elisaveta flushed but said with composure:

"Yes, he's interesting to listen to; and it's no use stuffing one's ears."

"There, she admits it!" exclaimed Piotr angrily.

"Admits what?" asked Elisaveta in astonishment.

"That for the sake of this cold, vain egoist you are ready to forget every one."

"I've not noticed either his vanity or his egoism," said Elisaveta coldly. "I wonder how you've managed to know him so well—or so ill."

"All this is pitiful and absurd nonsense, only

an excuse for starting a quarrel," said Piotr angrily.

"Petya, you envy him," retorted Elisaveta with unaccustomed sharpness. Then, feeling that she had overstepped the mark, she added :

"Do forgive me, Petya, but really you are exasperating sometimes with your personal attacks."

"Envy him ? Why should I ? " he said hotly. "Tell me, what useful thing has he done ? To be sure, he has published a few tales, a volume of verses—but name me even a single work of his prose or verse that contains the slightest sense or beauty."

"His verses . . . " began Elisaveta.

But Piotr would not let her continue.

"Tell me, where is his talent ? What is he famous for ? All that he writes only seems like poetry. If you look at it closely you will see that it is bookish, forced, dry—it is diabolically suggestive without being talented."

Rameyev interrupted in a conciliatory tone :

"You're unjust. You can't deny him everything."

"Let us admit, then, that there's something in his work not altogether bad," continued Piotr. "Who is there nowadays who cannot put together some nice-sounding versicles ! Yet what is there really I should respect in him ? He's nothing but a corrupt, bald-headed, ridiculous, and dull-sighted person—yet Elisaveta considers him a handsome man ! "

"I never said anything about his being handsome," protested Elisaveta. "As for his corruption, isn't it purely town tattle ? "

She frowned and grew red. Her blue eyes flared up with small greenish flames. Piotr walked angrily out of the room.

"Why is he so annoyed?" asked Rameyev in astonishment.

Elisaveta lowered her head and said with childish bashfulness:

"I don't know."

She could not repress an ashamed smile at her timid words, because she felt like a little girl who was concealing something. At last she overcame her shame and said:

"He's jealous!"

CHAPTER XII

TRIRODOV loved to be alone. Solitude and silence were a holiday to him. How significant seemed his lonely experiences to him, how delicious his devotion to his visions. Some one came to him, something appeared before him, wonderful apparitions visited him, now in dream, now in his waking hours, and they consumed his sadness.

Sadness was Trirodov's habitual state. Only while writing his poems and his prose did he find self-oblivion—an astonishing state, in which time is shrivelled up and consumed, in which great inspiration consoles her chosen ones with divine exultation for all burdens, for all annoyances in life.

He wrote much, published little. His fame was very limited—there were few who read his verses and prose, and even among these but a few who acknowledged his talent. His stories and lyrical poems were not distinguished by any especial obscurity or any especial decadent mannerisms. They bore the imprint of something strange and exquisite. It needed an especial kind of soul to appreciate this poetry which seemed so simple at the first glance, yet actually so out of the ordinary.

To others, from among those who knew him, the public's ignorance of him appeared inexplicable. His capabilities seemed sufficiently great to awaken the attention and admiration of the crowd. But he, to some extent, detested people—perhaps

115

because he was too confident of his own genius—and he never made a definite effort to gratify them. And that was why his works were only rarely published.

In general, Trirodov did not encourage intimacies with people. He found it painful to look with involuntary penetration into the confusion of their dark, foggy souls.

He found himself at ease only in the company of his wife. Love makes kin of souls. But his wife had died a few years ago, when Kirsha was six years old. Kirsha remembered her; he could not forget her, and kept on recalling her. Trirodov for some reason associated his wife's death with the birth of his son, though there was no obvious connexion: his wife died from a casual, sharp illness. Trirodov thought:

" She bore, and therefore had to die. Life is only for the innocent."

After her death he always awaited her; there was for him the consoling thought:

" She will come. She will not deceive me. She will give a sign. She will take me with her."

And life became as easy to bear as a vacillant vision seen in dream.

He loved to look at his wife's portrait. It was painted by a celebrated English artist and hung in his study. There were also many photographic reproductions of her. It was his joy to muse of her and, musing, to delight in images of her handsome face and her lovely body.

Sometimes his solitude was broken by the intrusion of external life and external, unemotional love. A woman used to come in to him some-

116

times—a strange, undemanding woman who seemed to come from nowhere and to lead to nowhere. Trirodov had had relations with her for several months. She was an instructress in the local girls' school, Ekaterina Nikolayevna Alkina—a quiet, tranquil, cold creature with dark red hair and a thin face, the dull pallor of which emphasized the impressively vivid lips of her large mouth; it seemed as if all the sensuality and colour of the face had poured themselves into the lips and made them startlingly and painfully vivid and suggestive of sin. She had married and had parted from her husband. She had a son, who lived with her. She was an S.D.* and worked in the organization, but all this was merely incidental in her life. She met Trirodov in party work. Her comrades understood as by some intuition that in order to carry on negotiations with Trirodov, who did not permit himself any intimacy with them, it was necessary to choose this woman.

And now Alkina had come again, and began as always :

" I've come on business."

Trirodov regarded her with a deep, tranquil glance and answered her with the usual commonplaces of welcome.

Slightly agitated by hidden desires, Alkina spoke of the " business " in hand.

It had already been decided that the party orator who was to come to speak at the projected mass meeting would be quartered at Trirodov's : this was thought to be the least dangerous place. Alkina came to say that the orator was expected

* Member of the Social Democratic Party.

that evening. It was necessary to bring him to Trirodov's house in such a way that the town should not know anything about it. As soon as they had decided at what entrance he should be received Trirodov went out of the room to make the necessary arrangements. The agreeable consciousness of creative mystery filled him with joy.

When Trirodov returned Alkina was standing at the table and turning over the pages of a new book. Her hands trembled slightly. She glanced expectantly at Trirodov. She appeared to wish to say something meaningful and tender—but instead she resumed her remarks on business. She told him what was new in town, in her school, in the organization—about the confiscation of the local newspaper, about personalities ordered to leave town by the police, about the factory ferment.

" Who will be our own speakers at the mass meeting ? " asked Trirodov.

" Bodeyev, from the school, for one."

" I do not like his manner of speaking," said Trirodov.

" He's a good party workman," observed Alkina with a timid smile. " He's to be valued for that."

" You know, of course, that I am not much of a party man," said Trirodov.

Alkina was silent. She trembled lightly as she rose from her seat, then suddenly ceased to be agitated. Only her vivid lips, speaking slowly, seemed to be alive in her pale face.

" Giorgiy Sergeyevitch, will you love me a little ? "

118

Trirodov smiled. He sat quietly in his chair and looked at her simply and dispassionately. He did not answer at once. Alkina asked again with her sad and gentle humility :

" Perhaps you haven't the time, nor the desire ? "

" No, Katya, I shall be glad," answered Trirodov calmly. " You'll find it convenient in there," and he signified with his eyes the little neighbouring room which had no other exit.

Alkina flushed lightly and said :

" If you will permit me, I'd rather undress here. It would give me joy to have you look at me a long time."

Trirodov helped her to undo the clasps of her skirt. Alkina sat down on a chair, bent over, and began to undo the buttons of her boots. Then, with evident enjoyment at having freed her feet, she walked slowly across the floor towards the door and turned the key in the lock.

" As you know, I have but one joy," she said.

She gracefully threw off her clothes and stood before Trirodov with uplifted arms. She was sinuously slender, like a white serpent. Crossing the fingers of her upraised hands, she bent her whole body forward, so that she appeared more sinuously slender than ever, and the curve of her body almost resembled a white ring. Then she relaxed her arms, stood up erect, all tranquil and self-possessed, and said :

" I want you to take a good look at me. I haven't grown old yet, have I ? And not altogether faded ? "

Trirodov surveyed her with admiration and said quietly :

" Katya, you are as handsome as always."

Alkina was mistrustful.

" It's true, isn't it, that clothes have too long cramped my body and injured the skin. How can my body be handsome ? "

" You are graceful and flexible," answered Trirodov. " The lines of your body are somewhat elongated but wholly elastic. If any one were to measure your body he would find no error in its proportions."

Alkina scrutinized herself attentively and went on incredulously :

" The lines are good—but the colour ? I believe you once said that Russians often have unpleasant complexions. When I look on the whiteness of my body I am reminded of plaster of paris, and I begin to weep because I am so ugly."

" No, Katya," asserted Trirodov. " The whiteness of your body is not like plaster of paris. It is marble, slightly rose-tinged. It is milk poured into a pink crystal vase. It is mountain snow lit up with the last glow of sunset. It is a white reverie suffused with rose desire."

Alkina smiled joyously and flushed lightly as she asked him :

" Will you take a few snapshots of me to-day ? Otherwise I shall weep, because I am so ugly and so meagre that you do not wish to recall sometimes my face and my body."

" Yes," answered Trirodov, " I have a few films ready."

Alkina laughed gleefully and said :

" Now kiss me."

She bent over Trirodov and almost fell into his arms. The kisses seemed tranquil and innocent ; it might have been a sister kissing a brother. How gentle and elastic her skin was under his hands ! Alkina pressed against him with a submissive, yielding movement. Trirodov carried her to the wide, soft couch. She lay in his arms timidly and quietly and looked straight into his eyes with a simple, innocent look.

When the sweet and deep minutes passed, followed by fatigue and shame, Alkina lay there motionlessly with half-closed eyes—and then said suddenly :

" I've been wanting to ask you, and somehow couldn't decide to. Do you detest me ? Perhaps you think me very shameless ? "

She turned her face towards him and looked at him with frightened, ashamed eyes. And he answered her with his usual resolution :

" No, Katya. Shame is often needed, in order that we may gain control over it."

Alkina once more lay back calmly, basking naked under his glances, as under the rays of the high Dragon. Trirodov was. silent. Alkina laughed quietly and said :

" My husband used to be so respectable, mean and polite. He never beat me—he was not a cultured man for nothing—and he never even used coarse words. If he had but called me a fool ! I sometimes think that I wouldn't have left him if our quarrels hadn't passed so quietly, if he had but beat me, pulled me by my hair, lashed me with something."

" Sweet ? " asked Trirodov.

" Life is so dull," continued Alkina. " One struggles in the nets of petty annoyances. If one could but cry out, but give wail to one's yearning, one's woe, one's unendurable pain ! "

She said this with a passion unusual to her and grew silent.

CHAPTER XIII

IT was drawing towards evening, and once more Trirodov was alone, tormented by his unceasing sadness. His mind was in a whirl. He was in a half-somnolent state, which was like the foreboding of a nightmare. His half-dreams and half-illusions were full of the day's impressions, full of burning, cruel reveries.

It had just grown dark. A fire was visible on a height near the town. The town boys were making merry. They had lit a bonfire, and were throwing the brands into the air; as they rose swiftly, the burning brands appeared like sky-rockets against the blue sky. And these beautiful flights of fire in the darkness gave joy and sadness.

Kirsha, silent as always, came to his father. He placed himself at the window and looked out with his dark, sad eyes upon the distant fires of St. John's Eve. Trirodov went up to him. Kirsha turned quietly towards his father:

" This will be a terrible night."

Trirodov answered as quietly:

" There will be nothing terrible. Don't be afraid, Kirsha. You had better go to sleep, my boy, it is time."

As if he had not heard his father, Kirsha went on:

" The dead will soon rise from their graves."

" The dead are already rising from their graves," replied Trirodov.

A strange feeling of astonishment stirred within

123

him, why did he speak of this ?   Or was it due to the urgency of the questioner's desire ?   Quietly, ever so quietly, half questioning, half relating, Kirsha persisted :

" The dead will walk on the Navii * footpath, the dead will speak Navii words."

And again, as though submitting to a strange will, not his own, Trirodov replied :

" The dead have already risen, they are already walking upon the Navii footpath, towards the Navii town, they are already speaking Navii words about Navii affairs."

And Kirsha asked :

" Are you going ? "

" I am going," said Trirodov after a brief silence.

" I am going with you," said Kirsha resolutely.

" You had better not go, dear Kirsha," said his father tenderly.

But Kirsha persistently repeated :

" I will spend this night with you there, at the Navii footpath. I will see and I will hear. I will look into dead eyes."

Trirodov said sternly :

" I do not wish to take you with me—you ought to remain here."

There was entreaty in Kirsha's voice :

" Perhaps mother will come by."

Trirodov, falling into deep thought, said finally :
" Very well, come with me."

The evening dragged on slowly and sadly. The father and son waited. It grew quite dark by the time they went.

They walked through the garden, past the

* See note on page 26.

124

closed greenhouse with its mysteriously glittering window-panes. The quiet children were not yet asleep. Quietly they swung in the garden upon their swings. Quietly clinked the swing rings, quietly creaked the wooden seats. Upon the swings sat the quiet children, lit up by the dead moon and cooled by the night breeze, and they swung softly and sang their songs. The night listened to their quiet songs, and the full, clear, dead moon also. Kirsha, lowering his voice so that the quiet children might not hear, asked:

" Why don't they sleep ? They swing on their swings neither upward nor downward, but evenly. Why do they do this ? "

" They must not sleep to-night," answered Trirodov, also in a whisper. " They cannot sleep until the dawn grows rosy, until the dawn begins to laugh. There is really no reason why they should sleep. They can sleep as well by day."

Again Kirsha asked:

" Will they go with us ? They want to go."

" No, Kirsha, they don't want anything."

" Don't want anything ? " repeated Kirsha sadly.

" They ought not to go with us unless we call them."

" Shall we call them ? " asked Kirsha joyously.

" We shall call one. Which one would you like ? "

Kirsha, after some thought, said:

" Grisha."

" Very well, we'll call Grisha," said Trirodov.

He turned in the direction of the swings, and called out:

125

" Grisha ! "

A boy, who resembled the sad-faced Nadezhda, quietly jumped down from his swing, and walked behind them, without approaching too closely. The other quiet children looked tranquilly after him, and continued to swing and to sing as before.

Trirodov opened the gate, and was followed by Kirsha and Grisha. The night hovered all around them, and the forgotten Navii footpath stretched in a black strip through the darkness.

Kirsha shivered—he felt the cold, heavy earth under his bare feet ; the cold air pressed against his bare knees, the cold moist freshness of the night blew against his half-bared breast. He heard his father ask in a low voice :

" Kirsha, are you not afraid ? "

" No," whispered Kirsha, as he breathed in the fresh aroma of the dew and the light mist.

The light of the moon was seductive with mystery. She smiled with her lifeless, tranquil face, and appeared to be saying :

" What was will be again. What was will happen more than once."

The night was peaceful and clear. They walked a long time—Trirodov and Kirsha, and some distance behind them the quiet Grisha followed. At last there appeared, quite near, peering through the mist, the low white cemetery wall. Another road cut across theirs. Quite narrow, its worn cobblestones gleamed dimly in the moonlight. The road of the living and the road of the dead crossed each other at the entrance of the cemetery. In the field near the crossing several mounds were visible—they were the unmarked graves of suicides and convicts.

The whole neighbourhood, bewitched with mystery and fear, seemed oppressed. The flat field stretched far—all enveloped in a light mist. Far to the left, the town fires showed their vague glimmers through the mist—and marked off by the wall of mist, the town seemed to be very distant, and to be guarding jealously from the fields of night the tumultuous voices of life.

An old witch, grey, and all bent, appeared from somewhere ; she swung a crutch and stumbled on in haste. She was mumbling angrily :

" It doesn't smell of our spirit. Strangers have come ! Why have they come ? What can strangers want here ? What are they seeking ? They'll find what they don't want to find. Ours will see them, and will tear them to pieces, and will scatter the pieces before all the winds."

Suddenly there was a weird rustle, there rose all about them the squeak of piping little voices, and the sounds of a confused scampering. At the crosspaths there darted in all directions, as thick as dust, countless hordes of grey sprites and evil spirits. Their running was so impetuous that they could have borne along with them every living, weak-willed soul. And it could already be seen that running in their midst were the pitiful souls of little people. Kirsha whispered in a voice full of fear :

" Quicker, quicker into the ring ! They will bear us away if we don't mark ourselves in."

Trirodov called quietly :

" Come here, come here, quiet boy, draw a circle around us with your nocturnal little stick."

They no sooner had succeeded in marking themselves in with the magic line than the dead began to pass down the Navii path. The throng of the dead, submitting to some evil malediction, walked towards the town. The spectres walked in the nocturnal silence and the traces they left behind them were light, curious, and hardly distinguishable. Whispered conversations were heard—lifeless words. The dead walked at random, without any defined order. At the beginning the voices merged into a general drone, and only afterwards, by straining one's ears, it was possible to distinguish separate words and whole phrases.

" Be good yourself, that's the chief thing."

" For mercy's sake—what perversion, what immorality ! "

" Plenty of food and plenty of clothes—what more can one want ? "

" I haven't sinned much."

" That's what they deserve. Kisses are not for them."

In the beginning all the dead fused into one dark, grey mass. But gradually, if one looked intently one could distinguish the separate corpses.

One nobleman who passed by had a cap with a red band on his head ; he was saying with calm and deliberation :

" The divine right of ownership should be inviolable. We and our ancestors have built up the Russian land."

Another of the same class, who walked beside him, remarked :

128

" My motto—autocracy, orthodoxy, and nationality. My credo—a strong redeeming power."

A priest in a black vestment swung a censer, and cried in a tenor voice :

" Every soul should submit to sovereign dominion. The hand that gives will not grow poorer."

A wise muzhik passed by muttering :

" We know everything, but are not saying anything just yet. When you don't know anything they leave you alone. Only you can't cover up your mouth with a handkerchief."

Several soldiers walked past together. They bawled their indecorous songs. Their faces were grey-red in colour. They stank of sweat, putrescence, bad tobacco, and vodka.

" I have laid down my stomach for my faith, my Tsar, and my Fatherland," a smart young colonel was saying.

After him came a thin man with the face of a Jesuit and cried out loudly :

" Russia for the Russians ! "

A stout merchant kept on repeating :

" If you don't cheat you can't sell your goods. Even a fur coat might be turned inside out. Your penny makes you well thought of anywhere."

An austere, freckled woman was saying :

" Beat me, seeing that I'm your woman, but there's no law that'll let you tie up with a girl so long as you've got a wife living."

A muzhik walked at her side, a dirty, ill-smelling fellow, who said nothing and hiccuped.

Once more there was a nobleman, large, stout, bristling, savage-looking. He ranted :

" Hang them ! Flog them ! "

129

Trirodov turned to Kirsha :

" Don't be afraid, Kirsha— these are dead words."

Kirsha silently nodded his head.

A mistress and her servant-maid walked together and exchanged quarrelsome words.

" God didn't make all the trees in the forest alike. I am a white bone, you are a black bone. I am a gentlewoman, you are a peasant-woman."

" You may be a gentlewoman, yet trash."

" Maybe trash, but still from the gentry."

Quite close to the magic line there was an apparent effort on the part of an elegantly dressed woman and a young man of the breed of dandies to emerge from the general throng. They had been only recently buried, and they exhaled the odour of fresh corpses. The woman coquettishly moved her half-putrefied lips and complained in a hoarse, creaking voice :

" They've forced us to walk with all these *Khams*.* They might have let us walk separately from all this common folk."

The dandy suddenly complained in a squeaking voice :

" Be careful, there, muzhik, don't nudge. What a dirty fellow ! "

The muzhik had evidently only just jumped out of his grave ; he was barely awake, and he had not yet realized himself or understood his condition. He was all dishevelled and in rags. His eyes were turbid. Curses and indecent words issued from his dead lips. He was angry because he had been disturbed, and he bawled :

" By what right ? You are lying there and not

* See note on page 44.

130

doing any one any harm, and are roused and made to walk along. What new rules have they got for us—disturbing the dead! You've only just found your earth—when up you must be and moving."

Unsteady on his feet, the muzhik continued to pour out his coarse abuse; when he saw Trirodov he opened his eyes wide and went straight to him. He was blindly conscious of being in the presence of a stranger and an enemy and he wished to destroy him. Kirsha trembled and grew pale. He clung to his father in fear. The quiet boy, retaining his tranquil sadness, stood at their side, like an angel on guard.

The muzhik touched the enchanted line. Pain and terror transpierced him. He stared with his dead eyes, but quickly lowered them; as he was unable to withstand the look of the living, he fell with his forehead to the ground just beyond the line and begged for mercy.

" Go ! " said Trirodov.

The muzhik rose to his feet and scampered away. But he soon paused, and again burst out into abuse; then ran farther.

Two lean, poorly dressed boys, with green faces, walked by. The rags which bound their feet hung loosely. One of them said :

" Do you understand ? They tormented me, tyrannized over me. I ran away and they caught me again—I had no strength left. I went to the garret and strangled myself. I don't know what I shall get for it now."

The other green boy replied :

" As for me, I was beaten with salted rods. My hands are quite clean."

131

"Yes, you are lucky," said the first boy enviously. "You will get a little golden wreath, but what will happen to me?"

"I will entreat the angels, the archangels, the cherubim and the seraphim for you—give me but your full name and address."

"My sin is quite a big one, and my name is Mitka Sosipatrov, from Nizhniya Kolotilovka."

"Don't be afraid," said the birched boy. "As soon as they let me in to the upper chambers, I will at once fall at the feet of the Virgin Mary until you are forgiven."

"Yes, do me this great favour."

Kirsha stood pale. His eyes sparkled. He trembled from head to foot and kept on repeating:

"Mamma, come to me! Mamma, come to me!"

A radiant apparition suddenly appeared in the throng, and Kirsha throbbed with joy. Kirsha's mother passed by—all white, all lovely, all gentle. She turned her tranquil eyes upon her dear ones and whispered:

"I will come."

Kirsha, transported with a quiet joy, stood motionless. His eyes gleamed like the eyes of the quiet angel who stood there on guard.

Again the dead throng moved on. A governor passed by. All his figure breathed might and majesty. Yet hardly awake, he grumbled:

"Make way for the Russian Governor! I'll have no patience with you. I will not permit it! You cannot frighten me. What! Feed the hungry, you say?"

He appeared, as it were, to awaken at these

words; he looked around him and said in great astonishment, as he shrugged his shoulders :

"What a strange disorder! How did I get into this crowd? Where is the police?"

Then he suddenly bawled out :

"Let the Cossacks come!"

In response to the Governor's cry a detachment of Cossacks came flying. Without noticing Trirodov and the children, they swept along past them and savagely flourished their *nagaikas*.* The dead, pressed from behind by the Cossacks' horses, became a confused, wavering mass, and answered with malignant laughter to the blows of the *nagaikas* upon their lifeless bodies.

The grey witch sat down on a near-by stone and shook with her hideous, creaking laughter.

* Whips.

CHAPTER XIV

ELISAVETA dressed herself up as a boy. She loved
to do this and she did it quite often; so tedious
is the monotony of our lives that even a change of
dress furnishes a diversion!

Elisaveta put on a white sailor-jacket with a
blue collar, and blue knee-breeches which revealed
the beauty and grace of her sunburnt lower limbs;
she put on a cap, took a fishing-rod and went to
the river. Elisaveta looked like a rather tall strip-
ling of fourteen in this dress.

It was quiet and bright on the river's bank.
Elisaveta sat down on a stone at the edge, lowered
her feet into the water, and watched the float. A
rowing-boat appeared. Elisaveta looked intently
and saw that it contained Stchemilov. The latter
called out:

" I say, my lad, if you belong here, can you
tell me if . . ."

Then he paused because Elisaveta was laughing.

" Well, who would have thought it—comrade
Elisaveta ? "

" You didn't recognize me, comrade ? " asked
Elisaveta with a merry laugh, as she approached
the landing-place where Stchemilov was already
fastening his boat.

" I must confess that I didn't know you at once,"
he replied, as he pressed her hand warmly. " I
have come for you. To-night we are to hold our
mass meeting."

134

"Is it really to-night?" asked Elisaveta.

She grew cold from agitation and confusion as she recalled that she had promised to speak that evening.

"Yes, to-night," said Stchemilov; "I hope you haven't changed your mind. You will speak, eh?"

"I thought it was to be to-morrow," she replied. "Just wait a moment. I'll get a small bundle of clothes. I will change at your place."

She quickly and gaily tripped up the bank. Stchemilov whistled as he sat waiting in the boat. Elisaveta soon reappeared, and deftly jumped into the boat.

It was necessary to row past the whole length of the town. No one on either bank recognized Elisaveta in her boy's attire. Stchemilov's house, a cabin in the middle of a vegetable garden, stood on a steep bank of the river, just along the edge of the town.

No one had yet arrived at the house. Elisaveta picked up a periodical which lay on the table and asked:

"Tell me, comrade, how do you like these verses?"

Stchemilov looked at the periodical, open at a page which contained Trirodov's verses. He smiled and said:

"What shall I say? His revolutionary poems are not bad. Nowadays, however, everybody writes them. As for his other works, they are not written about us. Noblemen's delights are not for us."

"It's a long time since I've been here," said Elisaveta. "What a mess you've got here."

135

"A house without a mistress," answered Stchemilov, rather confused.

Elisaveta began to put things in order and to clean and to scrub. She moved about with agile grace. Stchemilov admired her graceful limbs; it was fascinating to watch the play of the muscles under the brown skin of her calves. He exclaimed in a clear, almost ecstatic voice:

"How graceful you are, Elisaveta! Like a statue! I never saw such arms and legs."

"I feel embarrassed, comrade Aleksei. You praise me to my eyes as if I were a charming piece of property."

Stchemilov suddenly flushed with embarrassment; his habitual self-assurance appeared to have left him unexpectedly. He breathed heavily and stammered out in confusion:

"Comrade Elisaveta, you are a fine person. Don't be offended at my words. I love you. I know that for you social inequality is a silly thing; and you know that for me your money is of no account. Now if I am not repugnant to you . . ."

Elisaveta stood before him calm and yet sad, and as she dried her hands, grown red from the cold water, with a towel, she said quietly:

"Forgive me, comrade Aleksei—you are right about my views, but I love another."

She herself did not know how these words came to be spoken. Love another! So unexpectedly the secret of her heart revealed itself in superficial words. But did he love her, that other one?

They were both flustered. Stchemilov strove heroically to control his agitation. As he looked with his confused eyes into her clear blue ones he said :

"Forgive me, Elisaveta, and forget what I have said. I didn't guess right that time and did the wrong thing. I didn't think that you'd love him. Don't be angry at me and don't despise me."

"Enough, Aleksei," said Elisaveta tenderly. "You know how I respect you. We are friends. Give me your hand."

Stchemilov gave her hand a tight, comradely pressure, then bent down and kissed it. Elisaveta drew nearer to him and kissed his lips with a tranquil, innocent, delicious kiss, such as a sister gives a brother. Then she snatched up her bundle and ran into the passage, one of the doors of which led to a small storeroom where the literature was kept in a trunk under the floor.

She ran into Kiril on the way.

"Is Aleksei home, my lad ?"

"Yes," said Elisaveta ; " enter, comrade Kiril."

When Kiril heard the familiar voice and, lifting his eyes, saw plaits of hair wound around the lad's head, he was astonished. He was very much embarrassed upon recognizing Elisaveta. She hid herself behind the door of the storeroom, while Kiril blundered for a long time in the dark hall, unable in his confusion to find the door.

Others began to come in : there was the school-instructor Bodeyev, instructor Voronok of the town school, and the imported orator, who came accompanied by Alkina.

Elisaveta was attired by now in a simple dark blue dress.

"It's time to start," said Stchemilov.

.137

Once seated in the rowing-boat, the members of the party· became silent and slightly nervous. Only the new-comer was perfectly calm—he was used to it. Near-sighted, he looked indifferently out of his spectacles, now one side, now the other, and told bits of news while smoking one cigarette after another. He was young, tall, and flat-chested. He had a lean face, long, smooth, chestnut-coloured hair, and a scant beard. His flat round cap, reddish in the sun, gave him the look of an artisan.

It had begun to grow dark by the time they disembarked at the appointed place. There was still a half-verst to go through the wood on foot. The evening twilight seemed oppressed under the eternal vaults of the wood ; it hummed and rustled with barely audible noises and the sad whisperings of stealthy beings.

They gathered at last in a large glade in the midst of a tall, dense wood. The moon was already high in the sky, and the black shadows of the trees crept across half of the glade. The trees were intensely still and pensive, as if they wished to listen to the words of these people who had collected at their feet. But they really did not care to listen—they had their own life and were indifferent to all these people. And they suffered neither joy nor sadness at sheltering in their dark shade many young girls who were in love with the dream of liberation—among them Elisaveta, who was also in love with this dream, and who created for it a temple of young passion and embroidered into this dream's design the image of a living man in a mysterious house. She was deliciously in love and painfully agitated by the

138

sudden acknowledgment she made of her love in her poignantly sweet words, " I love another."

In the dark shade of the trees were red glimmering cigarettes and pipes. The odour of tobacco mingled with the fresh, nocturnal coolness and gave it a sweet piquancy. Piquant also, in the nocturnal stillness, were the sounds of the young, eager voices. And these people had no concern with the mystery of the wood made audible in the silence. The people behaved as if they were at home. They sat about and walked and met each other and chatted. Sometimes, when the din of talk grew too loud, the leaders of the meeting uttered their warnings. Then the voices were lowered.

There were about three hundred people of all kinds—labouring men, young people from schools, young Jews, and very many girls. All the young Jews and Jewesses of the town had come. They were agitated more than the rest and their speech nearly always passed into a violent commotion. They awaited so much, they hoped so passionately ! They were so painfully in love with the dream of liberation !

Some of the instructresses from Trirodov's colony were also here, among them the sad Nadezhda and the ecstatic Maria. There were quite a number of schoolboys and schoolgirls present. These tried to act at ease, to show that it was not their first occasion of the sort. There were also many college students, both men and women. The young were burning with joyous unrest. But all who had gathered were intensely agitated. It was the sweet agitation of their dream of liberation ;

how tenderly and how passionately they were in love with it ! And in more than one young heart virginal passion flowed together with the dream of liberation ; young passionate love flamed with a great fire in the joy of liberation, making one of liberation and love, of revolt and sacrifice, of wine and blood—what delicious mystery in love thirsting and yielding ! And more than one pair of eyes sparkled at the sight of a beloved image, and more than one pair of lips whispered :

" And he's here ! "

" And she's here ! "

In the shade, under the trees, where indiscreet glances could not penetrate, impatient lips met in a quick, timid kiss. And the first words were :

" I'm not late, comrade ? "

" No, comrade Natalya, you are in time."

" Let us go over there, comrade Valentine.

The names were pronounced tenderly.

A man in a cap, black shirt,* and high boots, walked up to Elisaveta. He had a small black beard and moustache, and his face, which was both familiar and unfamiliar, had something in it that stirred her. He exclaimed :

" Elisaveta, you don't recognize me ? "

She recognized him at once by his voice. A warmth suffused her. She laughed and said joyously :

" I knew you by your voice alone. Your beard and moustache make you wholly unrecognizable."

" They are glued on," explained Trirodov.

* Members of the Social Revolutionary Party are supposed to wear black shirts, those of the Social Democratic Party red.

They conversed. He heard some one whisper behind his back:

"That is comrade Elisaveta. She's considered the first beauty in our town."

Trirodov was for some reason overjoyed at these words, partly because Elisaveta heard them and blushed so furiously that even the dim moonlight could not hide her blushes.

A few detectives had also managed to find their way here, and there was even one provocateur. These chattels alone knew that the police had information about the meeting and that the wood would shortly be encircled by the Cossacks.

Conversations were kept up among small groups for some time before the meeting opened. The agitators discussed matters with labouring men who were not in the party. The more interesting people were introduced to the invited speaker.

Stchemilov's loud voice rang out:

"Comrades, attention. I propose comrade Abram as chairman."

"Agreed, agreed," came suppressed voices from every side.

Comrade Abram took his place on a high stump of a hewn-down tree. The speeches began. Elisaveta was nervous until it came her turn to speak. She was troubled with pain and fear because she knew that Trirodov would hear her.

Proud, brave watchwords and bold instructions were heard. The provocateur also made a speech. He urged them to an immediate armed revolt. Some one's voice called out:

"Comrades—this man's a provocateur!"

There was a commotion. The provocateur

shouted something in his defence. He was promptly
jostled out.

Then Stchemilov spoke ; he was followed by the
invited orator. Elisaveta's agitation grew.

But when the chairman said, " Comrade Elisaveta, the word belongs to you," she suddenly
became calm and, having ascended the high stump
that served as the platform, began to speak. Her
deep, measured voice carried far. Some one
seemed to echo it in the wood—it was like a fantastic, restless din. A being beloved by her and
near to her sat there and listened ; her beloved,
near comrades also listened. Hundreds of attentive eyes followed her, and the dear friendly looks,
converging like lances under a shield, held her
very high in the pure atmosphere of happiness.

The sweet moments of joy passed by like a
short dream. She ended her speech and came
down among the audience, where she was received
with flattering comments and strong pressures of
the hand—sometimes, it must be confessed, a little
over-strong.

" I say, comrade, you'll break my hand. How
strong you are ! "

And his face would also break into a joyous smile.

The speeches ended. The songs began. The
wood re-echoed with proud, brave words, with a
song of freedom and revolt. Suddenly the song
stopped short, a confused murmur ran through
the crowd. Some one shouted :

" The Cossacks ! "

Some one shouted :

" Run, comrades ! "

142

Some one ran.   Some one shouted :
" Be calm, comrades ! "

The Cossacks had hid themselves in the wood
a couple of versts from the meeting. Many of
them had managed to take several drinks. As
they sat around their bonfires they began to sing
a gay, noisy, indecent song, but their officers
enjoined silence.

A spy came running ; he whispered something
to the colonel. Soon a command was given. The
Cossacks jumped quickly on their horses and rode
away, leaving the half-consumed bonfire behind
them. The dry faggots and the grass smouldered
a long time. The forest caught fire.*

" What's the matter ? " asked Elisaveta.
Some one whispered quickly :
" Do you hear, it's the Cossacks ! I wonder
which side they are coming from. It's hard to
tell which way to run."
" They are coming from town," said some one.
" The only thing to do is to go towards Opalikha."
The leaders began to give orders :
" Comrades, be calm. Scatter as quickly as
possible. Don't jostle. The road to Dubky is
clear."
A number of horses' heads suddenly appeared
from among the trees quiet close to Elisaveta,
and their dumb but good eyes looked on incom-
prehensibly. The crowd of young people began

* Forest fires are one of the numerous problems of Russia.
They seem to be difficult to put out, and sometimes go on for
weeks. Hence the numerous references in the following pages
to the constant odour of forest flames.

143

to run, and carried Elisaveta along with them. She was seized by a feeling of stupor. She thought :

" What's the use of running ? They'll overtake us and drive us wherever they will."

But she had not enough strength to pause. They were all running, and she with them. Another detachment of Cossacks appeared in front of them. Cries and wails went up from the crowd, which began to scatter in all directions. The Cossacks came on, as it were, in a broad chain.

Many managed to break through, some with blood-stained faces and torn clothes. The others were driven forward from the rear and the sides and gradually became a compact mass. It was evident that the Cossacks were trying to get the crowd into the middle of the glade. Those who had broken through the ring at the very beginning had some hope of escape. There were about a hundred people in the ring. They were driven towards the town, and those who tried to escape were lashed with the *nagaika*.

A few shots resounded in the distance. The provocateur fired the first shot—into the air. This aroused the anger of the Cossacks, who began to shoot at those who ran.

Elisaveta and Alkina managed to escape the first ring together. But they could hear all around them the cries of the Cossacks. They paused and pressed close to an old oak, not knowing which way to turn. They were joined by Trirodov.

" Follow me," he said to them ; " I think I can find a less dangerous place."

" What has become of our invited speaker ? " asked Alkina.

144

" Don't worry about that," was the impatient reply ; " he was the first to be attended to. He's out of danger now. You'd better go on quickly."

He walked confidently through the bushes and they followed him.

The sounds made by the patrols of Cossacks were heard on every side. Suddenly the runners were confronted by the figure of a Cossack who stepped out from the bushes. He aimed his *nagaika* at Elisaveta, but she, falling headlong, escaped the brunt of the blow. The Cossack bent down, caught Elisaveta by her plait of hair, and began to drag her after him. Elisaveta cried out from pain. Trirodov pulled out a revolver and shot him almost without taking aim. The Cossack cried out and let his victim go. All three then made their way through the bushes. A deep hollow cut their progress short.

" Well, we are almost out of danger here," said Trirodov.

They lowered themselves, almost rolled down to the bottom of the hollow. Their faces and hands bore scratches and their clothes were torn. On one of the sloping sides of the hollow they found a deep recess made by the rains, and now obscured by the bushes ; and here they hid themselves.

" Presently we'll make for the river-bank," said Trirodov. " We are quite close to it."

Suddenly they heard the crackle of breaking twigs above them, followed by a revolver-shot and out-cries. A running figure defined itself in the dark.

" Kiril ! " called Elisaveta in a whisper, " come here."

Kiril heard her, and threw himself through the

145

bushes in the direction of the hiding-place. Elisaveta could now see, quite close to her, his fatigued, desperate eyes. There was a loud, near report of a revolver. Kiril reeled; there was the sound of breaking twigs as he fell heavily and rolled down the hollow.

Presently a running Cossack came down precipitately from above. He brushed so closely past them that a twig caught by his body struck Alkina's shoulder. But Alkina did not stir; pale, slender, and calm, she stood tightly pressing her body against the almost perpendicular wall of their refuge. The Cossack bent over Kiril, examined him attentively, then muttered as he straightened himself:

"Well, there's no breath left in him. You're done for, my clever chap."

Then he turned to climb back again. When the rustle of the parted bushes ceased Trirodov said:

"Now we must walk carefully along this hollow until we come to the river. There is a bend in the river here in the direction of the town—we are bound to get somewhere almost across from my place. Then we must find our way to the other side somehow or other."

Slowly and cautiously they made their way through the thick growths of the hollow. They walked in the dark—Trirodov and the two with him, his chance one and his fated one, sent him by the two Moiræ, Aisa and Ananke.*

* These two Greek Fates are important and recurring symbols in Sologub's philosophy. The world of Aisa is the world of chaos and chance, in which man is too often lost in trying to emerge from it. The people who belong to Ananke are those who, acting of necessity, define their world clearly and conquer chaos. Theirs is the immutable truth. See also Introduction.

The bushes became moist and a fresh breeze blew from the river. Then Alkina came close to Trirodov and whispered to him :

" If you are glad that she loves you, tell me, and I will share your gladness."

Trirodov pressed her hand warmly.

The quiet, dim river lay before them. Beyond it the labours and dangers of life created by the dream of liberation awaited them.

Soon the mist would rise above the river under the cold and witching moon—soon the misty veil of fantasy would lighten the tedious and commonplace life, and behind the veil of mist there would rise in dim outlines another kind of life, creative and unattainable.

CHAPTER XV

THAT night the streets of Skorodozh were alive with noises—which gradually died away. The frightened townsmen sprang from their warm beds, and peering through the half-opened blinds into the dark streets saw those who had been caught in the woods led away in the custody of the Cossacks. Then when the stamp of horses' hoofs and the hum of human voices subsided, the residents quietly went back to their beds, and were soon asleep. Lady Godiva would have been highly pleased with such modest people: they looked, yet did not show themselves, and did not hinder.

They went to bed again, and muttered something to their wives. The freedom-loving bourgeois grumbled:

" They won't let you sleep. The horses' hoofs make such a noise. They might employ bicycles instead of horses."

The night passed like a nightmare for many. It seemed to grip all life with a cold apprehensiveness, and burdened one's soul with a hate towards the earthly life which suffered agony from its bondage to the flaming, exultant Dragon. Why did he exult? Was it because we beings of the earth are evil and cruel, and love to torment, to see drops of blood and tears?

Our dark, earthly nature is suffused with a cruel voluptuousness. Such is the imperfection

148

of the human breed that a single human vessel contains all the deepest ecstasies of love and all the lowest delights of lust, and the mixture is poisoned with shame and with pain—and with the desire for shame and pain. From one fountain come both the gladdening raptures and the gladdening lusts of the passions. We torment others only because it gives us joy.

After the agonies on the way from the wood, after a search had been made, many of the prisoners were dispatched to prison. Others were set free.

A restless, sluggish, and unfriendly morning rose over the city. From the wood, just beyond the town, came the half-pleasant, half-disagreeable odour of a forest fire.

The news about the two dead victims, Kiril and another workman, Kliukin, a family man, soon spread. Their comrades were excited.

The corpses had been taken to the mortuary of the town hospital. A large crowd, grave, silent, and resolute in mood, had gathered quite early near the mortuary. It mostly consisted of labouring men, and their wives and children. The large square in front of the hospital, with its dirty, unpaved spots, its trampled grass, its grey, gloomy little shops, appeared oppressed by an atmosphere of early morning fatigue. The slant rays of the rising Dragon, veiled with a light mist, fell upon the scowling faces of the crowd as indifferently as upon the fence or the closed gates. The Ancient Dragon is not our sun.

The faces of those who stood near the closed gates were scowling. No one was permitted to enter the hospital. Within, preparations were going on for a secret burial of the victims. Tumultuous voices of anger rose in the crowd.

A detachment of Cossacks soon appeared on the scene. They came on quickly, and paused near the crowd. The beautiful smooth horses trembled sensitively. The riders were handsome, sun-burnt, black-eyed, and black-browed; their black hair, not cut in the military fashion, was visible from under their high hats. The women in the crowd looked at them now and then with involuntary admiration.

The tumult increased, the crowd continued to grow. The whole square was alive with people. There seemed to be imminent danger of a bloody collision.

Trirodov went that morning to the chief of the rural police and to the officer of the gendarmerie. He wished to convince them that a secret burial would only add to the workers' excitement. The chief listened to him in a dull way, and kept on repeating :

" Impossible. I can't . . ."

He gazed down persistently. This caused his neck to look tight, poured out like copper. And he kept on turning his ring round his finger as if it were a talisman protecting him from hostile calumny.

The colonel of the gendarmes proved easier to deal with. In the end Trirodov succeeded in obtaining an order for the surrender of the bodies of the dead men to their families.

The chief of the rural police arrived in the square. The crowd greeted him with discordant

150

and angry cries. He stood up in his trap and motioned with his hand. Every one grew silent. He addressed them:

"Would you like to bury them yourselves? Very well, you shall have them. Only be careful that nothing happens which shouldn't happen. In any case, the Cossacks will be present, in an emergency. And now I will see that the bodies of your comrades are delivered to you."

CHAPTER XVI

THE sun was already high when Elisaveta awoke. She quickly recalled all that happened the night before. She took but little time in dressing and, urged by a suppressed excitement, was soon on the way to Trirodov in her carriage. Trirodov met her at the gates. He was returning from town, and he told her briefly about his conferences with the authorities. Elisaveta said resolutely :

" I want to see the family of the dead man."

" I don't know where they live. We shall have to see Voronok first. He has all the information."

" Shall we find him at home now ? "

" I think so," said Trirodov. " If he's at home we'll all start together."

They drove off. The dusty road trailed behind the rapid wheels, and revealed vistas of depressing commonplaceness. The light dust, stirred by the wheels into the sultry air, trailed behind the carriage like a long serpent. The high flaming Dragon looked down from his inaccessible sky with furious eyes upon the impoverished earth. There was a thirst for blood in the hot glister of his rays, and there was a soaring exultation because men had shed some priceless drops of the wine of life. In the midst of these open, heat-swept spaces, Trirodov, drawn at this moment into the crowded town life, was addressing his companion in dull, everyday words :

" They searched many houses early this morning.

152

They found a great deal of literature at Stchemi-lov's. He's been arrested."

He also repeated the rumour of whippings at the police-station. Elisaveta was silent.

Voronok's house was situated in a very convenient place, somewhere between the centre of the town and the factory section. This house had many visitors because Voronok was an assiduous worker in the local Social Democratic Party. His chief function was to carry on propaganda among the working men and the young, and incidentally to instil into them party views and a true understanding of the aims of the working classes.

Young boys used to come to Voronok, his pupils from the town school, and these brought their comrades and acquaintances with them—those whom they met at home or by chance. They were for the most part charming, sincere, and intelligent youngsters, but very dishevelled and very self-conscious. Voronok taught them very heartily and with good results. They assimilated his teachings : a sympathy towards the working proletariat, a hate towards the satiated bourgeois, a consciousness of the irreconcilability of the interests of the two classes, and a few random facts from history. The ragamuffins from the town school invariably opened every visit to Voronok by complaining against the school rules and the inspector. They complained chiefly about trifles. They would say with an injured air :

" They compel us to wear official badges upon our caps."

" They treat us as if we were little children."

153

" They brand us, so that every one may know that we are the boys of the town school."

" They force us to cut our hair; why should our hair worry them ? "

Voronok sympathized with them fully. This helped him to keep them in a state of revolt. Their no less unkempt friends, who did not go to school, also found something to complain about—if not against their parents, then against the police, indeed against anything that occurred to them. But their complaints did not contain quite that poison and steadiness which was instilled into the schoolboys with all the force of a school. Voronok used to give both classes pamphlets that cost a kopeck and were intensely strict in their party purity.

The younger of the working men also used to come to Voronok's house. There were still others, a ragged, grumbling lot, who appeared to carry an air of eternal injury with them, as if they had lost all capacity for smiling and jesting. Voronok took great pains to read the pamphlets with them, and to explain to them anything that was not especially clear. Regular hours were allotted for these readings and conversations. By such means Voronok succeeded in developing the desired mood in his visitors ; all the party shibboleths were assimilated by them quickly and thoroughly. He also gave them books for home reading. Many used to buy this literature occasionally.

In this manner, a flood of books and pamphlets continually poured through Voronok's house. Sometimes he selected whole libraries, and sent them by trustworthy people through the villages.

154

Elisaveta and Trirodov found Voronok at home. He did not much resemble a party workman; he was gracious, spoke little, and produced the impression of a reserved, well-trained man. He always wore starched linen, a high collar, a fashionable tie and a bowler hat. He had his hair trimmed short, and his beard was most neatly brushed.

" I will go with you, with pleasure," said Voronok amiably.

He seized his thin cane, put on his bowler hat, took a cursory glance of himself in the mirror, and said again :

" I'm ready. But perhaps you'd like to rest ? "

They declined, and the three of them started off. The painful silence of the bright streets hovered about them stealthily and expectantly. They seemed strangers among these wooden huts, depressing fences, and the tottering little bridges. They wanted to ask :

" Why are we going ? "

But this only seemed to bring them closer, and to make the quick beats of their hearts more friendly. The whole picture of the life of the poor was here in all its sordidness ; dirty, malicious children played here, and abused each other, and wrangled ; a drunkard reeled ; grey buckets swung on a grey wooden yoke across the shoulders of a grey woman in a worn grey dress.

There was everyday commonplaceness in the poverty of the house, where lay the hastily prepared yellow corpse. A pale-faced woman stood at its head, and wailed quietly and ceaselessly. Three pale, sandy-haired children came in and looked at the visitors ; their gaze was at once strange

155

and stupid, neither joyous nor sad, but dulled for ever.

Elisaveta went up to the woman. The blooming, rosy, graceful girl stood at the side of the pale, tear-eyed woman, and was quietly saying something to her; the latter was nodding her head and crooning unnecessary, belated words. Trirodov turned quietly to Voronok:

" Is any money needed ? "

Voronok whispered back:

" No, his comrades will bury him. We'll make a collection among ourselves. Afterwards the family will· need some money."

The day of the funeral arrived. The factories stopped work. There was a clear sky, and under it the turbulent crowd; the light currents of incense streamed in the air, and its sumptuous aroma mingled with the light odour of the smoke that came from the forest cinders. The schoolboys struck and went to the funeral. Some of the schoolgirls came also. The more timid ones remained in school.

The children from Trirodov's colony decided to come. They brought two wreaths with them. The quiet children came also. They kept by themselves and were silent.

The entire town police were present at the funeral. Even police from outlying districts were here. As always, petty provocateurs lurked among the crowd.

The crowd moved calmly and solemnly. Above it the wreaths swung, the red flowers glimmered vividly, the red ribbons fluttered. The Cossacks
156

rode alongside. There was austerity and suspicion in their looks—they were prepared to suppress any demonstration. The chanting of a prayer could be heard. Each time the subsided chant was renewed, the Cossacks listened with great intentness. No—it was only the prayer again.

Elisaveta and Trirodov walked with the crowd behind the coffin. They spoke of that which enraptures those who seek rapture and frightens those who seek repose. Poignant were Elisaveta's impressions as she stepped upon the sharp cobblestones of the dusty, littered pavement.

The road was long. The austere harmony was kept up for some time. At last the cemetery was reached. Some dejected moments were passed in waiting by the church. The last services were pronounced hurriedly.

The Cossacks moved about in bustling fashion, and as before formed a circle around the throng.

The coffin was carried out of the church. The wreaths swung once more above the crowd, which moved on chanting.

Suddenly the women's lament grew louder—the women's lament above the grave. The instructor Bodeyev then stood at the head of the coffin. He began in his shrilly-thin, but far-carrying voice :

" Comrades, we have gathered to-day at the grave of our brother . . ."

The colonel of the gendarmes went up to him, and said sternly :

." It is forbidden. I must ask you to do without speeches or demonstrations."

Bodeyev asked in astonishment :

" But why ? "

157

"No, I must ask you not to. It is forbidden," said the colonel dryly.

Bodeyev shrugged his shoulders and remarked as he moved away:

"I submit to brute strength."

"To the law," the officer in the blue uniform corrected him sharply.

The dead man's comrades, crowding near the grave, followed one another with handfuls of soil, which they threw on the coffin. The damp, heavy soil struck the coffin with a hollow sound.

The grave was being filled up. Every one stood silently, and as silently left the spot.

Then suddenly a voice was heard.

And in an instant the whole crowd began to sing words of a proud, melancholy, revolutionary song. The Cossacks looked on morosely. The command was given. The Cossacks quickly mounted their horses. The singing stopped abruptly.

Once outside the cemetery gates, Elisaveta said:

"I am hungry!"

"Let's go to my place," suggested Trirodov.

"Thank you," said Elisaveta. "But I'd rather go to some tavern."

Trirodov looked at her in astonishment, but made no objection. He understood her curiosity.

The tavern was crowded and noisy. Trirodov and Elisaveta sat down near the window, at a small table covered with a dirty, spotted cloth. They ordered cold meat and light beer.

At one of the tables, a young man in a red shirt

sat drinking. He was in a boastful mood. Behind his ear stuck a cigarette. The fellow intruded upon his neighbours, and shouted :

" Who's drunk ? "

" Well, who ? " asked a young working man at the next table contemptuously.

" I am drunk ! " exclaimed the drunkard in the red shirt. "And who am I, do you know, eh ? "

" Yes, who are you ? What sort of a bird are you ? " asked the young working man in the black calico blouse derisively.

" I am Borodulin ! " said the drunkard, and there was an expression on his face as if he had pronounced a famous name.

His neighbours roared with laughter, and shouted coarse, derisive words. The fellow in the red shirt cried angrily :

" What do you think ? Is Borodulin, in your opinion, a peasant ? "

The working man in the black blouse began to get annoyed. His lean cheeks grew red. He sprang from his place, and shouted angrily :

" Well, who are you ? Answer."

" I'm a peasant on my passport. An army reserve man. But that's not all, I assure you," said Borodulin.

" Well, who then are you ? " repeated the young working man angrily, as he took a step towards him.

" And do you know what I am on my card ? Can you guess ? " asked Borodulin.

He blinked, and tried to look important. The comrades of the young working man tried to

159

dissuade him from pursuing his inquiries, and whispered as they drew him away :

"Don't waste your time on him. He's a nobody."

"I'm a detective, that's what I am!" said Borodulin with his important air.

The working man in the black blouse spat contemptuously and walked back to his table. Borodulin went on :

"You think I'm out of my senses. No, old chap, you're mistaken. I'm an experienced man. What do you think of me now? I'm a detective. I can arrest any one!"

The men at the neighbouring tables listened to him and exchanged glances. Borodulin went on boasting.

"Suppose I put the police on to you?" asked a merchant at one of the middle tables angrily. His small black eyes sparkled.

Borodulin burst out laughing, and shouted :

"I have the police in the hollow of my hand. That's where I have them."

The customers grumbled. Threats were heard :

"You'd better go away while you're still whole."

He paid his bill and left. Suddenly the sound of a crowd gathering in the street was heard. From the window Elisaveta and Trirodov could see the fellow in the red shirt sauntering backwards and forwards in the street, only a few paces from the tavern, and annoying the passers-by. He could be heard shouting :

"I'll report you! I'll arrest you! Hand over your ten kopecks."

160

Many, afraid of him, acceded to his request. Borodulin clutched at every passer-by. He threw off the men's caps, he pinched the women, while he pulled young boys by the ear. The women ran from him shrieking. The more timid men also ran. The bolder ones paused in menacing attitudes. These Borodulin did not dare to molest. Small boys ran behind him in a crowd, laughing and hooting. Borodulin grumbled.

"You'd better look out. Do you know who I am?"

"Well, who are you?" asked a young fellow whom he jostled. "You're a pothouse plug."

A crowd formed round them. Their faces were morose and unfriendly. Borodulin was afraid, but he showed a bold front and boasted. He shouted:

"Two or three of you will be necessary!"

A sudden attack was made upon Borodulin. A young robust fellow sprang forward from the crowd with a shout, an enormous cobblestone in his hand.

"What's this dog showing his teeth for?"

He hit Borodulin on the head with the stone. It was unfortunately too well aimed. Borodulin fell. Others attacked him as he lay there. The workman who hit him with the stone made his escape.

Elisaveta and Trirodov were looking out of the window. Trirodov exclaimed:

"The Cossacks!"

The people in the street scattered in all directions. The mutilated corpse lay in a pool of blood on the pavement.

161

CHAPTER XVII

OSTROV caused Trirodov a great deal of annoyance. More than once Trirodov returned to the earlier circumstances of their acquaintance and to their recent meeting at Skorodozh.

The week having elapsed, Ostrov paid Trirodov another visit. That whole week Ostrov could not get rid of his confusion and uneasiness. The details of his meeting with Trirodov became absurdly entangled in his memory. He kept on forgetting the day of the week it was. The week passed rather quickly for him. This was possibly due to his having made several interesting acquaintances. He had become quite a noticeable personage about town.

Ostrov made his visit late on Tuesday evening. He was received at once, and led into a chamber on the ground floor. Trirodov came in almost immediately. Not a little astonished, he asked unwillingly :

" Well, what can I do for you, Denis Alekseyevitch ? "

" I've come for the money," said Ostrov gruffly. " To receive the promised relief at your bountiful hands."

" I did not expect you until Wednesday," replied Trirodov.

" Why Wednesday when Tuesday is just as good ? " said Ostrov with a savage smile. " Or do you find it so hard to part with your cash ?

Have you become a bourgeois, Giorgiy Sergeye-vitch ? "

Trirodov suddenly appeared to recall something as, with a tinge of derision in his smile, he asked :

" I beg your pardon, Denis Alekseyevitch, I thought you were coming to-morrow, as was arranged. I haven't the money ready for you."

Ostrov was annoyed. His broad face grew dark. He exclaimed, his eyes red with anger :

" You asked me to come in a week, and I've come in a week. You don't expect me to come here forty times, do you ? I have other business. You've promised me the money, and so hand it over. You must loosen your purse-strings whether you like it or not."

He grew more savage with every word. In the end he struck the small round white table that stood on slender legs in front of him with his stout fist. Trirodov answered calmly :

" It is now Tuesday. That means the week is not up yet."

" What do you mean it isn't up ? " said Ostrov. " I came to see you on Tuesday. Do you count eight days in a week, in the French fashion ? You won't come off so easily."

" You came here on Wednesday," replied Trirodov. " And this is why I haven't the money ready for you."

Ostrov was unable to grasp the situation. He looked at Trirodov with some perplexity, and showed his irritation.

" What do you mean by saying that you haven't it ready ? Why should you get it ready ? All you've got to do is to take it out of your safe, count it out, and give it to me—that's the whole method of procedure. It isn't as if it were a lot of money—it's a mere trifle."

"It may be a trifle for some people. It isn't at all a trifle for me," said Trirodov.

"Don't pretend that you're poor! Some one might think you were a forsaken orphan! What do you expect us to believe?"

Trirodov rose from his seat, looked with stern intentness into Ostrov's eyes, and said resolutely:

"In a word, I can't give you the money to-day. Try to come here to-morrow about this time."

Ostrov rose involuntarily from his chair. He experienced a strange sensation, as if he were being lifted from his seat by his collar and forcibly led to the door. He fired his parting shot:

"Only don't think that you can pull wool over my eyes to-morrow. I'm not the sort of a chap whom you can feed on promises."

His small eyes gleamed malignantly. His broad jaws trembled savagely. His feet seemed to carry him to the door of themselves.

"No," answered Trirodov, "I do not intend to fool you. You will get your money to-morrow."

Ostrov came at the same hour next evening. This time he was led into Trirodov's study.

"Well," asked Ostrov rather impudently, "do you mean to give me the money? Or will you play the same farce once more?"

Trirodov pulled a bundle of bank-notes out of a drawer in his writing-table, and said as he gave them to Ostrov:

164

" Please count them. There should be two thousand."

Ostrov whistled and said gruffly :

" That's too little. I asked for much more."

" That's all you'll get," said Trirodov resolutely. " It ought to last you quite a while."

" Perhaps you will add a trifle," said Ostrov with a stupid smile.

" I can't," said Trirodov coldly.

" I can't leave town on this money," said Ostrov in a threatening voice.

Trirodov frowned, and looked sternly at Ostrov. New thoughts began to take shape in his mind, and he said :

" You won't find it to your advantage to remain, and everything you do here will be known to me."

" Very well, I'll go away," said Ostrov with a stupid smile. He took the money, counted it carefully, and put it into his greasy pocket. He was about to take his leave, but Trirodov detained him.

" Don't go yet. We'll have a talk."

At the same instant a quiet boy in his white clothes appeared from some dark corner. He paused behind Trirodov's chair, and looked at Ostrov. His wide dark eyes, looking out of his pale face, brought Ostrov into a state of painful dread. He lowered himself slowly into the chair near the writing-table. His head felt giddy. Then a strange mood of nonchalance and submission took possession of him. His face bore an expression of apathetic readiness to do everything that he might be commanded to do by some

165

one stronger than himself—whose will had conquered his. Trirodov looked attentively at Ostrov and said :

" Well, tell me what I want to know. I wish to hear from your own lips what you are doing here, and what you are up to. You couldn't have done much in such a short time, but you surely have found out something. Speak ! "

Ostrov sniggered rather stupidly, fidgeted as if he were sitting on springs, and said :

" Very well, I'll tell you something interesting and won't charge you a penny for it."

Trirodov, without taking off his heavy, fixed gaze from Ostrov's face, repeated :

" Speak ! "

The quiet boy looked with his eyes full of intense questioning straight into Ostrov's eyes.

" Do you know who killed the Chief of Police ? " asked Ostrov.

Trirodov was silent. Ostrov's whole body twitched as he kept up his absurd sniggering.

" He killed him and went away," went on Ostrov. " He made his escape by taking advantage of the confusion and the darkness, as the newspapers would say. The police have not caught him to this day, and the authorities do not even know who he is."

" And do you know ? " asked Trirodov in a cold, deliberate voice.

" I know, but I won't tell you," replied Ostrov rather venomously.

" You shall tell me," said Trirodov with conviction. Then he added in even a more loud, determined, and commanding voice :

" Tell me, who killed the Chief of Police ? "

Ostrov fell back into his chair. His red face became tinged with a sudden grey pallor. His eyes, now bloodshot, half closed like those of a prostrate doll with the eye mechanism in its stomach. There was witheredness, almost lifelessness, in Ostrov's voice :

" Poltinin."

" Your friend ? " asked Trirodov. " Well, go on."

" He is now being sought for," went on Ostrov in the same lifeless way.

" Why did Poltinin kill the Chief of Police ? "

Ostrov resumed his stupid snigger, and said :

" It's a matter of very delicate politics. That means, it simply had to be done. I won't tell you why. Indeed, I couldn't tell you if I really wished to. I don't know myself, I can only venture to guess. But what is a guess worth ? "

" Yes," said Trirodov, " it is quite true that it is impossible for you to know this. Continue your tale."

" This same affair," said Ostrov, " is a very profitable article for us just now. Indeed, an article in the budget, as they say."

" Why ? "

Trirodov's face did not reveal any astonishment, as Ostrov went on :

" We have Potseluytchikov among us, a very lively individual."

" A thief ? " asked Trirodov abruptly.

Ostrov smiled almost consciously, and said :

" Not exactly a thief, still one's got to be careful with him. An able man in his way."

Ostrov's eyes assumed a frankly insolent expression. Trirodov asked:

"What sort of relation has he to this article in your budget?"

"We send him out to the rich men of the place."

"To blackmail them?" asked Trirodov.

Ostrov replied with complete readiness:

"Precisely. Let us suppose that he comes to Mr. Moneybags. 'I have,' he tells him, 'a thing to tell you in confidence, a thing of great personal interest to you.' Left alone with Mr. Moneybags he says to him: 'Five hundred roubles, if you please!' The other, it goes without saying, is up on his hind legs. 'What for? What sort of demand is this?' 'I mean what I say,' says the other chap. 'Otherwise,' he says, 'I will put your eldest son in gaol. I can prove that your eldest son has had something to do with the murder of the gallant Chief of Police.'"

"They give?" asked Trirodov.

"Some give, some escort you out of the door," replied Ostrov.

"A lovely crowd!" observed Trirodov contemptuously. "And what may you be planning now?"

With the same involuntary obedience Ostrov told Trirodov how their company was conspiring to steal a miracle-performing ikon from a neighbouring monastery. The plan was to burn the ikon and to sell the precious stones with which it was covered. It was a difficult affair, as the ikon was under guard. But Ostrov's friends were counting on taking advantage of one of the summer feasts, when the monks, escorting distinguished pilgrims, would have drunk freely. The thieves had still a month in which to make preparations for the theft; they meant to make use of this time by becoming friendly with the monks, and in this way familiarize themselves with all the conditions.

Trirodov, having listened without interrupting, said to Ostrov:

"Forget that you have told me all this. Goodbye."

Ostrov gave a start. He appeared as if he had just awakened. Without comprehending the causes of his oppressive confusion he bade his host goodbye and left.

Trirodov decided that the bishop of the local diocese must be warned of the contemplated theft of the miracle-performing ikon.

Bishop Pelagius lived in the monastery in which the ikon of the Mother of God, so revered by the people, was preserved. The relics of an old sainted monk were preserved in the same monastery. Men came from all ends of Russia to worship these holy relics. That was why this monastery was considered wealthy.

Trirodov thought for a long time as to how he might best inform the bishop of the contemplated theft. The thought of writing an anonymous letter was repugnant to him. He decided that it was better to speak to the bishop in person, or to write him a letter with his real name. But then the question remained as to how to explain his own knowledge of the conspiracy. He himself might be suspected as an accomplice of the criminals. As it was, the local townsmen had none too friendly an eye for Trirodov.

He dreaded entangling himself in this dark affair. He already began to feel vexed with himself for his strange curiosity that impelled him to question Ostrov about his affairs. It would have been better perhaps if he were ignorant of the conspiracy. In any case, Trirodov saw clearly that it was impossible for him to maintain silence. He thought that the dark aspects of monastic life did not justify the evil deed planned by Ostrov's companions. Besides, the consequences of this deed might well prove very dangerous.

Trirodov decided that there was nothing left for him to do but to pay a visit to the monastery. Once on the spot, he thought that some opportunity of informing the bishop would occur to him. But as this visit was very unpleasant to him, he delayed it a very long time.

CHAPTER XVIII

TRIRODOV at last realized that he was in love with Elisaveta. He knew too well the nature of this delicious and painful emotion. It had come again and once more filled the world with light. He had looked enigmatically upon this broad, eternally inaccessible world, full of past memories and past people. But his love of Elisaveta meant his love and acceptance of the world, the whole world.

This emotion aroused dismay in Trirodov. To the perplexities of the past, not yet thrown off his shoulders, and to those of the present begun with a strange, as yet unmeasured influence, were to be added the perplexities of the future, of a new and unexpected bond. And was not love in itself a means for realizing one's dreams?

Trirodov made effort to crush this new love in himself, and to forget Elisaveta. He tried to keep away from the Rameyevs, not to come to their house—but with each day his love only increased. His thoughts and musings of Elisaveta grew more and more persistent. They became interwoven with one another and grafted themselves on to his soul. More and more a pencil in his hand guided itself to outline on paper now her austere profile—softened by the youthful joy of liberation—now her simple costume, now a rapid sketch of her shoulders and neck, or the knot of her broad belt.

Again and again a strong hope awakened in

171

him that he might strangle and crush the gentle blossom of his delicious love. Several days had already passed without his visiting the Rameyevs. He did not even come on those days on which they grew accustomed to expect him.

Elisaveta thought this a deliberate incivility, and it hurt her feelings. But whenever Piotr abused him she defended him. Her imagination began to evoke more and more frequently the features of his face : his deep, observing glance ; his proud, ironic smile ; his pale face, clean-shaven like an actor's, and cold like a mask. How sweetly and how bitterly she was in love with him—her sweet vision betrayed itself in the gleam in her eyes.

Rameyev had grown fond of Trirodov, and he missed his presence. He found it a pleasant diversion to chat with Trirodov, and even to wrangle with him sometimes. He made two calls at Trirodov's house, and did not find him in. Rameyev wrote several invitations. He received courteous but evasive replies expressing regret at not being able to come.

One evening Rameyev growled at Piotr :

" He stopped coming because of your rudeness."

Piotr replied sharply :

" Let him stay away. I'm very glad."

Rameyev looked at him sternly, and said :

" But I'm not glad. There's one interesting man in this wilderness, and we frighten him away."

Piotr excused himself. He felt uneasy. He walked out of the house alone, aimlessly, wishing only to escape his own relatives.

The sunset blazed for a long time, tormented itself with its unwillingness to die; it lingered on as if it were its last day, and at last expired. The whole sky became blue—exquisitely blue. But to the north-west an edge of it was translucently green. The quiet stars trembled in the blue heights. The moon, which had looked for some time a pale white in the luminous clearness, now rose yellow and distinct. Almost total darkness covered the earth. There was a coolness along the bank of the river—after the hot day. There was an odour of a forest fire, and it, too, softened its unpleasant, malignant bitterness in the dark evening coolness. A green-haired, green-eyed water-nymph bathed near the low, dark dam; she splashed about in the water, which struck the obstruction with a brittle sound, and in rhythmic response to it the stream laughed most sonorously.

Piotr walked quietly upon the path along the river-bank, and thought of Elisaveta sadly and languorously—or rather, he recalled her—evoked her in vision—involuntarily yielded himself to the melancholy play of the nervous fantasies of his brain. The peaceful silence of the evening, so much at one with him, said to him without words, yet comprehensibly, that the pitch of his soul was too quiet, too feeble for Elisaveta, who was so strong, so erect, and so simple.

He had so little audacity—so little daring. He only believed in Christ, in Antichrist, in his love, in her indifference—he only believed! He only sought for the truth, and could not create it—he could evoke neither a god from nonentity, nor a devil from dialectical argument; neither a conquering love from carnal emotions, nor a conquering hate from stubborn " Noes." And he loved Elisaveta ! He had loved her a long time, with a jealous and helpless love.

He loved ! What sadness ! The languor of the springtide and the joyousness of the morning breeze—the distant ringing of bells—tears in one's eyes—and she will smile—pass by—the dear one ! What sadness ! How dark everything is upon this earth—love as well as indifference.

Suddenly Piotr saw Trirodov quite near him. Trirodov was walking straight upon Piotr, as if he did not see him ; he moved quickly, almost automatically, like a mechanical doll. He held a hat in the hand that hung loose at his side— his face was pale—he had a wild look—his eyes were aflame. He uttered disconnected words. He walked so impetuously that Piotr had no time to turn aside. They came face to face, almost colliding with one another. Trirodov gave a start when he saw that he was not alone. His face had an expression of fright. Piotr got out of his way awkwardly, but Trirodov walked rapidly up to him, and looked intently as he turned his own back to the moonlight. Piotr, involuntarily yielding to this movement, also turned round. The moon now looked straight into Piotr's handsome face, which seemed pale and strange in the cold, lifeless light.

Trirodov began in a trembling, agitated voice :

" Ah, that is you ? "

" As you see," said Piotr in a tone of derision.

" I didn't expect to meet you here," said Trirodov. " I took you for . . ."

174

But he did not finish. Piotr, somewhat vexed, asked him :

"For whom ? "

Without replying to the question Trirodov inquired :

"But where ? . . . There's no one here. You didn't hear . . . ? "

"I wasn't trained to eavesdropping," replied Piotr; "all the more since these fragments of poetry are inaccessible to me."

"Who talks of eavesdropping ? " exclaimed Trirodov. "No, I thought that you had unwillingly heard some words which might have sounded strange, enigmatic, or terrible in your ears."

"I came here by chance," said Piotr. "I was taking a mere stroll, and was not here to listen to any one."

Trirodov looked attentively at Piotr; then lowered his head with a sigh, and said quietly :

"Forgive me. My nerves are in a bad state. I have grown accustomed to living with my fantasies, and in the peaceful society of my quiet children. I love seclusion."

"Where did your quiet children come from ? " asked Piotr somewhat contemptuously.

But Trirodov continued as though he had not heard.

"Please forgive me. I too often accept for reality that which exists only in my imagination. Perhaps always. I live devoted to my dreams."

There was so poignant a sadness in these words and in the way they were uttered that Piotr felt an involuntary pity for Trirodov. His hate

175

strangely vanished—as the moon vanishes at the rising of the sun.

Trirodov said with quiet sadness:

" I have so many strange whims and ways. It is in vain that I go to see people. It is far better for me to be alone with my innocent, quiet children, with my secrets and dreams."

" Why better ? " asked Piotr.

" I sometimes feel that people interfere with me," said Trirodov. " They weary me in themselves—and no less with their petty, commonplace affairs. And what are they to me ? There is only one thing of which I can be sure—that is myself. It is a great task to be with people. They give me so little, and for that they thirstily and malignantly drink my whole soul. How often have I left their company exhausted, humiliated, crushed. What a holiday for me my solitude is, my sweet solitude ! If it were only with some one else ! "

" Still you would rather it were with some one else ! " replied Piotr with sudden malice.

Trirodov looked at him steadily and said :

" Life is tragic. She destroys all illusions with the power of her pitiless irony. You know, of course, that Elisaveta's soul is a tragic soul, and that a great boldness is necessary in order to approach her, and to say to her the great Yes of life. Yes, Elisaveta . . ."

Piotr's voice trembled as he shouted in jealous rage :

" Elisaveta ! Why do you mention Elisaveta ? "

Trirodov looked steadily at Piotr. He asked rather slowly—in a strangely sounding voice :

" You are not afraid ? "

176

"What is there to be afraid of?" replied Piotr morosely. "I am not at all a tragic person. My path is clear to me, and I know who guides me."

"You don't know that," said Trirodov. "Besides, Elena is lovely. He who fears to take the grand and the terrible, he who loves tender melodies, for him there is Elena."

Piotr was silent. Some sort of new—perhaps alien—thoughts swarmed in his head. He listened to them, and suddenly said:

"You haven't visited us for a long time, and you are very much liked in our house. You would be welcome. You may come when you like, and you may talk or be silent, as suits your mood."

Trirodov smiled in response.

Piotr Matov returned home quite late in a dazed state of mind. Every one had already sat down to supper. Elisaveta glanced at him curiously—as if she expected another person there instead of him.

"I've come late," said Piotr confusedly. "I don't know how I managed to wander off so far."

He could not understand why he was so flustered. He barely recognized Elisaveta dressed up as a boy in her sailor jacket and short breeches. She sat so erect there, and smiled her abstract, indifferent smile.

Elena, blushing for some unknown reason, moved silently closer—and there was a strange timorousness in her movement—a timorous desire. Piotr complied with her wish, and sat down at her side. She looked at him tenderly, lovingly. Her glances touched him. He thought:

" Why do I not love Elena ? Or is it she alone that I really love ? Perhaps some mistake of the will had dimmed my eyes ? "

He conversed with her gently and tenderly, and as he looked at her again and again, a new love took spark in him. It was as if by some prodigious power the strange being at the riverbank had instilled this new love into him. Elena's heart beat joyfully.

CHAPTER XIX

AFTER that evening Trirodov, suppressing his devotion to quiet loneliness, once more began to visit the Rameyevs. He resisted no longer the all-powerful, desire to see Elisaveta, to look into the depth of her blue eyes, to listen to the golden sonorousness of her words, and to feel the breathing and the witchery of her fresh, primitive strength. It was so pleasant to look upon her simple attire, upon the trusting openness of her shoulders, upon the light tan of her feet, and upon the austere outlines of her face.

Elisaveta's sunlit depth became transformed for Trirodov into a blue, fathomless height. Elisaveta's love grew stronger ; to grow stronger was its desire, and it wished to surmount all intolerable obstacles.

Rameyev looked at Elisaveta and Trirodov, and he was consumed by a strange, mature joy. He seemed to think :

" They will marry and bring me grandchildren."

There were already certain hours in which they expected him. He and Elisaveta often remained alone. Something in their natures drew them apart from other people, whether strangers or kin. They would go off somewhere into a neglected part of the garden, where under the spread net of superb black poplars the agreeable aroma of thyme reached them with a gentle poignancy—and here they loved to chat with one another.

179

Had he been alone instead of with Elisaveta, he could not have expressed his thoughts more simply or more candidly. They spoke of so many things—they tried, as it were, to contain the whole world within the rigid bounds of rapid words.

As they strolled along the high bank of the river, under the broad shadows of the mighty black poplars and strange black maples, and listened to the loud, cheerful twitter of the birds that came to the bushes, Elisaveta said :

" The sensation of existence and of the fullness and joy of life is delicious. A new sky seems to have opened above my head, and for the first time the violets and the lilies of the valley besprinkled with their first dew have begun to bloom for me ; and for the first time May-drinks made from herbs by young housewives taste delicious."

Trirodov smiled sadly and said :

" I feel the heavy burden of life. But what's to be done ? I don't know whether life can be made more easy and tranquil."

" Why desire ease and tranquillity in life ? " asked Elisaveta. " I want fire and passion, even if I perish. Let me become consumed in the fire of rapture and revolt."

" Yes," said Trirodov, " it is necessary to discover all the possibilities and forces within oneself, and then a new life may be created. I wonder if life is necessary ? "

" And what is necessary ? " asked Elisaveta.

" I don't know," answered Trirodov sadly.

" What do you desire ? " she asked again.

" Perhaps I desire nothing," said Trirodov. " There are moments when I seem to expect nothing

180

from life; I do what I do unwillingly, as if it were a disagreeable action."

"How do you live then?" asked Elisaveta in astonishment.

He replied:

"I live in a strange and unreal world. I live—but life goes past me, always past me. Woman's love, the fire of youth, the stirring of young hopes, remain for ever within the forbidden boundaries of unrealized possibilities—who knows?—perhaps unrealizable."

The sad, flaming moments of silence were marked by the heavy beats of Elisaveta's heart. She felt intensely vexed by these sad words of weakness and of dejection, and she did not believe them. But Trirodov went on speaking, and his beautiful but hopelessly sad words sounded like a taunt to her:

"There is so much labour and so little consolation. Life passes by like a dream—a senseless, tormenting dream."

"If only a radiant dream! If only a tempestuous dream!" exclaimed Elisaveta.

Trirodov smiled and said:

"The time of awakening is drawing nearer. Old age comes with its depression; and the empty, meaningless life wanders on towards unknown borders. You ask yourself, and it seems hopeless to find a worthy answer: 'Why do I live in this strange and chance form? Why have I chosen my present lot? Why have I done this?'"

"Well, who is at fault here?" asked Elisaveta.

Trirodov replied:

"The conscience, ripened to universal fullness, says that every fault is my fault."

181

"And that every action is my action," added Elisaveta.

"An action is so impossible!" said Trirodov. "A miracle is impossible. I wish to break loose from the claims of this dull existence."

"You speak of love," said Elisaveta, "as of a thing unrealized. But you had a wife."

"Yes," said Trirodov sadly. "The short moments passed by rapidly. Was there love? I cannot say. There was passion, a smouldering—and death."

"Life will again bring its delights to you," said Elisaveta confidently.

And Trirodov answered:

"Yes, it will be a different life, but what's that to me? If one could only be quite different, and simple—say a small child, a boy with bare feet, with a fishing-rod in his hands, his mouth yawning good-naturedly. Only children really live. I envy them frightfully. I envy frightfully the simple folk, the altogether simple folk, remote from these cheerless comprehensions of the intellect. Children live—only children. Ripeness already marks the beginning of death."

"To love—and to die?" asked Elisaveta with a smile.

She listened to the sound of these beautiful, sad words and repeated them quietly:

"To love—and to die!"

And as she listened again, she heard him say:

"She loved—and she died."

"What was the name of your first wife?" asked Elisaveta.

She was amazed at herself for uttering the word

"first," as there had been only one; and her face became suffused slowly with pink.

Trirodov fell into thought; he appeared not to have heard her question, and was silent. Elisaveta did not repeat it. He suddenly smiled and said:

"You and I feel ourselves to be living people here, and what can there be for us more certain than our life, our sensation of life? And yet it is possible that you and I are not living people at all, but only characters in a novel, and that the author of this novel is not at all concerned with its external verisimilitude. His capricious imagination had taken this dark earth for its material, and out of this dark, sinful earth he grew these strange black maples and these mighty black poplars and these twittering birds in the bushes and us."

Elisaveta looked at him in astonishment and said with a smile:

"I hope that the novel will be interesting and beautiful. Let it even end in death! But tell me, why do you write so little?"

With unexpected passion, almost with exasperation, Trirodov replied:

"Why should I write volumes of tales on how they fell in love and why they fell out of love, and all that? I write only that which comes from myself, that which has not yet been said. So much has already been said; it is far better to add a simple word of one's own than write volumes of superfluities."

"Eternal themes are always one and the same," said Elisaveta. "Do they not constitute the content of great art?"

"We never originate," said Trirodov. "We always appear in the world with a ready inheritance. We arc the eternal successors. That is why we are not free. We see the world with others' eyes, the eyes of the dead. But I live only when I make everything my own."

And while these two spent their hours in conversing, Piotr usually made his way somewhere to the top of the house. He sometimes descended with his eyes red—red from tears or from the vigorous, high wind. His days dragged on miserably. His hate and jealousy of Trirodov now and again tormented him.

Piotr sometimes made unpleasant, pitiful scenes before Elisaveta. He loved her and he hated her. He would have killed her—had he dared ! And he had not the force to hate either Elisaveta or Trirodov to the bitter end.

When he learned to know Trirodov better his hate lost something of its venom, his malice no longer irritated him like nettles. He looked with curiosity upon them and began to understand. The agony of his unconscious fury was replaced by a clear contemplation of the separating abyss ; and this made him even more miserable.

He decided to go away ; he made the decision again and again, but always remained there— restless and yearning.

As for Misha, he fell quite in love with Trirodov. He liked to remain with Elisaveta in order to talk about him.

One evening Piotr came to Trirodov's house.

He did not like to go there, for such antagonistic feelings wrestled in his soul ! But common courtesy made the visit necessary.

Again a discussion was started. In Piotr's opinion revolution was to the detriment of religion and culture. It was a tedious, unnecessary discussion. But Piotr could never resist uttering malicious words against the extremes of the " liberating movement."

He felt awkward during the whole visit. He wished to handle something all the time and to be doing something. His restlessness tormented him in a strange way. Now he picked up one trifle from the table, now another, and put it down again. He took a prism in his hand. Trirodov trembled. He said something quietly and inaudibly. Piotr did not hear, but kept on looking in astonishment at the heavy prism in his hand ; and as he turned it over and over he wondered at the reason of its weight. Trirodov trembled nervously. Piotr, in turning the prism rather awkwardly, struck it against the edge of the table. Trirodov shivered, shouted something incoherently, and, snatching the prism from Piotr's hands, said in an agitated voice :

" Please put it down ! "

Piotr looked in astonishment at Trirodov, who was visibly confused. Piotr smiled unwillingly and asked :

" Why, what is it ? "

" How should I tell you ! " said Trirodov. " It is connected with . . . Please forgive my sharpness. I thought you were going to drop it, and I wanted to . . . It seems like a whim. . . . Of

185

course it is really nothing . . . but it is connected with an old episode in my life. Really, I don't know why I keep these ugly things on my table. But there are such intimate memories . . . you understand . . . Still, I'm so very sorry . . ."

Piotr listened in perplexity. Suddenly he realized that it was rude to be silent for so long, and he made haste to say, not without embarrassment :

" Please don't think about it. I quite well understand that there are things which . . . But if you find it difficult or unpleasant to speak about it, then please . . ."

Trirodov said a few more incoherent, confused words of apology to Piotr and thanked him. He breathed a sigh of relief when Stchemilov was announced.

Piotr let loose his irritation at the new-comer with the ironic question :

" Again free ? For how long ? "

" I've skipped," answered Stchemilov calmly. " I'm leading an illegal life now."

Piotr soon left.

" To-day ? " asked Stchemilov. " Here ? "

" Yes, we'll meet here to-day," replied Trirodov.

" He hasn't left yet, and there are several matters and reports to attend to. It is necessary to arrange a meeting and to let various people know about it."

" You have a convenient house here," said Stchemilov. " May I help myself ? " he added, pointing at the box of cigars as he lounged back comfortably on the large sofa. " Most convenient,"
186

he repeated, as he lit his cigar. " They don't suspect us as yet, but if they should pay you a visit, there are so many exits and entrances here and out-of-the-way nooks . . . Very convenient indeed. It is easy to hide things here—no comparison at all with my little trunk."

CHAPTER XX

THE town was in a state of unrest : strikes were
in the air, patriotic demonstrations were held. Its
outer environs were visited by suspicious-looking
characters; these distributed proclamations, mostly
of an illiterate nature, in the villages.. The
proclamations threatened incendiarism if the
peasants did not revolt. The incendiaries were
to be "students," discharged from the factories
on account of the strikes. The peasants believed
the announcement. In some of the villages
watchmen were engaged to catch the incendiaries
at night.

Ostrov began to play a noticeable rôle in town.
He quickly squandered the money he received from
Trirodov in drink and in other ways. He did not
dare as yet to visit Trirodov again, but appeared
to be in an expectant mood, and remained in
town.

It was here that Ostrov met his old friend
Yakov Poltinin.

Yakov Poltinin and two other members of the
Black Hundred were sent from the capital at the
request of Kerbakh and Zherbenev. The apparent
purpose of this request was to establish a connexion
between the local section of the All-Russian Black
Hundred union—organized by Kerbakh, Zherbenev,
and Konopatskaya, the wife of a general—with
the central office of the organization. The actual
purpose, however, as understood by all these
188

respected folk, though they ventured to do little more than hint of it to one another, was to establish—with the help of the trio—a patriotic movement ; in short, to strike a blow at the *intelligentsia.*

Yakov Poltinin took Ostrov with him to visit the families of the patriots. A company of suspicious characters was in town—ready to do anything they were bidden. Yakov Poltinin led Ostrov also among this company.

In the course of the company's friendly carouse at Poltinin's apartments in a dirty little house on the outskirts of the town, the idea of stealing the sacred ikon came into some one's mind. Poltinin said :

" There's no end of precious stones on it of all sorts—diamonds, sapphires, and rubies. It took hundred of years to collect them. Little Mother Russia, orthodox Russia, has done her best."

The thief Potseluytchikov affirmed :

" It's certainly worth not less than two million."

" You're putting it on rather thick," declared Ostrov incredulously.

" Not at all," said Poltinin with a knowing look. " Two million is putting it mildly—it's more likely worth three."

" And how are you going to dispose of it ? " asked Ostrov.

" I know how," said Poltinin confidently. " Of course you'd get a trifle compared with its real value—still we ought to get a half-million out of it."

This was followed by blasphemous jests.

Yakov Poltinin had for some time entertained the secret ambition of accomplishing something on a grand scale, something that would cause a lot of talk. It is true the murder of the Chief of Police created a deep impression. Still, it was hardly as important as the affair he had in mind. To steal and destroy the miracle-working ikon— that would be something to crow about ! Poltinin said :

" The Socialist Revolutionaries are certain to be blamed for it. Expropriation for party purposes— why not ? As for us, no one will even suspect us."

" The priests will never get over it," declared Molin, a former instructor, who was a drunkard and a thief—a jail-bird deprived of his legal rights.

The friends began preparations for the projected theft. Now one of them, now another, developed the habit of frequenting the monastery. Ostrov especially received an eager welcome there. He pleased, by his external piety, the older monks who were in authority. There were a number of convivial monks who were especially fond of Ostrov. The monks advised him to join the local union of the Black Hundred. They said that it would be pleasing to God. They engaged him in religious and patriotic conversations and invited him to drink with them.

Poltinin and Potseluychikov were also well received in the monastery.

Strange threads are woven into the relations of people at times. Although Piotr Matov met Ostrov under unfriendly circumstances, Ostrov managed to scrape up an acquaintance even with him. It reached a point when Piotr even agreed to make a journey with Ostrov to the monastery.

Glafira Pavlovna Konopatskaya, the rich widow of a general, was an energetic, power-loving woman, and enjoyed considerable influence in town. She was a most generous contributor to the various enterprises of the Black Hundred. Her house served as the meeting-place of the local branch of this All-Russian organization as well as of another secret society, which bore the elaborate name of " The Union of Active Combat with Revolution and Anarchy."

The initiation ceremony of the union was very elaborately exulting. Especial efforts were made to attract working men. Each new member was presented with a badge, a Browning revolver, and a little money.

The local patriots used to say about Glafira Pavlovna's house :

" Here dwells the Russian spirit, here it smells of Russia ! " *

After the meeting it usually smelt of vodka and shag.

Some of the working men joined these unions for material reasons, others from ignorance. The Black Hundred had but a few members from among the working class by conviction. The Union of Active Combat attracted people who served now one side, now the other, people like Yakov Poltinin, and even two or three confirmed revolutionaries. They accepted the Brownings and handed them over to members of revolutionary organizations. Members of the union did not find this out until quite late.

Kerbakh and Zherbenev were the most frequent

* A line from a poem by Pushkin.

guests at Glafira Pavlovna's cosy, hospitable house.
Evil tongues made slander of this, and associated
her name now with Kerbakh, now with Zherbenev.
But this was a calumny. Her heart had only a
place for a young official who served as a private
secretary to the Governor.

Once after dinner at Konopatskaya's, Kerbakh
and Zherbenev were telling Glafira Pavlovna about
Ostrov. Kerbakh was the first to broach the
subject :

" I have in view a man whom I should like to
call to your attention."

" I too know a lively chap," said Zherbenev.

Kerbakh, annoyed at the interruption, looked
none too amiably at Zherbenev, and went on :

" He didn't at all please me at first."

" My friend also did not appeal to me at the
beginning," said Zherbenev, who would not stay
repressed.

" To look at him you might think that he's a
cut-throat," said Kerbakh.

" That describes my man too," announced Zherbenev, as if he were announcing something gay
and pleasant.

" But at heart," went on Kerbakh, " he is an
ingenuous infant and an enthusiastic patriot."

" Well, well, and mine's like that too," chimed
in Zherbenev.

Glafira Pavlovna smiled graciously at both of
them.

" Whom are you talking about ? " asked Kerbakh
at last, rather annoyed at his companion.

Zherbenev replied :

" There is a chap here—what's his name ? You
192

remember we met him at the pier some time ago. He was rather interested in Trirodov."

" You mean Ostrov ? " ventured Kerbakh.

" That's the fellow," said Zherbenev.

" I also meant him," said Kerbakh.

" Excellent ! " exclaimed Zherbenev. " We seem to agree about him. So you see, Glafira Pavlovna, we ought to invite him into our union. He would be a most useful man. Once mention Jews to him and he begins to howl like a dog on a chain."

" Of course we ought to have him," decided Glafira Pavlovna. " It is just such people that we want."

That was how Ostrov came to be admitted into the union. He worked very zealously on its behalf.

One of the chief functions of the Black Hundred was to lodge information against certain people. They informed the Governor and the head of the District Schools that Trirodov's wards had been at the funeral of the working men killed in the woods.

The colony established by Trirodov had for some time been a source of great annoyance and scandal to the townsfolk. Complaints had been lodged with the authorities even earlier. Ostrov communicated considerable information, mostly invented by himself or by the alert townsmen. The head of the schools sent an order to the Headmaster of the National Schools to make an investigation. The Governor took other measures. Clouds were beginning to gather over Trirodov's colony.

The union also made no little effort to arouse the hooligan part of the population against the Jews and against the *intelligentsia*.

The town was in a state of ferment. The Cossacks often paraded the streets. The working men eyed them with hostility. Some one spread rumours about town that preparations were being made for an armed revolt. Trifling causes led to tragic collisions.

One evening the Summer Garden was full of people; they were strolling or else listening to the music and to the songs in the open-air theatre. The evening was quiet and the sky still red. Just outside the rail-fence the dust was flying before the wind, and settled now on the pointed leaves of the acacia-trees, now on the small, light purple flowers near the road.

There was a rose-red glow in the sky; the road stretched towards it; and the grey of the dust mingling with the red glow produced a play of colour very agreeable to the eye.

A red giant genie broke his vessel with its Solomon's seal, freed himself, and stood on the edge of the town; he laughed soundlessly yet repugnantly. His breath was like the smoky breath of a forest fire. But he made sentimental grimaces, tore white petals from gigantic marguerites, and whispered in a hoarse voice which stirred the blood of the young:

"He loves me—he loves me not; he will cut me up—he will hang me."

But the people did not see him. They were looking at the sky and saying:

194

"How superb! I love nature! And do you love nature?"

Others looked on indifferently and thought that it did not matter. The lovers of nature bragged before these because they admired the splendid sunset and were able to enjoy nature. They said to the others:

"You, old chap, are a dry stick. I suppose you'd rather go to a stuffy room and play cards."

The promenaders strolled on, crowding and jostling each other; they were flaunting their gaiety. There was a cheerful hum, and young girls, amused by schoolboys and officials, giggled. Grey devilkins mingled with the crowd, and when the little jokers-pokers hopped on the girls' shoulders and poked their shaggy and ticklish little paws into the corsage under the chemise the girls raised piercing screams. They were dressed prettily and lightly, in holiday order. Their high breasts outlined under their coloured textures taunted the youths.

An officer of the Cossacks was among those on the promenade. He had had a drop too much, which made his face red. He was in a gay mood, and he began to boast:

"We'll cut their heads off, yes, of all of them!"

The petty tradesmen treated him to drinks, embraced him, and said to him:

"Cut their throats. Do us the favour. Make a good job of it. It will serve these anathemas right too! As for the women and the girls, give them a hiding—the hotter the better."

There was a continuous change of amusements,

each noisier and duller than the one before. Now in the theatre, now in the open, they played a stupid but obscene vaudeville piece, and vicious topical songs were sung (a thunder of applause); an animated chansonnette-singer screeched and pulled about with her naked, excessively whitened shoulders, and winked with her exaggeratedly painted eyes; a woman acrobat, raising her legs, attired in pink tights, above her head, was dancing on her hands.

Everything was as if the town were not under guard and as if the Cossacks were not riding about in the streets.

Suddenly some one in the depth of the garden raised a cry.

A frightful confusion spread among the crowd. Many darted impetuously towards the exit. Others jumped over the fence. Suddenly the crowd, with frenzied cries, came sweeping in retreat from the exits back into the depth of the garden.

Cossacks darted in from somewhere and, crying savagely, made their way along the garden paths. Their sudden appearance gave the impression that they were waiting somewhere near by for the command. Their knouts began to work rapidly. The thin textures upon the girls' shoulders were rent apart and delicate bodies were unbared, and beautiful blue-and-red spots showed themselves on the white-pink skin like quickly ripened flowers. Drops of blood, large like bilberries, splattered into the air, which had already quenched its thirst on the evening coolness, on the odour of the foliage and the aroma of artificial scents. Delicately shrill, loud sobs were the accompaniment

196

to the dull, flat lashings of whips across the bodies.

They threw themselves this way and that way, they ran where they could. Several were caught—ragged young men and girls with short hair. Two or three of the girls were caught and beaten in error : they were from the most peaceful, even respected, families in town. These were afterwards permitted to go free.

The hooligans were making merry in a dirty, ill-smelling beerhouse. They were celebrating something or another, were jingling their money, discussing future earnings, and laughing uproariously. One table was especially absorbed in its noisy gaiety. There sat the celebrated town-rowdy Nil Krasavtsev with three of his friends. They drank, and sang hooligan songs, then paid their bill and went out. One could hear their savage outbursts :

" The Jew dogs are rebels, they are against the Tsar."

" The Jews want to get hold of everything for themselves."

" It wouldn't be a bad thing to cut up a Jewess ! "

" The Jews want to take over the whole earth."

It had grown dark. The hooligans went into the main street, the Sretenka. It was very quiet, and only a few passers-by were to be met with ; people stood here and there at their gates and talked. A Jewish widow sat at the gate of a house and chatted with her neighbour, a Jewish tailor. Her children, a whole throng of them, one smaller than the other, played about here, deeply wrapt in their own affairs.

Nil walked up to the Jewess and shouted :

" You dog of a Jew, pray to God for the orthodox Tsar ! "

" What do you want of me ? " cried the Jewess. " I'm not touching you ; you had better go away ! "

" What's that you say ? " shouted the hooligan.

A broad knife was lifted in the darkness and, gleaming, came down in a swoop, piercing the old woman. She gave a quick, shrill cry—and fell back dead. The Jew, terrified, ran away, filling the night air with his piteous wails. The children began to whimper. The hooligans marched off, laughing uproariously.

CHAPTER XXI

MIDDAY. It was quiet, innocent, and fresh in the depth of the wood, at the edge of the hollow—and the outer heat penetrated hither only by an infinite coiling as of a scaly serpent impotent at last and deprived of its poison.

Trirodov had found this place for himself and Elisaveta. More than once they came here together—to read, to talk, and to sit a while at the moss-covered stone, out of which, like a strange corporeal ghost, grew up all awry a slender quaking ash. Elisaveta, dressed in her simple short skirt, her long sunburnt arms and part of her legs showing, seemed so tall, so erect, and so graceful at this moss-covered stone.

Elisaveta was reading aloud—poems! How golden her voice sounded with its seductive, sun-like sonorousness! Trirodov listened with a slightly ironical smile to these familiar, infinitely deep and lovely words, so seemingly meaningless in life. When she finished Trirodov said:

"A man's whole life is barely enough to think out a single idea properly."

"You mean to say that each should choose for himself but a single idea."

"Yes. If people could but grasp this fact human knowledge would take an unprecedented step forward. But we are afraid to venture."

And coarse life already hovered near them behind their backs, and was about to intrude upon them. Elisaveta gave a sudden faint outcry at the unexpectedness of an unseemly apparition. A dirty, rough-looking man, all in tatters, was almost upon them ; he had approached them upon the mossy ground as softly as a wood fairy. He stretched out a dirty, horny hand, and asked, not at all in a begging voice :

"Give a hungry man something to buy bread with."

Trirodov frowned in annoyance, and without looking at the beggar took a silver coin out of the pocket of his waistcoat. He always kept a trifle about him to provide for unexpected meetings. The ragged one smiled, turned the coin, threw it upward, caught it, and hid it adroitly in his pocket.

"I thank your illustrious Honour most humbly," he said. "May God give you good health, a rich wife, and assured success. Only I want to say something to you."

He grew silent, and assumed a grave, important air. Trirodov frowned even more intensely than before, and asked stiffly :

"What is it you wish to tell me ? "

The ragged one said with frank derision in his voice :

"It's this. You were reading a book, my good people, but not the right one."

He laughed a pathetic, insolent laugh. It was as if a timorous dog suddenly began to whine hoarsely, insolently, and cautiously.

Trirodov asked again in astonishment :

"Not the right one, why not ? "

The ragged one began to speak with awkward

200

gestures, and he gave the impression that he was able to speak well and eloquently, and that he merely assumed his stupid, unpolished manner of speaking.

"I had been listening to you a long time. I was behind the bush there. I was asleep, I must confess—then you came—chattered away, and waked me. The young lady read well. Clearly and sympathetically. One could see at once that it was from the heart. Only I don't like the contents, and all that's in this book."

"Why don't you like it?" asked Elisaveta quietly.

"In my opinion," said the ragged one, "it isn't your style. It doesn't fit you somehow."

"What sort of book ought we to read?" asked Elisaveta.

She gave a light, forced smile. The ragged one sat down on a near-by stump, and answered in no undue haste:

"I am not thinking of you alone, honourable folk, but of all those who parade in fancy gaiters and in velvet dresses, and look scornfully at our brothers."

"What book?" again asked Elisaveta.

"It's the gospels that you ought to read," he replied, as he looked attentively and austerely at Elisaveta, his glance taking in her entire figure from her flushed face down to her feet.

"Why the gospels?" asked Trirodov, who suddenly grew morose. He appeared to be pondering over something, and unable to decide; his indecision seemed to torment him.

The ragged one replied slowly:

201

" I will tell you why; you'll find the true facts there. We will take it easy in paradise, while the devils will be pulling the veins out of you in hell. And we shall look on coolly, and applaud gaily with our hands. It ought to prove entertaining."

He burst out into loud, hoarse laughter—but it seemed more assumed than joyous, and rather abject and hideous. Elisaveta shivered.

" What a wicked person you are! Why do you think that ? " said Elisaveta reproachfully.

The ragged one glanced at her crossly, and looked fixedly into her deep blue eyes; then he said with a broad smile :

" Why am I wicked ? And are you two good ? Wicked or not, the thing is to be just. But I may tell you, sir, that I like you," he said as he turned suddenly to Trirodov.

" Thank you for your good opinion," said Trirodov with a slightly ironical smile, " but why should you like me ? "

He looked attentively at the ragged one. Then suddenly he felt depressed and apprehensive, and he lowered his eyes. The other slowly lit his foul-smelling pipe, stretched himself, and began after a brief silence :

" Other gentlemen's mugs are mostly gay, as if they had gorged themselves on a pancake with cream, or had successfully forged their uncle's will. But you, sir, seem to have the same lean mug always. I have been observing you some time now. It's evident that you have something on your soul. At least a capital crime."

Trirodov was silent. He lifted himself on his

202

elbow and looked straight into the man's eyes with such a fixed, strange expression in his unblinking, commanding, wilful eyes.

The ragged one grew silent, as if he had been congealed for a moment. Then, as if frightened, he suddenly shook himself. He shrank and stooped, and as he took his cap off he revealed an unkempt, tousled head of hair; he mumbled something, slipped away among the bushes, and disappeared quietly—like a fairy of the wood.

Trirodov looked gloomily after him—and was silent. Elisaveta thought that he deliberately avoided looking at her. She was intensely embarrassed, but made an effort to control herself. She laughed, and said with assumed gaiety :

" What a strange creature ! "

Trirodov turned upon her his melancholy glances and said quietly :

" He talks like one who knows. He talks like one who sees. But no one can know what happened."

Oh, if one could only know ! If one could only change that which once had happened !

Trirodov recalled again during these days the dark history of Piotr Matov's father. Trirodov had carelessly entangled himself in this affair, and now it compelled him to have dealings with the blackmailer Ostrov.

Piotr's father, Dmitry Matov, had fallen into a trap which he had set for others. He had joined a secret revolutionary circle. There they soon discovered his relations with the police, and they decided to detect him and kill him.

One of the members of the circle, the young physician Lunitsin, took the rôle of betrayer upon himself. He promised to obtain for Dmitry Matov important documents involving many of the members. They made a bargain at a moderate figure. The meeting at which the documents were to be exchanged for the money was designated to take place in a small borough close to the town in which Trirodov then lived.

At the appointed hour Dmitry Matov got out of his train at a little station. It was late in the evening. Matov wore blue spectacles and a false beard, as was agreed upon. Lunitsin waited for him a few .yards from the station, and led him to a very solitary spot where was situated the house hired for the purpose.

A supper had been prepared there. Matov ate heartily and drank much wine. His companion began to invent stories about certain suspicious movements he had heard of lately. Little by little Matov grew candid, and began to boast of his connexions with the police, and of the great number of people he had skilfully betrayed.

The door leading to the next room was hung with draperies. Three people were hiding in that room—Trirodov, Ostrov, and the young working man Krovlin. They were listening. Krovlin was intensely excited. He kept on repeating in indignant whispers :

" Oh, the scoundrel ! The wretch ! "

Ostrov and Trirodov managed to restrain him with great difficulty.

" Be silent. Let him babble out everything," they said to him.

At last Matov's impudent boastfulness was too much for Krovlin, who jumped out from his hiding-place, and shouted :

" So that's how it is ! You've betrayed our men to the police ! And you have the face to confess it ! "

Dmitry Matov grew green with fear. He shouted to his companion :

" Kill him ! He has been listening to us ! Shoot quick ! He mustn't live. He will give us both up ! "

At this moment two other men appeared from the same place. Lunitsin aimed his revolver straight at Matov's forehead, and asked :

" Who ought to be killed, traitor ? "

Matov then understood that he had been caught in a trap. But he still made efforts to wriggle out of it, and called all his skill and his insolence to his assistance. They tried him for treachery. At first he defended himself. He said that he had deceived the police, and that he had entered into relations with them merely to get important information for his comrades. But his protestations soon grew weaker. Then he began to beg for mercy. He spoke of his wife and of his children.

Matov's entreaties failed to impress any one. His judges were adamant. His fate was decided. The sentence of hanging was passed unanimously.

Matov was bound. The noose was already thrown about his neck. Then Trirodov intervened :

" What are you going to do with him ? It will be difficult to take him away, and it is dangerous to leave him here."

"Who will come here?" said Lunitsin. "At best only by chance. Let him hang here until he's found."

"Let us bury him here in the garden, like a dog," suggested Krovlin.

"Give him to me," said Trirodov. "I will dispose his body in such a way that no one will find it."

The others assented eagerly. Ostrov said with a scornful smile:

"Will you try your chemistry on him, Giorgiy Sergeyevitch? Well, it's all the same to us. A bad man ought to be punished—make even a skeleton of him for your use if you like."

Trirodov drew a flagon containing a colourless liquid from his pocket.

"Now this will put him to sleep," he said.

He injected with a small syringe several drops of the liquid under Dmitry Matov's skin. Matov gave a feeble cry and fell heavily to the floor. In a few moments the body lay before them, blue and apparently lifeless. Lunitsin examined Matov and said:

"He's done for."

The men left one by one. Trirodov alone remained with Matov's body. Trirodov took off Matov's clothes and burned them in the stove. He made several more injections of the same colourless liquid.

The night passed slowly. Trirodov lay on the sofa without taking his clothes off. He slept badly, tormented by oppressive dreams. He awoke several times.

Dmitry Matov lay in the next room on the floor.

206

The liquid, injected into his blood, acted strangely. The body contracted in proper proportion, and wasted very quickly. Within several hours it lost more than half of its weight, and assumed very small dimensions; it became very soft and pliant. But all its proportions were faithfully preserved.

Trirodov made up the body into a large parcel, covered it over with plaid, and bound it with straps. It resembled a pillow wrapped up in plaid. Trirodov left by the morning train for home, carrying with him Dmitry Matov's body.

At home Trirodov put the body into a vessel containing a greenish liquid compounded by himself. Matov's body shrunk in it even more. It had become barely more than seven inches long. But as before all its proportions remained inviolate.

Then Trirodov prepared a special plastic substance, in which he wrapped Matov's body. He pressed it compactly into the form of a cube, and placed it on his writing-table. And thus a thing that once had been a man remained there a thing among other things.

Nevertheless Trirodov was right when he told Ostrov that Matov had not been killed. Yes, notwithstanding his strange form and his distressing immobility, Dmitry Matov was not dead. The potentiality of life slept dormant in that solid object. Trirodov thought more than once as to whether the time had not come to rehabilitate Matov and return him to the world of the living.

He had not decided upon this before. But he was confident that he would succeed in doing this without hindrance. The process of rehabilitation required a tranquil and isolated place.

In a little more than a year at the beginning of the summer Trirodov decided to begin the process of rehabilitation. He prepared a large vat over six feet in length. He filled it with a colourless liquid, and lowered into it the cube containing Matov's body.

The slow process of rehabilitation began. Unperceived by the eye, the cube began to thaw and to swell. It needed a half-year before it would thaw out sufficiently to permit the body to peer through.

CHAPTER XXII

SONYA SVETILOVITCH was badly shaken by the hard, cruel events of that night in the woods. She fell ill, and remained two weeks in an unconscious state. It was feared that she would die. But she was a strong girl and conquered her illness.

Scenes from that nightmarish occasion passed before the poor girl in her heavy delirium. Grey, ferocious demons, with dim, tinny eyes, came to her, taunted her, and acted without reason. There was no place in which to hide from the hideous frenzy.

Deep oppression reigned in the Svetilovitch house. Sonya's mother wept, and bewailed her lot. Sonya's father spoke of the matter warmly and eloquently, with gesticulations, to his friends in his study—and inevitably got into a state of indignation. Sonya's little brothers discussed plans of vengeance. Fräulein Berta, the governess of Sonya's younger sister, made censorious remarks about barbarous Russia.

All the acquaintances of the Svetilovitches were also indignant. But their indignation assumed only platonic forms. Perhaps it was impossible for it to have been otherwise. To be sure, all the more or less independent people in town paid the Svetilovitches visits of sympathy. Even the liberal Inspector of Taxes came. He was a patient of Doctor Svetilovitch's, and came during the reception hour to express his interest; incident-

ally he asked advice about his physical indisposi-
tions and paid no fee—in view of its being a visit
of sympathy.

Sonya's father, Doctor Sergey Lvovitch Svetilovitch, was a member of the Constitutional Democratic Party; among his own he was regarded
as belonging to the extreme left wing. Like his
friend Rameyev, who was a Cadet of more moderate
views, he was a member of the local committee.

Doctor Svetilovitch thought he ought to protest
against the improper actions of the police. He
lodged complaints with the Governor and the
District Attorney, and wrote circumstantial peti-
tions to both—his chief concern being that no
offending expression of any sort should enter into
them.

Doctor Svetilovitch was an extremely correct
and loyal man. Other people around him, if
placed in unusual circumstances, might lose their
presence of mind and forget their principles;
others around him, friends or enemies, might act
incorrectly and illegally; but Doctor Svetilovitch
always remained faithful to himself. No circumstance, no earthly or heavenly power, could
swerve him from the path which he acknowledged
as the only true one, in so far as it conformed to
Constitutional Democratic principles. The problem
of expedience of conduct concerned Doctor Svetilovitch but little. The important thing was to be
correct in principle. He always placed, however,
the responsibility for the result this procedure
achieved upon the shoulders of those who wished
to follow along other lines. That was why Doctor
Svetilovitch enjoyed extraordinary respect in his
210

own party. Great weight was attached to his opinions, and in the matter of tactics his declarations were indisputable.

Several days after Doctor Svetilovitch presented his petition he had a call from an inspector of the police, who handed him, with a request for a receipt, a grey, rough paper impressed at the upper left-hand corner with the stamp of the Skorodozh governing authorities, together with a packet from the District Attorney. This last contained a white solid-looking page of foolscap folded in four, handsomely engraved with the District Attorney's seal. Both the grey rough paper and the solid-looking page of foolscap contained approximately in the same words the answers to the complaints of Doctor Svetilovitch. These informed Doctor Svetilovitch that a very careful investigation had been made in connexion with his complaints ; in conclusion, it was affirmed that Doctor Svetilovitch's evidence as to the illegal actions of the police, and as to the subjection of the girls caught in the woods to blows, was not borne out by facts.

At last Sonya began to improve. The members of the family and acquaintances tried not to recall the sad incident of that night before Sonya. Only indifferent and pleasant matters were mentioned in the poor girl's presence in order to divert her. A number of visitors were invited one evening for this purpose. Some were asked by letter, others by Doctor Svetilovitch in person. He visited the Rameyevs and Trirodov in his carriage, which was harnessed to a pair of stout ponies.

In inviting Trirodov, Doctor Svetilovitch asked him to read something from his own work at the gathering, something that would not make Sonya unpleasantly reminiscent. Trirodov agreed to this quite heartily, although he usually avoided reading his own work anywhere.

As Trirodov was preparing to leave his house that evening and was putting on a coloured tie, Kirsha said to him with his usual gravity :

" I should not go to the Svetilovitches' to-night if I were you. It would be much wiser to remain at home."

Trirodov, not all astonished by this unexpected advice, smiled and asked :

" Why shouldn't I go ? "

Kirsha held his father's hand and said sadly :

" There have been many detectives of late poking their noses about here. What can they want here ? It's almost certain they will make a search of Svetilovitch's house to-night—I have a presentiment."

" That's nothing," said Trirodov with a smile, " we have got used to everything. But, dear Kirsha, you are very inquisitive—you look in everywhere, even where you shouldn't."

" My eyes see, and my ears hear," replied Kirsha, " is that my fault ? "

In the pleasant, well-appointed drawing-room of the Svetilovitches, in the lifeless light of three electric globes with lustrous bronze fittings, the green-blue upholsterings of the Empire furniture seemed illusively beautiful. The dark curves of the grand piano were gleaming. Albums were
212

lying on a little table under the leaves of a palm. The portrait of an old man with a long, white moustache smiled down youthfully and cheerfully from its place on the wall above the sofa. The visitors gathered in the midst of these attractive surroundings, as if there were nothing to mar them. They spoke a great deal, with much heat and eloquence.

Most of the visitors were local Cadets. Among those present were three physicians, one engineer, two legal advocates, the editor of a local progressive newspaper, a justice of the peace, a notary, three gymnasia instructors, and a priest. Nearly all came accompanied by women and girls. There were also several students, college girls, and grown-up schoolboys from the higher gymnasia classes.

The young priest, Nikolai Matveyevitch Zakrasin, who sympathized with the Cadets, gave lessons in Trirodov's school. He was considered a great freethinker among his colleagues, the priests. The town clergy looked askance at him. And the Diocesan Bishop was not well disposed towards him.

Father Zakrasin had completed a course in the ecclesiastical academy. He spoke rather well, wrote something, and collaborated not only in religious but also in worldly periodicals. He had wavy, dense, not over-long hair. His grey eyes smiled amiably and cheerfully. His priestly attire always appeared new and neat. His manners were restrained and gentle. He did not at all resemble the average Russian priest; Father Zakrasin seemed more like a Catholic prelate who had let his beard grow and had put on a golden

213

pectoral cross. Father Zakrasin's house was bright, neat, and cheerful. The walls were decorated with engravings, scenes from sacred history. His study contained several cases of books. It was evident from their selection that Father Zakrasin's interests were very broad. In general he liked that which was certain, convincing, and rational.

His wife, Susanna Kirillovna, a good-looking, plump, and calm woman, who was wholly convinced of the justice of the Cadets' cause, was now sitting quietly on the sofa in the Svetilovitch drawing-room, and expounding truths. Notwithstanding her Constitutional Democratic convictions, she was a real priest's spouse, a housewifely, loquacious, timorous creature.

Priest Zakrasin's sister, Irina Matveyevna, or Irinushka as every one called her, was a parish-school girl who had been won over to the cause by the priest's wife; she was young, rosy, and slender, and greatly resembled her brother. She got excited so often and so intensely that she constantly had to be appeased by the elders, who regarded her youthful impetuosity with benevolent amusement.

Rameyev was there with both his daughters, the Matov brothers, and Miss Harrison. Trirodov was there also.

There was almost a spirit of gaiety. They talked on various subjects—on politics, on literature, on local matters, etc. Sonya's mother sat in the drawing-room and discussed women's rights and the works of Knut Hamsun. Sonya's mother liked this writer intensely, and loved to tell about

214

her meeting with him abroad. There was an auto-graphed portrait of Knut Hamsun upon her table and it was the object of much pride for the whole Svetilovitch family.

At the tea-table in the small neighbouring room, which was called the "buffet," Sonya—surrounded by young people—was pouring out tea. In Doctor Svetilovitch's study they spoke of the recent unrest in near-by villages. There were incendiary fires on various estates and farms belonging to the landed gentry. There were several cases in which the bread granaries belonging to certain hoarders were broken into.

Sonya's mother was asked to play something. She refused a long time, but finally, with evident pleasure, went to the grand piano, and played a selection from Grieg. Then the notary took his turn at the instrument. Irinushka, blushing furiously, sang with much expression the new popular song to his accompaniment:

> *Once I loved a learnèd student,*
> *I admit I wasn't prudent ;*
> *On the day I married him*
> *The village feasted to the brim.*
>
> *Vodka every one was drinking,*
> *All were doing loud thinking—*
> *How to make the masters toil,*
> *And amongst us share their soil.*
>
> *Suddenly there came a copper*
> *Right into our hut a-flopper !*
> *" I'll send you both to Sakhalin ***
> *For raising this rebellious din."*

* Siberian island famous for its prison.

" Well, my dear one, quick, get ready,
Mind that you walk 'long there steady,
For your charming words, my sweet,
A gaol is waiting you to greet."

Do you think I was agitated?
No, not me—I was most elated.
Then the muzhiks stepped right in
And chucked him out on the green.

This song was an illustration appropriate to the discussions on village tendencies. It achieved a great success. Irinushka was profusely praised and thanked for it. Irinushka blushed, and regretted that she knew no other songs of the same kind.

Then Trirodov read his story of a beautiful and exultant love. He read simply and calmly, not as actors read. He finished reading—and in the cold polite praises he felt how remote he was from all these people. Once more, as it frequently had happened before, there stirred in his soul the thought: " Why do I come to see these people ? "

" There is so little in common between them and me," thought Trirodov. Only Elisaveta's smile and word consoled him.

Afterwards there was dancing—then card-playing. It was as always, as everywhere.

CHAPTER XXIII

No one else was expected. The dining-room table was being set for supper. Suddenly there was a loud, violent bell-ring. The housemaid ran quickly to answer it. Some one in the drawing-room remarked in astonishment :

" A rather late visitor."

Every one suddenly felt depressed for some reason. There was an air of ominous expectancy. Were robbers about to break in ? Was it a telegram containing an unpleasant announcement ? Or would some one come in panting and exhausted and divulge a piece of terrible news ? But the words they addressed to each other were of quite a different nature.

" But who can it be at such a late hour ? " said one woman to another.

" Who else can it be but Piotr Ivanitch ! "

" That's so ; he likes coming late."

" Do you remember—once at the Taranovs ? "

Piotr Ivanitch, approaching at that moment, overheard the remark.

" You are unfair to me, Marya Ivanovna ! I've been here a long time," said he.

" Forgive me, but who, then, can it be ? " said Marya Ivanovna in confusion.

" We'll soon know. Let's take a look."

The inquisitive engineer put his head out into the hall and stumbled upon some one in a grey uniform who was walking impetuously towards the drawing-room.   Some one whispered in suppressed horror :

" The police ! "

When the maid, in response to the ring, opened the door, several men filed into the hall, awkwardly jostling one another—house-porters,* gendarmes, detectives, an Inspector of the police, an officer of the gendarmerie, two petty constables.   The maid stood speechless with fright.   The police inspector shouted at her :

" Get back to the kitchen ! "

A detachment of policemen and porters remained outside under the command of the Inspector of the constabulary.   They watched to see that no one entered or left the Svetilovitch house.

Altogether about twenty policemen entered the house.   For some unknown reason they were armed with rifles with fixed bayonets.   Three hideous-looking men in civilian clothes kept close to the policemen.   These were the detectives.   Two policemen stationed themselves at the entrance, two others ran to the telephone, which was attached to a wall in the hall.   It was evident that everything had been arranged beforehand by a manager expert in such matters.   The rest of the men tumbled into the drawing-room.   The Inspector of the police stretched his neck and, assuming a tense red expression and bulging his eyes, shouted very loudly.

" Don't any one dare to move from his place ! "

And he looked round in self-satisfaction at the officer of the gendarmerie.

The men and the women remained transfixed

* Usually brought along as witnesses.

218

in their places, as if they were acting a tableau. They were looking silently at the new-comers.

The policemen, awkwardly holding their rifles, tramped with their ponderous boots on the parquet-floor and made their way about the rooms. They paused at all the doors, looked at the visitors timorously and savagely, uneasily pressed the barrels of their rifles, and tried to look like real soldiers. It was evident that these zealous people were ready to fire at any one whomsoever at the first suspicious movement : they thought that a band of conspirators had gathered here.

All the rooms were overrun with these strangers. It began to smell of bad tobacco, sweat, and vodka. Many of them drank to keep their courage up : they were afraid of a possible armed resistance.

A gendarme placed his Colonel's voluminous portfolio on the grand piano in the drawing-room. The Colonel, stepping forward to the middle of the room, so that the light of the centre cluster of lamps fell almost directly upon his bald forehead and upon his bushy, sandy-haired moustache, pronounced in an official tone :

" Where's the master of this house ? "

He made a determined effort to give the impression that he did not know Doctor Svetilovitch or the others. Actually he knew nearly all of them personally. Doctor Svetilovitch walked up to him.

" I am the master of this house. I am Doctor Svetilovitch," he said in a no less official tone.

The Colonel in the blue uniform then announced :

" M. Svetilovitch, it is my duty to make a search of your house."

219

Doctor Svetilovitch asked :

" Under whose authority are you doing this ? And where is your warrant for carrying out the search ? "

The Colonel of the gendarmerie turned towards the piano and rummaged in his portfolio, but produced nothing. He said :

" I assure you I have an order. If you have any doubts you can call up on the telephone."

Then the Colonel turned to the Inspector of the police and said :

" Please collect them all in one room."

All, except Doctor Svetilovitch, were compelled to go into the dining-room, which now became crowded and uncomfortable. Armed constables were placed at both doors—the one entering the hall and the other the dining-room—as well as in all the corners. Their faces were dull, and their guns seemed unnecessary and absurd in these peaceful surroundings—but then the guests felt even more uncomfortable.

A detective looked out from time to time from the drawing-room door. He looked searchingly into the faces. The look he had on his disagreeable face with its white eyebrows and eyelashes gave the impression that he was sniffing the air.

In the drawing-room the Colonel of the gendarmerie was saying to Doctor Svetilovitch :

" And now, M. Svetilovitch, will you be so good as to tell me with what object you have arranged this gathering ? "

Doctor Svetilovitch replied with an ironic smile :

" With the object of dancing and dining, nothing more. You can see for yourself that we are all peaceable folk."

220

"Very well," said the Colonel in an authoritative, rude tone. "Are the names and families of all gathered here with the object you state known to you?"

Doctor Svetilovitch shrugged his shoulders in astonishment and replied:

"Of course they are known to me! Why shouldn't I know my own guests? I believe you know many of them yourself."

"Be so good," requested the Colonel, "as to give me the names of all your guests."

He produced a sheet of paper from his portfolio and placed it on the piano. The Colonel wrote the names down as Doctor Svetilovitch gave them. When the doctor stopped short the Colonel asked laconically:

"All?"

"Doctor Svetilovitch answered as briefly:

"All."

"Show us into your study," said the Colonel.

They went into the study and rummaged among everything there. They turned over all the books and disarranged the writing-table. They looked through the letters. The Colonel demanded:

"Open the bookcases, the bureau drawers."

Doctor Svetilovitch answered: "The keys, as you see, are in their places in the locks."

He put his hands into his pockets and stood by the window.

"Will you be good enough to open them?" said the Colonel.

"I can't do this," replied Doctor Svetilovitch. "I do not consider it obligatory to help you in your searches."

Pride filled his Cadet's soul. He felt that he was behaving correctly and valiantly. What was the consequence? The uninvited guests opened everything themselves and rummaged where they pleased. A constable put aside all those books which looked suspicious. Several of these books had been published in Russia quite openly and sold no less openly. They took several books wholly innocent in their contents, simply because they thought they detected a rebellious note in their titles.

The Colonel of the gendarmerie announced:

"We will take the correspondence and the manuscripts with us."

Doctor Svetilovitch said in vexation:

"I assure you there's nothing criminal there. The manuscripts are very necessary to my work."

"We'll have a look at them," said the Colonel dryly. "Don't be concerned about them, they will be kept in safety."

Then they rummaged the other rooms. They searched the beds to see if there were any concealed fire-arms.

When he returned into the study the Colonel of the gendarmerie said to Doctor Svetilovitch:

"Well, try and see if you can find the papers of the strike committee."

"I have no such papers," replied Doctor Svetilovitch.

"S-so! Now," said the Colonel very significantly, "tell us frankly where you keep the weapons concealed."

"What weapons?" asked Doctor Svetilovitch in astonishment.

The Colonel replied with an ironic smile :

" Any sort that you may have about—revolvers, bombs, or machine-guns."

" I haven't any kind of weapons," said Doctor Svetilovitch with an amused laugh. " I haven't even a gun for hunting. What kind of weapon can I possibly have ? "

" We'll have a look ! " said the Colonel in a meaningful voice.

They turned the whole house upside down. Of course they found no weapons of any kind.

While all this was going on Trirodov was reading in the dining-room his own verses and some which were not his. The constables listened in a dull way. They did not understand anything, but waited patiently to see if any rebellious words were mentioned, but their waiting remained unrewarded.

The Inspector of the police then entered the dining-room. Every one looked guardedly at him. He said solemnly, as if he were announcing the beginning of an important and useful work :

" Gentlemen, now we must subject all those present to a personal examination. One at a time, please. Suppose we begin with you," said he, turning to the engineer.

The face of the Inspector of the police expressed a consciousness of his personal dignity. His movements were sure and significant. It was evident that he not only was not ashamed of what he was saying and doing, but that he had not the slightest comprehension that there was anything in this to be ashamed of. The engineer, a young and handsome man, shrugged his shoulders, smiled

223

contemptuously and went into the study, being directed there by an awkward motion of the red-palmed paw of the Commissary of the rural police.

The priest's wife found herself an arm-chair in the dining-room, but she was not any more comfortable in it. Terrified in her arm-chair, she trembled like jelly. With pale lips she whispered to the parish-school girl she had won over to the cause :

" Irinushka, dearest, think of it—they are going to search us ! "

" The parish-school girl, Irinushka, looking slender, fresh, and red, like a newly washed carrot, moved her ears in her fright—a faculty which her companions envied her intensely—and whispered something to the priest's wife.

The constable looked savagely at the priest's wife and at the parish-school girl, and cried out in a shrill, somewhat hoarse voice, which resembled the crowing of a cock :

" I must very humbly ask you not to whisper."

The constables with the guns pricked up their ears. Their sudden zeal made them perspire. The priest's wife and the parish-school girl almost fainted from fright, but the girl at once recovered herself and began to get angry ; she was now even more angry than she had been frightened a little while ago. Small tears gleamed in her eyes ; small drops of perspiration appeared on her cheeks and on her forehead. The angry girl's face grew even redder, so that now she resembled no longer a carrot but a wet beetroot. The only person in the room to be refreshingly and youthfully indignant, and all aflame with a deep anger, she looked truly beautiful in her ingenuous exasperation.

"Here is something new!" she cried. "Whispering is forbidden! Are you afraid that we will say something against you, that we will hurt you?"

At this moment all the Cadets and their wives and daughters, who were sitting around the table and against the walls, turned their horrified faces at the parish-school girl, and all together hissed at her. They would have laid hands on her, some one would have gagged her mouth—but not one of them dared to make a move. They sat motionless, looked at the parish-school girl with eyes dilated with fear, and hissed.

The parish-school girl, overcome with fright, grew silent. Only the hissing could be heard in the dining-room. Even the constables began to smile at the friendly hissing of the Cadets of both sexes.

When they had finished hissing, Irinushka said almost tranquilly:

"We didn't whisper anything criminal. I only said about you, Mr. Constable, that you were fascinatingly handsome with your dark hair."

When she saw that the Rameyev sisters were laughing, Irinushka turned to Elisaveta:

"You do agree with me, Vetochka, that the constable is a fascinatingly handsome man?"

The constable flushed. He was not sure whether the blushing girl was laughing at him or in earnest. In any case he frowned, vigorously twirled his dark moustache, and exclaimed:

"I must humbly ask you not to express yourself."

Later, at home, Irinushka was scolded for her behaviour, regarded as untactful by Priest Zakrasin.

225

The priest's wife was especially angry. Poor Irinushka even cried several times.

But this was later. At this particular instant the Inspector of the police and the Colonel of the gendarmerie were sitting in Doctor Svetilovitch's study and were examining the guests one by one; they turned their pockets inside out and, for some unknown reason, deprived their owners of letters, notes, and notebooks.

Rameyev was in a quiet, genial mood. He laughed on being searched. Trirodov made an effort to be calm and was a little sharper than he wished to be.

The women were searched in one of the bedrooms. A police-matron was brought for this purpose. She was a dirty, cunning sycophant. The contact of her coarse hands was repulsive. Elisaveta felt uncomfortably unclean after she had passed through the policewoman's paws. Elena shivered with fear and nausea.

Those who had been searched were not permitted to enter the dining-room but were led into the drawing-room. Nearly all the searched ones were proud of this. They looked as if they were celebrating a birthday.

No one was arrested. They began to draw up the official report. Trirodov quietly addressed a gendarme, but the latter replied in a whisper :

" We are not permitted to enter into conversation with any one. Those scoundrelly spies are watching us, so that we shouldn't speak with liberals. They are quick to inform against us."

" You are in an unfortunate business," said Trirodov.

226

The Inspector of the police read the official report aloud. It was signed by Doctor Svetilovitch, the Inspector, and the witnesses.

When the uninvited guests left, the hosts and the invited guests sat down to supper.

It was presently discovered that the beer prepared for the occasion had been consumed. At the same time the cap of one of the guests had disappeared. Its owner was very much disturbed. The cap became almost the sole topic of conversation.

On the next day there was much talk in town about the search at the Svetilovitches, the consumed beer, and especially about the lost cap.

Not a little was said in the newspapers about the beer and the cap. One newspaper in St. Petersburg devoted a very heated article to the stolen cap. The author of the article made very broad generalizations. He asked:

" Is it not one of those caps with which we were preparing to throw back the foreign enemy ? Is not all Russia seeking now its lost cap and cannot be consoled ? " *

Much less was said and written about the consumed beer. For some reason or other it did

* I have it on the authority of one who was of the party that it actually took place at the house of a celebrated living poet in St. Petersburg. The lost cap belonged to Dmitry Merezhkovsky, who immediately wrote a much-discussed article in an important newspaper under the title of " What has become of our Cap ? " The above is an actual quotation from it. The sarcastic remark about " throwing back the enemy " is aimed at those " patriots " who used to say that all Russians had to do to repel foreign enemies was to throw their caps at them.—TRANSLATOR.

not offend people so much. In accordance with our general custom of placing substance above the form, it was found that the stealing of the cap deserved the greater protest, inasmuch as it is more difficult to get along without a cap than without beer.

CHAPTER XXIV

ONCE more alone! He sat in his room, musing of her, recalling her dear features.

There was an album before him—portrait after portrait of her—naked, beautiful, calling to love, to the sweet solace of love. Would this white breast cease heaving? Would these clear eyes grow dim?

She died.

Trirodov closed the album. For a long time he remained immersed in thought. Suddenly there was a rustling behind the wall, which gradually grew louder—it seemed as if the whole house were alive with the movements of the quiet children. Some one knocked on the door; Kirsha entered, distraught. He said:

"Father, let us go into the wood as fast as we can."

Trirodov looked at him in silence. Kirsha went on:

"Something terrible is happening. There, near the hollow, by the spring."

Elisaveta's blue eyes appeared to him suddenly as in a flame. Where was she? Was she in a difficulty? And his heart fell into the dark abyss of fear.

Kirsha made haste. He almost cried in his agitation.

They went on horseback. They whipped up their horses. They feared they might be too late.

Again the quiet, dark, intensely pensive wood. Elisaveta walked alone—tranquil, blue-eyed, simple in her dress, harmonious in the graceful harmony of her deep experiences. She fell into thought—she recalled things and mused upon them. Her dreams were revealed in the gleam of her blue eyes. Dreams of happiness and of passionate love were interwoven with a different, greater love; and these melted into one another in the fiery longing for noble activity and sacrifice.

What did she not recall? What did she not dream of?

Sharp swords were being forged. To whose lot would they fall?

The high standard of solitary freedom was fluttering.

Youths and maidens!

There, in the dark halls of his house, proud plans were being made.

What a beautiful environment of naked beauty!

There were the children—happy and beautiful —in the wood.

There were the quiet children in his house— radiant and lovable and touched with such sadness.

There was the strange Kirsha.

Portraits of his first wife—naked and beautiful.

Elisaveta's blue eyes gleamed dreamily.

She recalled the details of the previous evening— the remote room in Trirodov's house, the small gathering in it, the long discussions, the subsequent labours, the measured knock of the typing-machine, the damp pages put into portfolios.

Then she thought how she, Stchemilov, Voronok and some one else walked out into the various streets of the town to paste up the bills. They put the paste on while still walking. They always took a look round first to see that no one was in sight. Then they would pause and quickly stick the bill on the fence. They would go on farther. . . . The effort had been successful.

Elisaveta did not think where she was going; she had walked quite far out of her way, to a place that she had not been to before. She imagined that the quiet children were keeping guard over her. She walked trustfully in the forest silence, yielding her bare feet to the caresses of the moist forest grasses, and now listened, now ceased listening, in delicious drowsiness.

Something rustled behind the bushes, some one's nimble feet were running behind the light undergrowth.

Suddenly she heard a loud laugh—almost at her ears; it broke into her sweet reverie with such a violent suddenness—like the trumpet of an archangel calling to wake the dear dead on Judgment Day. Elisaveta felt some one's hot breath on her neck. A rough, perspiring hand caught her by her bared forearm.

It was as if Elisaveta had suddenly awakened from a pleasant dream. She raised her frightened eyes and paused like one bewitched. Two vigorous ragged men stood before her. They were both handsome young fellows; one of them was astonishingly handsome, swarthy, black-eyed. Both were barely covered by their dirty rags, the openings in which showed their dirty, perspiring, powerful bodies.

The men were laughing and crying insolently:

" We've caught you this time, pretty one ! "

" We'll fondle you to your heart's content—you shan't forget us so soon ! "

They drew closer and closer to her and blew their hot breath upon her. Elisaveta suddenly came to herself, tore herself away with a quick movement and began to run. A horror akin to wonder swung the resounding bell in her breast—her heavily beating heart. It hindered her running, and there was a beating of sharp little hammers under her knees.

The two men quickly overtook her, and as they obstructed her passage they laughed insolently and said :

" Ah, my beauty ! Don't make a fuss ! "

" You won't get away anyway."

They jostled one another as they pulled Elisaveta about, each towards himself ; and acted altogether awkwardly, as if they did not know who should begin and how. Their sensual panting bared their white teeth, vigorous as those of a wild beast. The beauty of the half-naked, swarthy man tempted Elisaveta—it was a sudden piquant temptation acting like a poison.

The handsome man, his voice hoarse with agitation, shouted :

" Tear her clothes ! Let her dance naked before us, and make our eyes glad."

" She hasn't much on ! " the other responded with a gay laugh.

He caught the broad collar of Elisaveta's dress with one hand and jerked it forward ; he thrust the other hand, large, hot, and perspiring, under her chemise and pressed and squeezed her taut young breast.

"Two men against one woman—aren't you ashamed?" said Elisaveta.

"Don't be ashamed, my lass, and lie down on the grass," exclaimed the handsome, swarthy one, with a laugh very much like a horse's neigh. His white teeth gleamed, his eyes flamed with desire, as he tore Elisaveta's clothes with his hands and his teeth. The red and the white roses of her body were soon bared.

The sensual breathing of the assailants was horrible and repugnant to her, and she found it no less horrible and repugnant to look at their perspiring faces, at the gleaming of their enkindled eyes. But their beauty was tempting. In the dark depths of her consciousness a thought struggled —to yield herself, to yield willingly.

Her dress and chemise, flimsy of texture, ripped with a barely audible noise. Elisaveta struggled desperately, and shouted something—she did not remember what.

All her clothes were already torn, and soon the last shreds of her very light garments fell from her naked body. And in the struggle the rags of the two clumsily moving men ripped with a loud, splitting sound, their sudden nakedness rousing them even more.

There was seductiveness for Elisaveta in the nakedness of these impetuous bodies. She taunted them:

"The two of you can't manage one girl."

She was strong and agile. It was difficult for them to conquer her. Her naked body struggled and wriggled itself out of their arms. The blue arch of her teeth on the naked shoulder of the

233

handsome, swarthy man grew red quickly. Drops of dark blood spurted on to his naked torso.

" Wait, you carrion-flesh," he cried in a hoarse voice, " I will . . ."

The powerful but awkward pair grew more and more exasperated. They were enraged and intoxicated by her extraordinary resistance, by the falling away of their rags and their sudden nakedness. They beat Elisaveta, in the beginning with their fists, later with quickly severed branches, or with those which already lay on the ground. The sharp fires of pain stung her naked body and tempted her with a burning temptation to yield herself willingly. But she did not yield herself. Her loud sobs resounded for some distance around her.

The struggle continued for a long time. Elisaveta already began to weaken, and the raging passions of the two men had not yet exhausted themselves. Naked and savage, the lips of their wry mouths grown blue, their blood-inflamed eyes gleaming dimly, they were on the point of drawing her down to the ground.

Suddenly the white, quiet boys came running in a swarm into the glade, lightly and noiselessly, like a rapid, light summer shower. They appeared so quickly from among the bushes and threw themselves on the savage pair ; they surrounded them, cast themselves upon them, threw them down, cast a sleeping spell upon them, and dragged them away into the depth of the dark hollow. And they left the naked bodies sprawling helplessly on the rough grasses.

The rapid, noiseless movements of the quiet boys put Elisaveta into a mood verging on oblivion, half painful and half sweet.

What happened in that thicket seemed like a heavy and incredible dream to Elisaveta—a sudden and cruel whim of the undependable Aisa. And for a long time a dark horror nestled in her soul, merging with senseless laughter—the exulting smile of pitiless irony. . . .

Elisaveta came to herself. She saw above her the green branches of the birches and the lovely pale faces. She lay in the refreshing grass encircled by quiet children. She could not recall at once what had happened to her. Her nakedness was incomprehensible to her—but she felt no shame.

Her eyes paused for a moment on some one's neatly combed fair hair. She recognized Klavdia, the dissembling instructress. She stood under the tree, her arms folded, and looked with her grey eyes gleaming with envy at Elisaveta's naked body; it was as if a grey spider was spinning across her soul a grey web of dull oblivion and tedious indifference.

"Clothes will be here in a moment," said one of the boys quietly.

Elisaveta closed her eyes and lay tranquilly. Her head felt somewhat dizzy. Fatigue overcame her. Beautiful and graceful she lay there—as perfect as the dream of Don Quixote. . . .

They were dark, long-drawn-out moments, and there fell in their midst from the gradually darkening sky a brief interval of great comprehension. And this brief interval became like an age—from birth until death. Early next morning Elisaveta clearly recalled the course of this strange, vivid life — the sad lofty road, the life of Queen Ortruda.*

And when, suffocating, Ortruda was dying . . .

The rush of light feet in the grass awakened Elisaveta. Light, adroit hands dressed her. The quiet boys helped her to rise. Elisaveta rose and looked around her : a light green Grecian tunic draped her tired body within its broad folds. Elisaveta thought :

" How shall I manage to walk so far ? "

And as if in answer to her question, she suddenly caught sight of a light trap under the trees. Some one said :

" Kirsha will drive you home."

In her strange dress Elisaveta returned home. She sat silently in the trap. She did not even notice Trirodov. She was trying to recall something. Through the dark horror and senseless laughter there shone clearer and clearer the recollection of another life lived through momentarily— the life of Queen Ortruda.

* The second of the novels under the general head of " The Created Legend " deals with the previous existence of Elisaveta when she was the Queen Ortruda of the United Isles in the Mediterranean, and her consort was Prince Tancred, now Trirodov. She died from suffocation in a volcanic eruption, after a vain effort to help her people. The author draws a curious parallel, not only with regard to these two characters, but has also a revolution as the background ; it is a rather veiled effort to describe over again the events which took place in Russia in 1905.—TRANSLATOR.

CHAPTER XXV

THE quiet boy Grisha stood within the enclosure of enchanted sadness and mystery. His face was pale and reposeful, and there was a keen, quiet sparkle in his cool, sky-blue eyes.

The early evening sky was growing bluer—a blue reposefulness was pouring itself out upon the earth and extinguishing the ruby-coloured flames of the sunset. And silhouetted against the blueness of the heights birds were flying about. Why should they have wings, these earthly, preoccupied creatures ?

As he stood there in the quiet of the enclosure, Grisha felt himself drawn by the fragrance of the lilies of the valley, no less innocent than he, the quiet, blue-eyed Grisha. It was as if some one were calling him outside the enclosure, towards the poor life which tormented itself in the blue and mist-enveloped distance, calling him despairingly and agonizingly — and he both wished and did not wish to go. Some one's voice, full of distress, called him wearily to life outside.

How can calls of distress be resisted ? When will the tranquil heart forget earthly travail wholly and for always ?

At last Grisha walked out of the gate. He took a deep breath of the sharp but delicious outside air. He walked quietly upon the narrow, dusty path. His light footprints lay behind him, and

237

his white clothes glimmered brightly, in quiet movement, against the dim verdure and the grey dust. Before him, barely visible, rose the white, lifeless, clear moon, powerless to enchant the tedious earthly spaces.

Then the town began—the grey, dull, tiresome town, with its dirty back yards, consumptive vegetable gardens, broken-down hedges, bathhouses, and sheds, and all manner of ugly projections and depressing amorphousness—all of it resembling a hopeless ruin.

Egorka, the eleven-year-old son of a local commoner, stood by the hedge of one of the vegetable gardens. What had been red calico once made up his torn shirt; but his face!—it was like that of an angel in a tawny mask covered with spots of dirt and dust. Wings are for light feet, but what can the earth do? Only dust and clay cling to light feet.

Egorka had come out to play. He waited for his companions, but for some reason none of them was to be seen. He stood alone there, now listening to this, now looking at that. He suddenly espied on the other side of the hedge an unknown quiet boy, who—all in white—was looking at him. Egorka asked in astonishment :

" Where do you come from ? "

" You can never know," said Grisha.

" Don't be too sure of that ! " shouted Egorka gaily. " Maybe I do know. Now tell me."

" Would you like to know ? " asked Grisha with a smile.

It was a tranquil smile. Egorka was about to stick his tongue out in response, but changed his mind for some reason. They began to converse, to exchange whispers.

Everything around them lapsed into deep quiet, and nothing appeared to give heed to them—it was as if the two little ones went off into quite another world, behind a thin curtain which no one could rend. So motionless stood the birches bewitched mysteriously by three fallen spirits. Grisha asked again :

" Yes, you would like to know ? "

" Honest to God, I'd like to ; here's a cross to prove it," said Egorka rather quickly, and he crossed himself with an oblique movement of the joined fingers of his dirty hand.

" Then follow me," said Grisha.

He turned lightly homewards, and as he walked he did not stop to look round at the meagre, tiresome objects of this grey life. Egorka followed the white boy. He walked quietly and marvelled at the other. He thought for a while, then he asked :

" Are you not one of God's angels ? Why are you so white ? "

The quiet boy smiled at these words. He said with a light sigh :

" No, I am a human being."

" You don't mean it ? An ordinary boy ? "

" Just like you—almost like you."

" How clean you are ! I should say you washed yourself seven times a day with egg-soap ! You walk about barefoot, not at all like me, and the sunburn doesn't seem to stick to you—there's only a cover of dust on your feet."

The aroma of violets came from somewhere,

and it mingled now with the dry smell of the flying dust, now with the sickly, half-sweet, half-bitter odour of the smoke of a forest fire.

The two boys avoided the tiresome monotony of the fields and the roads, and entered the dark silence of the wood. They passed by glades and copses and quietly purling streams. The boys strode along narrow footpaths, where the gentle dew clung to their feet. Everything appeared wonderful in Egorka's eyes, used only to the raging turbulence of a malignant yet dull and grey life. The time lingered on, running and consuming itself, wreathed in a circle of delicious moments, and it seemed to Egorka that he had come into some fabulous land. He slept somewhere at night, and he felt intensely happy on opening his eyes next morning, having been awakened by the twitter of birds which shook the dew from the pliant tree-limbs ; then he played with the cheerful boys and listened to music.

Sometimes the white Grisha left Egorka all by himself. Then he again reappeared. Egorka noticed that Grisha kept apart from the others, the cheerful, noisy children ; that he did not play with them, and that he spoke little—not that he was afraid, or deliberately turned aside, but simply because it seemed to arrange itself, and it was natural for him to be alone, radiant and sad.

Once Egorka and Grisha, on being left by themselves, went strolling together through a little wood which was all permeated with light. The wood grew denser and denser.

They came to two tall, straight trees. A bronze rod was suspended between them, and upon the

rod, on rings, hung a dark red silk curtain. The
light breeze caused the thin draperies to flutter.
The quiet, blue-eyed Grisha drew the curtain aside.
The red folds came together with a sharp rustle
and with a sudden flare as of a flame. The opening
revealed a wooded vista, all permeated with a
strangely bright light, like a vision of a transfigured
land. Grisha said :

" Go, Egorushka—it is good there."

Egorka looked into the clear wooded distance :
fear beset his heart, and he said quietly :

" I am afraid."

" What are you afraid of, silly boy ? " asked
Grisha affectionately.

" I don't know. Something makes me afraid,"
said Egorka timidly.

Grisha felt aggrieved. He sighed quietly and
then said :

" Well, go home, then, if you are afraid here."

Egorka recalled his home, his mother, the town
he lived in. He did not have a very happy time
of it at home—they lived poorly, and he was
whipped often. Egorka suddenly threw himself
at the quiet Grisha, caught him by his gentle, cool
hands, and cried :

" Don't chase me away, dear Grisha, don't chase
me from you."

" Am I chasing you away ? " retorted Grisha.
" You yourself don't want to come."

Egorka got down on his knees and whispered
as he kissed Grisha's feet :

" I pray to you angels with all my strength."

" Then follow me," said Grisha.

Light hands descended on Egorka's shoulders

241

and lifted him from the grass. Egorka followed Grisha obediently to the blue paradise of his quiet eyes. A peaceful valley opened before him and the quiet children played in it. The dew fell on Egorka's feet, and its kisses gave him joy. The quiet children surrounded Egorka and Grisha and, all joining hands in one broad ring, carried the two boys with them in a swiftly moving dance.

" My dear angels," shouted Egorka, twirling and rejoicing, " you have bright little faces, you have clean little eyes, you have white little hands, you have light little feet ! Am I on earth or am I in Paradise ? My dear ones, my little brothers and little sisters, where are your little wings ? "

Some one's near, sweet-sounding voice answered him :

" You are upon the earth, not in Paradise, and we have no need of wings—we fly wingless."

They captivated, bewitched, and caressed him. They showed him all the wonders of the wood under the tree-stumps, the bushes, the dry leaves— little wood-sprites with rustling little voices, with spider-webby hair, straight ones and hunch-backed ones ; little old men of the wood ; the shadow-sprites and little companion spirits ; bantering little sprites in green coats, midnight ones and daylight ones, grey ones and black ones ; little jokers-pokers with shaggy little paws ; fabulous birds and animals—everything that is not to be seen in the gloomy, everyday, earthly world.

Egorka had a splendid time with the quiet children. He did not notice how a whole week had passed by—from Friday to Friday. And suddenly he began to long for his mother. He heard her calling him at night, and as he woke in agitation he called :

" Mamma, where are you ? "

There was stillness and silence all around him—it was an altogether unknown world. Egorka began to cry. The quiet children came to comfort him. They said to him :

" There's nothing to cry about. You will return to your mother. And she will be glad, and she will caress you."

" She may whip me," said Egorka, sobbing.

The quiet children smiled and said :

" Fathers and mothers whip their children."

" They like to do it."

" It seems wicked to beat any one."

" But they really mean well."

" They beat whom they love."

" People mix everything up—shame, love, pain."

" Don't you be afraid, Egorushka—she's a mother."

" Very well, I'll not be afraid," said Egorka, comforted.

When Egorka took leave of the quiet children Grisha said to him :

" You had better not tell your mother where you have passed all this time."

" No, I won't tell," replied Egorka vigorously, " not for anything."

" You'll blab it out," said one of the girls.

She had dark, infinitely deep eyes ; her thin, bare arms were always folded obstinately across her breast. She spoke even less than the other quiet children, and of all human words she liked " no " most.

243

"No, I shan't blab anything," asserted Egorka. "I shan't even tell any one where I have been; I shall put all these words under lock and key."

That same evening when Egorka left with Grisha, his mother suddenly missed him. She shouted a long time and cursed and threatened; but as there was no response she became frightened. "Perhaps he's been drowned," she thought. She ran among her neighbours, wailing and lamenting.

"My boy's gone. I can't find him anywhere. I simply don't know where else to look. He's either drowned in the river or fallen into a well— that's what comes of mischief-making."

One neighbour suggested:

"It's most likely the Jews have caught him and are keeping him in some out-of-the-way spot, and only waiting to let his Christian blood and then drink it."

This guess pleased them. They said with great assurance:

"It's Jews' work."

"They are again at it, that accursed breed."

"There's no getting rid of them."

"What a wretched affair!"

They all believed this. The disturbing rumour that the Jews had stolen a Christian boy spread about town. Ostrov took a most zealous share in disseminating the rumour. The markets were filled with noisy discussions. The tradesmen and dealers, instigated by Ostrov, bellowed loudly their denunciations. Why did Ostrov do this? He knew, of course, that it was a lie. But latterly, acting on the instructions of the local branch of the Black Hundred, he had been engaged in provocatory work. The new episode came in handily.

The police began an investigation. They looked for the boy, but without success. In any case, they found a Jew who had been seen by some one near Egorka's house. He was arrested.

It was evening again. Egorka's mother was at home when Egorka returned. There was a radiant sadness about him as he walked up to his mother, kissed her and said :

" Hello, mamma ! "

Egorka's mother assailed him with questions :

" Oh, you little wretch ! Where have you been ? What have you been doing ? What unclean demons have carried you away ? "

Egorka remembered his promise. He stood before his mother in obstinate silence. His mother questioned him angrily :

" Where have you been ? tell me ! Did the Jews try to crucify you ? "

" What Jews ? " exclaimed Egorka. " No one has tried to crucify me."

" You just wait, you young brat," shouted his mother in a rage, " I'll make you talk."

She caught hold of the besom and began to tear off its twigs. Then she stripped the boy of his light clothes. Still wrapt in his radiant sadness, Egorka looked at his mother with astonished eyes. He cried plaintively :

" Mamma, what are you doing ? "

But, already seized by the rough hand, the little body that had been washed by the still waters

245

began to struggle on the knees of the harshly crying woman. It was painful, and Egorka sobbed in a shrill voice. His mother beat him long and painfully, and she accompanied each blow with an admonition :

" Tell me where you've been ! Tell me ! I won't stop until you tell me."

At last she stopped and burst out into violent crying :

" Why has God punished me so ? But no, I'll yet beat a word out of you. I'll give it to you worse to-morrow."

Egorka was shaken less by the physical pain than by the unexpected harshness of his reception. He had been in touch with another world, and the quiet children in the enchanted valley had reconstructed his soul on another plane.

His mother, however, loved him. Of course, she loved him. That was why she beat him in her anger. Love and cruelty go always together among humankind. They like to torment, vengeance gives them pleasure. But later Egorka's mother took pity on him ; she thought she had flogged him too hard. And now she walked up quietly to him.

Egorka lay on the bench and moaned softly, then he grew silent. His mother smoothed his back awkwardly with her rough hands and left him. She thought he had gone to sleep.

In the morning she went to wake him. She found him lying cold and motionless on the bench, his face downward. And his radiance was gone from him—he lay there a dark, cold corpse. The horrified mother began to wail :

246

"He's dead! Egorushka, are you really dead? Oh, God—and his little hands are quite cold!"

She dashed out to her neighbours, she aroused the whole neighbourhood with her shrill cries. Inquisitive women soon filled the house.

"I struck him ever so lightly with a thin twig," the mother wailed. "Then my angel lay down on the bench, cried a little, then grew quiet and went to sleep, and in the morning he gave up his soul to God."

Held by a heavy, death-like sleep, Egorka lay there motionless and to all appearances lifeless, and listened to his mother's wailing and to the discordant clamour of voices. And he heard his mother keening over him:

"Those accursed Jews have sucked out all his blood! It was not the first time that I beat my little darling! It used to be that I'd beat him and put a bit of salt on afterwards, and nothing would come of it—and here I've hit him with a little twig and he, my handsome darling, my little angel . . ."

Egorka heard her groans and wondered at his fettered helplessness and immobility. He seemed to hear the noise of some one else's body—he realized that it was his own as it was put on the floor to be washed. He had an intense longing to stir, to rise, but he could not. He thought:

"I have died: what are they going to do with me now?"

And again he thought:

"Why is it that my soul is not leaving my body? I do not feel that I have arms or legs, yet I can hear."

He wondered and waited. Then, with a sudden powerless exertion, he tried to wake from his death-like sleep, to return to himself, to run away from the dark grave—and again his helpless will drooped, and again he waited.

And he heard the sounds of the funeral chant, and noted the blueness of the little cloud of incense-smoke and the fragrance that was wafted by the quietly sounding swings of the smoky censer.

CHAPTER XXVI

Egorka was buried. His mother wept long over his grave in long-drawn-out wails, then went home. She was convinced that her boy would be far better off there than upon the earth, and was consoled. But such truly Russian people as Kerbakh, Ostrov, and others would not be consoled. They let loose evil rumours. The report spread :

"The Jews have tortured a Christian boy. They've cut him up with knives and used his blood in their *matzoth*." *

The slanderers were not deterred by the consideration that the Jewish Passover had taken place very much earlier than the running away of Egorka from his mother.

The townsmen were agitated—those who believed as well as those who did not believe the tale. Demands were made for an investigation and the opening of the grave.

Elisaveta came to Trirodov's house early in the day and remained there long. Trirodov showed her his colony. The quiet boy Grisha accompanied them, and looked with the blue reposefulness of his impassionate eyes into the blue flames of her rapturous ones, soothing the sultriness and passion of her agitation.

Her light, ample dress seemed transparent—the perfect outlines of her body showed clearly ; the

* Unleavened bread of the Passover.

red and white roses of her breast and shoulders were visible. Her sunburnt feet were bare—she loved the affectionate contact of the earth and the grass.

It was all like a paradise—the twittering of the birds, the hubbub of the children, the rustle of the wind in the grass and in the trees, the murmur of the brook in the wood. Everything was innocent, as in Paradise—girls, scantily dressed, came up, spoke to them, and were not ashamed. Everything was chaste, as in Paradise. And cloudless, the sky shone above the forest glades.

Towards evening Elisaveta sat at Trirodov's. They read poems. Elisaveta loved poems even before she met Trirodov. Who else should love them if not girls? Now she read poems avidly. Whole hours passed by quickly in reading, and the poems gave birth in her to sweet and bitter emotions and passionate dreams.

Perhaps this was so because she was in love; in love she had found a new sun for herself, and she led a new dance round it of dreams, hopes, sorrows, joys, enchantments, and raptures. And, flaunting a rainbow of radiance, this round dance, this flaming circle of impetuous emotions, was full of a rich music and vivid colour.

Trirodov caused her to fall in love with the verses of the new poets. She found such enchantments and such disillusions in the fragile music of new poetry, written so happily and so elusively, with a lightness and transparency like those of the dresses that she now loved to wear.

With the harmony of their souls thus achieved, why should they not love one another?
250

Once, after they had read together some beautiful love-poems, Trirodov remarked :

" Love says ' No ' to the world, the lyrical ' No '—marriage says ' Yes ' to it, the ironic ' Yes.' To be in love, to strive, yet not to possess—that is the poetry of love, sweet but illusive. Externally love contradicts the world and conceals its fatal discord. To be together, to say ' Yes ' to some one, to yield oneself—that is the way in which life reveals its irreconcilable contradictions. And how to be together when we are such solitary souls ? And how to yield oneself ? Mask after mask falls off, and it is terrible to see Janus-faced actuality. A weariness comes on—what has become of love, that love which had prided itself on being stronger than death ? "

" You have had a wife," said Elisaveta. " You loved her. Everything here is reminiscent of her. She was beautiful."

Her voice became dark, and the blue flashes under the moist eyelids lit up with a jealous flame. Trirodov smiled and said sadly :

" She left life before the time had come for weariness to make its appearance. My Dulcinea did not want to become Aldonza."

" Dulcinea is loved," said Elisaveta, " but the fullness of life belongs to Aldonza becoming Dulcinea."

" But does Aldonza want that ? " asked Trirodov.

" She wants it, but cannot realize it," said Elisaveta. " But we will help her, we will teach her."

Trirodov smiled affectionately—if sadly—and said :

" But he, like the eternal Don Juan, always

251

seeks Dulcinea. And what is to him the poor earthly Aldonza, poisoned by the dream of beauty?"

"It is for that that he will love her," replied Elisaveta; "because she is poor and has been poisoned by the exultant dream of beauty. The basis for their union will be creative beauty."

The night came: a darkness settled outside the windows, full of the whisperings of sad, pellucid voices. Trirodov walked up to the window. Elisaveta soon stood beside him—and almost at the same instant their eyes fixed themselves upon the distant, dimly visible cemetery. Trirodov said quietly:

"He has been buried there. But he will rise from his grave."

Elisaveta looked at him in astonishment and asked:

"Who?"

Trirodov glanced at her like one suddenly awakened and said slowly:

"It is a boy who has not yet lived, and who is still chaste. His body contains all possibilities and not a single achievement. He is like one created to receive every energy directed at him. Now he is asleep in his tight coffin, in a grave. He will awake for a life free from passions and desires, for clear seeing and hearing, for the establishment of one will."

"When will he awake?" asked Elisaveta.

"When I wish it," said Trirodov, "I will wake him."

The sound of his voice was sad and insistent—like the sound of an invocation.

"To-night?" asked Elisaveta.

" If you wish it," answered Trirodov quietly.

" Must I leave ? " she asked again.

" Yes," he answered, just as simply and as quietly as before.

She bid him good-bye and left. Trirodov again walked up to the window. He called some one in a voice of invocation and whispered :

" You will awake, dear one. Wake, rise, come to me. I will open your eyes, and you will see what you have not yet seen. I will open your ears, and you will hear what you have not yet heard. You are of the earth—I will not part you from the earth. You are from me, you are mine, you are I ; come to me. Wake ! "

He waited confidently. He knew that when the sleeper had awakened in his grave they would come to him—the wise, innocent ones—and would tell him.

Kirsha walked into the room quietly. He walked up to his father and asked :

" Are you looking at the cemetery ? "

Trirodov laid his hand silently on the boy's head. Kirsha said :

" There is a boy in one of the graves who is not dead."

" How do you know ? " asked Trirodov.

But he knew what Kirsha's answer would be. Kirsha said :

" Grisha told me that Egorka was not quite dead. He is asleep ; but he will awake ! "

" Yes," said Trirodov.

" And will he come to you ? " asked Kirsha.

" Yes," was the answer.

" When will he come ? " asked Kirsha again.

253

Trirodov said with a smile :

" Rouse Grisha and ask him whether the sleeper has yet begun to wake in his grave."

Kirsha walked away. Trirodov looked in silence at the distant cemetery, where the dark, bereaved night stooped sadly over the crosses.

" And where are you, my happy beloved ? "

A quiet rustle made itself audible behind the doors : the little house-sprites moved quietly near the walls, and whispered and waited.

Awakened by a low sigh, Grisha arose. He walked out into the garden and stood listening with downcast eyes near the railing. He was smiling, but without joy. Who knew whether the other would rejoice ?

Kirsha walked up to him and, indicating the cemetery with a movement of his head, asked :

" Is he alive ? Has he awakened ? "

" Yes," said Grisha. " Egorushka is sighing in his grave ; he's just awakened."

Kirsha ran home to his father and repeated to him Grisha's words.

" We must make haste," said Trirodov.

He again experienced an agitation with which he had been long familiar. He felt in himself an ebb and flow as of some strange power. A kind of marvellous energy, gathered by some means known to himself alone, issued slowly from him. A mysterious current passed between himself and the grave where the boy who had departed from life lay in the throes of death-sleep ; it cast a spell upon the sleeper and caused him to stir.

Trirodov quickly descended the stairway into

the room where the quiet children slept. His light footsteps were barely audible, and his feet felt the cold that came from the planked floor. The quiet children lay upon their beds motionlessly, as if they did not breathe. It seemed as if there were many of them, and that they slept eternally in the endless darkness of that quiet bedchamber.

Trirodov paused seven times, and each time one of the sleepers awoke at his one glance. Three boys and four girls answered his call. They stood there tranquilly, looked at Trirodov and waited.

" Follow me ! " said Trirodov.

They walked after him, the white quiet ones, and the rustle of their light footsteps was barely heard.

Kirsha waited in the garden—and he seemed earthly and dark among the white, quiet children.

They walked quickly upon the Navii path like gliding, nocturnal shadows, one after another, the whole ten of them, with Grisha leading. The dew fell upon their naked feet, and the ground under their feet was soft, warm, and sad.

Egorka awoke in his grave. It was dark and somewhat stuffy. His head felt oppressed as under a weight. There sounded in his ears the persistent call :

" Rise, come to me."

Fear assailed him. His eyes looked but did not see. It was hard to breathe. He recalled something, and all that he recalled was like a horrible delirium. Then came the sudden awful realization :

" I am in a grave, in a coffin."

He groaned, and his heart began to thump. His

throat, as if clutched by some one's fingers, shivered convulsively. His eyes dilated widely, and the flaming darkness of the nailed-up coffin swept before them. As he tossed about in the tight coffin, tormented by his dread, Egorka moaned, and whispered in a dull voice :

" Three house-sprites, three wood-sprites, three fallen sprites ! "

The gate to the burial-ground was open. Trirodov and the children entered. They were among the poor graves—simple little mounds and wooden crosses. It was gloomy, damp, and quiet. There was a smell of grass—a graveyard reverie. The crosses gleamed white in the mist. A poignant silence hovered there, and the whole cemetery seemed filled with the dark reverie of the dead. Poignant feelings were re-experienced deliciously and painfully.

Nowhere does the soil feel so near to one as in a graveyard—it is the sacred soil of repose. They walked quietly, the whole ten of them, one after another, and felt the coolness and the softness of the ground under their bare feet. They passed near a grave. The little mound was quiet and poor, and it seemed as if the earth were crying, wailing, and suffering.

The boys, dimly discernible in the darkness against the lumps of black earth, began to dig the grave. The little girls stood very quietly, one at each of the four sides, and seemed engrossed in the nocturnal silence. The watchmen slept like the dead, and the dead slept, keeping a powerless watch over their graves.

Slowly the little coffin began to show. The low moan became audible. The boys already jumped into the grave. They bent over the poor little coffin. Though it was half-covered with earth, the boys already felt the tremors of its cover under their feet.

The cover, hammered down with nails, yielded easily to the exertions of the small, childish hands, and fell to the side against the grave's earthen wall. The coffin opened as simply as the door of a room opens.

Egorka was already losing his consciousness. When the boys first looked at him he was lying on his side. He stirred faintly.

He breathed in the air as if with short, broken sighs. He shivered. He turned over on his back.

The fresh air blew into his face like a young rapture of deliverance. There was a sudden instant of joy—and it went out like a flame. Why indeed, should he rejoice? The tranquil, unjoyous ones bent over him.

Again to live? His soul felt strange, quiet, indifferent. Some one said affectionately over him:

" Rise, dear one, come to us ; we will show you that which you have not seen and will teach you that which is secret."

The stars of the far sky looked into his eyes, and some one's near, affectionate eyes bent over him. Many, many gentle, cool hands stretched out to him ; they took him, helped him up and lifted him out.

He stood in a circle. They looked at him. His arms again folded themselves across his breast,

as in the grave—as if the habit had been assimilated for ages. One of the little girls rearranged
them and straightened them out.

Suddenly Egorka asked :

" What is this ?   A little grave ? "

Grisha replied :

" This is your grave, but you will be with us
and with our master."

" And the grave ? " asked Egorka.

" We will fill it up again," replied Grisha.

The boys began to fill up the grave. Egorka
looked on in quiet astonishment as lumps of earth
fell into the grave and the little mound kept on
growing. The ground was smoothed down and
the cross placed as before. Egorka walked up to
it and read the inscription :

" Boy Giorgiy Antipov."

Then the year, month, and date of his death.

He was faintly astonished, but an ominous
indifference already made captive his soul.

Some one touched his shoulder and asked something. Egorka was silent. He looked as if he
did not understand.

" Come to me," said Trirodov quietly to him.

The little girl who always said " No " took
Egorka by the hand and led him away. They
went back by the same road as they came. The
darkness closed after them.

Egorka remained with the quiet children. He
had no passport, and his life was different.

CHAPTER XXVII

TRIRODOV returned home. Like one returned from a grave, he felt happy and light-hearted. His heart was consumed with exultation and resolution. He recalled the talk he had had that day with Elisaveta. There rose before him the proud, joyous vision of life transfigured by the force of creative art, of life created by the proud will.

If love, or what seemed like love, came to him, why should he resist it ? Whether it was a true emotion, or an illusion, was it not all the same ? The will, exulting above the world, would determine everything as it wanted. It would have the power to erect a beautiful love over the helplessness of the exhausted senses.

That which has so long weighed in the scales of consciousness, that which has so long and so desperately wrestled in the dark region of the unconscious now stood at a clear decision. Let the word " Yes " be said. Once more Yes. For a new grief ? For a glorious triumph ? It was all the same. If only he believed in her—and she in him. So much did one mean to the other now.

Trirodov sat down at the table. He smiled, and for a few moments seemed lost in thought. Then he wrote quickly upon a light blue sheet of paper :

" Elisaveta, I want your love. Love me, dear one, love me. I forget my knowledge, I reject my doubts, I become again as simple and as humble as a communicant of a radiant kingdom, like my dear children—and I only want your nearness and your kisses. Upon the earth, dear to our heart, I will pass by, in simple and joyous humility, with bare feet, like you—in order that I may come to you as you come to me. Love me.

" Your GIORGIY."

There was a slight rustle behind the door. It seemed as if the whole house were filled with the quiet children.

Trirodov sealed the letter. He wished to take it at once and leave it on the sill of her open window. He walked quietly, immersed in the wood's darkness—and his feet felt the contact of warm moss, the dew-wet grass, and the simple, rough, beloved earth. A refreshing breeze blew from the river in the night coolness, but now and then there came a sickly, pungent gust of the forest fire.

Elisaveta could not fall asleep. She rose from her bed. She stood by the window, and yielded her naked body to the transparent embraces of the nocturnal breeze. She thought of something, mused of something. And all her thoughts and musings joined in one dancing circle around Trirodov.

Should she wait ? He was a weary, sad man, and he would not say the sweet words for fear of appearing ridiculous, and of receiving a cold answer.

"Why should I wait?" she thought. "Or don't I dare decide my fate like a queen, to call him to me, and to demand his love? Why should I remain silent?"

And she decided:

"I will tell him myself—I love you, I love you, come to me, love me."

Elisaveta whispered the delicious words, entrusting her passionate reveries to the nocturnal silence. The dark eyes of the nocturnal guest who brought tempting reveries were aflame. The quiet splashing laughter of the water-nymph behind the reeds under the moon mingled with the quiet, delicious laughter of the nocturnal enchantress who had flaming eyes, burning lips, and a naked body formed from the coils of white flame. Her flaming body was like Elisaveta's body, and the black lightnings of the invisible sorceress were like the blue lightnings of Elisaveta's eyes. She tempted Elisaveta, and called to her:

"Go to him, go. Fall naked at his feet, kiss his feet, laugh for him, dance for him, tire yourself out for his sake, be a slave to him, be a thing in his hands—cling to him, and kiss him, and look into his eyes, and yield yourself up to him. Go, go, hurry, run, he is approaching even now—do you see him? It is he who has just come out of the wood—do you see? It is his feet that show white in the grass. Fling the door wide open and run as you are to meet him."

Elisaveta saw Trirodov coming. Her heart began to beat with such pain and such delight.

She walked away from the window. She waited. She heard his footsteps on the sand under the window. Something flashed through the window and fell on the floor. The footsteps retreated.

Elisaveta picked up the letter, lit a candle, and read the beloved blue sheet of paper. The nocturnal enchantress whispered to her:

"He's going away. Hurry. You will know how sweet are the first kisses of love. Go to him, run after him, don't look for tiresome robes."

Elisaveta impetuously flung the door open on the veranda, and ran down the broad steps into the garden. She ran after Trirodov and shouted:

"Giorgiy!"

It was like the outcry of passionate desire. Trirodov paused, saw her, impetuously white and clear in the moonlight. Elisaveta fell into his arms and kissed him and laughed, and kept on repeating without end:

"I love you, I love you, I love you."

And they kissed, and they laughed, and said something to one another. The red and white roses of her strong, graceful body were chaste and uncrumpled. The words they said to one another were chaste and sacred. The chaste moon looked down on them, and the stars also, as they spoke the words that bound them to one another. There were vows and rites not less durable than any other kind. There were smiles, kisses, tender words—in these consist the eternal rite and the eternal mystery.

The sky began to lighten and a new dew fell on a new dawn, and when the sunrise had extended its rapturous flames the sun rose—only then they parted.

Elisaveta returned to her room. But she could not sleep. She went into Elena's room. Elena had only just awakened. Elisaveta lay down at her side under the bed-cover, and told her about her great love, her great joy. Elena rejoiced and laughed and kissed her sister without end.

Then Elisaveta put on her morning dress, and went to her father—to tell him about her joy, her happiness.

As for Trirodov, oppressed by morning fatigue, he walked home across the moist grass—and his soul was filled with perplexity and dread.

Later in the day he drove to the Rameyevs. He brought as a gift to Elisaveta a photograph he had taken of his first wife—upon her nude body was a bronze belt, its ends coming down to the knees being joined up in the front; upon her dark hair was a narrow round strip of gold. A slender, graceful body—a melancholy smile—intense dark eyes.

"Father knows," said Elisaveta. "Father is glad. Let us go to him."

When Elisaveta and Trirodov were once more alone, a dark thought came into Elisaveta's mind. She became pensively sad, and asked:

"What of the sleeper in the grave?"

"He has awakened," replied Trirodov. "He's in my house. We've dug up his grave just in time to save his mother from having any qualms of conscience."

"What do you mean?"

263

Trirodov explained :

" Early this morning the coroner had the grave dug up. They found the empty coffin. Luckily, I found out about this in time, before new stupid talk might arise, and gave them the necessary explanation."

" What of the boy ? " asked Elisaveta.

" He will remain with me. He does not wish to go to his mother, and he is not particularly necessary to her—she will receive money for him."

Trirodov said all this in a dry, cold voice.

The news that Elisaveta would become Trirodov's wife acted differently on her relatives. Rameyev liked Trirodov, and was glad because of the closer connexion ; he was a little sorry for Piotr, but thought it was well that the matter had come to a decision, and Piotr would no longer torment himself by entertaining false hopes. Nevertheless Rameyev was disturbed for some unknown reason.

Elena loved Elisaveta and shared her joy. She loved Piotr, and was, therefore, even more glad ; she pitied him—and, therefore, loved him even more. She loved him so deeply, and entertained such hopes of his love, that her pity for him became serene and radiant. She looked at Piotr with loving eyes.

Piotr was in a state of despair. But Elena's eyes aroused in him a sweet agitation for a new love. His wearied heart thirsted, and suffered intensely from deceived hopes.

Misha was strangely distraught. He flushed,

and ran off more than usual with his fishing-rod to the river; there he wept. Now he impetuously embraced Elisaveta, now Trirodov. He felt ashamed and bitter. He knew that Elisaveta did not even suspect his love, and that she looked at him as at an infant. Sometimes in his helplessness he hated her. He said to Piotr:

" I shouldn't walk about with a long face if I were you. She is not worthy of your love. She puts on airs. Elena is much better. Elena is a dear, while the other fancies all sorts of things."

Piotr walked away from him in silence. And it was well that there was some one who did not scold, and with whom it was possible to ease his soul. Misha, too, wanted to be with Elisaveta, and it made him feel ashamed and depressed.

Miss Harrison did not express her opinion. Many things had already shocked her, and she grew accustomed to bear herself indifferently to everything that happened here. Trirodov, in her opinion, was an adventurer, a man with a doubtful reputation, and a dark past.

Elisaveta was the most tranquil of all.

Piotr's gloomy appearance disturbed Rameyev. He wanted to comfort him if only with words. Luckily, people believe even in words! They must believe in something.

Rameyev and Piotr happened to find themselves alone. Rameyev said:

" I must confess that I once thought Elisaveta loved you. Or that she might love you, if you wished it strongly."

Piotr said with a gloomy smile:

"I too may be pardoned for the error. All the more since M. Trirodov does not lack lovers."

"Any one may be pardoned for mistakes," answered Rameyev calmly, "though they may be painful enough sometimes."

Piotr grumbled something. Rameyev continued:

"I have been observing Elisaveta very attentively of late. And listen to what I say—pardon me for my frankness—I have come to the conclusion that you'd be better off with Elena. Perhaps you have also erred in your feelings."

Piotr replied with a bitter smile:

"Why, of course—Elena is more simple. She doesn't read philosophic books, she doesn't wear over-classical frocks ; and doesn't detest any one."

"Why drag self-love into everything ?" asked Rameyev. "Elena is not as simple as you think. She is a very intelligent girl, though without pretensions to a deep and broad outlook—and she is good, attractive, and cheerful."

"In fact, quite a match for me," observed Piotr with an ironic smile.

"As for that," said Rameyev, "you are not limited to choosing a charming wife from among my daughters."

"That's not so easy," said Piotr with dejected irony. "But I see no need of insisting. Besides, the same thing might happen with Elena. She might come across a more brilliant match. And there are not a few charlatans in this world of the Trirodov brand."

"Elena loves you," said Rameyev. "Surely you have noticed it ?"

266

Piotr laughed. He assumed a gaiety—or did he actually feel gay and joyous at the sudden thought of the charming Elena? Of course she loved him! But he asked:

"Why do you think, my dear uncle, that I need a wife at all costs? May God be with her!"

"You are in love generally, as is common in your years," said Rameyev.

"Perhaps," said Piotr, "but Elisaveta's choice revolts me."

"Why should it?" asked Rameyev.

"For many reasons," replied Piotr. "For one thing, he presented her with a photograph of his dead wife, a naked beauty. Why? Is it right to make universal that which is intimate?* She revealed her body to her husband, and not for Elisaveta and for us."

"You would do away with many fine pictures if you had your way," said Rameyev.

"I am not so simple as not to be able to make a distinction," replied Piotr animatedly. "In the one case it is pure art, always sacred; in the other there is an effort to inflame the feelings with pornographic pictures. And don't you notice it yourself, uncle, that Elisaveta has poisoned herself with this sweet poison, and has become terribly passionate and insufficiently modest?"

"I do not find this at all," said Rameyev dryly.

* In a poem in prose which serves as an introduction to his Complete Works, Sologub says: "Born not the first time, and not the first to complete a circle of external transformations, I simply and calmly reveal my soul. I reveal it in the hope *that the intimate part of me shall become the universal*."—TRANSLATOR.

" She is in love—so what's to be done ? If there is sensuality in people, what is to be done with nature ? Shall the whole world be maimed in order to gratify a decrepit morality ? "

" Uncle, I did not suspect you of being such an amoralist," said Piotr in vexation.

" There is morality and morality," replied Rameyev, not without some confusion. " I do not uphold depravity, but nevertheless demand freedom of thought and feeling. A free feeling is always innocent."

" And what will you say of those naked girls in his woods—is that also innocent ? " asked Piotr rather spitefully.

" Of course," replied Rameyev. " His problem is to lull to sleep the beast in man, and to awaken the man."

" I have heard his discourses," said Piotr, showing his annoyance, " and I do not believe them in the slightest. I'm only astonished that others can believe such nonsense. And I don't believe either in his poetry or in his chemistry. He has too many secrets and mysteries, too many cunning mechanisms in his doors and his corridors. Then there are his quiet children—that I do not understand at all. Where have they come from ? What does he do with them ? There is something nasty behind it all."

" That's a work of the imagination," answered Rameyev. " We see him often, we can always go to him, and we haven't seen or heard anything in his house or in his colony to confirm the town tattle about him."

Piotr recalled the evening that he met Trirodov

on the river-bank. His sad but determined eyes suddenly flared up in Piotr's memory—and the poison of his spite grew weaker. He seemed affected as by a strange bewitchment, as if some one persistently yet quietly urged him to believe that the ways of Trirodov were fair and clean. Piotr closed his eyes—and the radiant vision appeared before him of the semi-nude girls of the wood, who filed past him, and sanctified him by the serenity and the peace of their chaste eyes. Piotr sighed and said quietly, as if fatigued:

"I have no cause to say these malicious words. Perhaps you are right. But it is so hard for me!"

Nevertheless this conversation did much to soothe Piotr. Thoughts about Elena returned to him oftener and oftener, and became more and more tender.

It so happened that, acting upon some unspoken yet understood agreement, every one tried to direct Piotr's attention to Elena. Piotr submitted to this general influence, and was affectionate and gentle with Elena. Elena expectantly waited for his love; and at night, turning her blazing face and loosened locks in the direction of the nymph's laughter, she would whisper:

"I love you, I love you, I love you!"

And when left alone with Piotr, she would look at him with love-frightened eyes, all rosy like the spring, and pulsating with expectancy; and with every sigh of her tender breast, and with all the life of her passionate body she would repeat the same unspoken words: "I love you, I love you,

269

I love you." And Piotr began to understand that he had met his fate in Elena, and that whether he willed it or not he would grow to love her. This presentiment of a new love was like a sweet gnawing in a heart wounded by treacherous love.

CHAPTER XXVIII

THE local police department was not very skilful in tracking down thieves and murderers. And it did not occupy itself much with this ungrateful business. It had other things to think of in those turbulent days. Instead, it turned its ill-disposed attention to Trirodov's educational colony —thanks to the efforts of Ostrov and his friends and patrons.

The neighbourhood of Trirodov's estate began to teem with detectives. They assumed various guises, and though they employed all their cunning to escape observation they did not succeed in fooling any one. Of limited intelligence, they fulfilled their duties without inspiration, tediously, greyly, and dully.

Soon the children learned to recognize the detectives. Even at a distance they would say at the sight of a suspicious character :

" There goes a detective ! "

Upon seeing him again they would say :

" There goes our detective ! "

Of the uniformed police the first to make inquiries at Trirodov's colony was a sergeant. He was fairly drunk It happened on the same day that Egorka returned home to his mother.

The sergeant entered the outer courtyard, the gates of which happened to have been left open by chance. A strong smell of vodka came from him. With the suspicious eye of an inexperienced

271

spy he examined the barns, the ice-cellar, and the kitchen. He wondered stupidly at the cleanliness of the yard and the tidiness of the new buildings.

The sergeant was about to enter the kitchen in order to talk with some one about the business on which he had been sent, when quite suddenly he saw a young girl, one of the instructresses, Zinaida. She walked without haste in the yard, in a white-blue costume that reached to her knees. Zinaida had a cheerful, simple, sunburnt face. Her strong, bare arms swung lightly as she walked. It seemed as if the graceful girl were carried upon the earth without visible effort.

The chaste openness of her chaste body naturally aroused hideous thoughts in the half-drunken idiot. And was it possible to be otherwise in our dark days ? Even in the tale of a poet in love with beauty, the nudity of a chaste body calls out the judgment of hypocrites and the rage of people with perverted imaginations, as if it were the arrogant nudity of a prostitute. The austere virtue of these people is attached to them externally. It cannot withstand any kind of temptation or enticement. They know this, and cautiously guard themselves from seduction. But in secret they console their miserable imaginations with unclean pictures of back-street lewdness, cheap, and regulated, and almost undangerous for their health and the welfare of their families.

The police sergeant, upon seeing the young girl, so lightly dressed, gave a lewd smile. His unclean desire stirred in his coarse body under its slovenly sweaty dress. He beckoned Zinaida to him with his crooked dirty finger and gave an idiotic laugh.

272

He pushed his faded cap down to the back of his head.

The young girl walked up to the police sergeant with a light easy gait. Thus walk queens of beloved free lands, barefoot virgins crowned with white flowers, queens of lands of which our too Parisian age does not know.

The police sergeant whiffed his shag, vodka, and garlic at Zinaida, and smiling lasciviously, so that the green and the yellow of his crooked teeth showed conspicuously, he said :

" Look-a-here, my pretty girl—d'ye live here ? "

Zinaida ingenuously marvelled at his red, dirty hands, at his red, provokingly perspiring face, his big, heavy, mud-bedraggled boots, and all those external tokens of the deformity of our poor, coarse life. They so quickly became unused to this deformity here in the valley of their beloved, innocent, tranquil life.

Zinaida replied with an involuntary smile :

" Yes, I live here in this colony."

The police sergeant asked :

" Are you the cook ? Or the laundress ? What a nice piece of sugar-candy you are ! "

He burst into a shrill, neighing laugh, and was about to begin his offensively affectionate tactics— he lifted his open, tawny hand, and aimed his forefinger with a black border on a thick yellow finger-nail towards a place where he might jab, pinch, or tickle the barefoot, bare-armed girl. But Zinaida, smiling and frowning at the same time, edged away from him and answered :

" I'm an instructress in this school—Zinaida Ouzlova."

The sergeant drawled out :

" An instructress ! You are fibbing ! "

He did not believe at first that she was an instructress. He thought that she was the cook, or the washerwoman, who had tucked up her dress in order to wash, scour, or cook more conveniently ; and that she was joking with him. But after he had scrutinized her face more intently, a face such as a cook does not have, and her hands, such as a washerwoman does not have—he suddenly believed.

With astonishment and curiosity Zinaida eyed this strange, coarse, offensively affectionate creature with the heavy sabre in a black sheath dangling about his legs, and asked :

" And who are you ? "

The sergeant replied with a very important air :

" I am the local police sergeant."

He tried to look dignified.

" What is it you want here ? " asked Zinaida.

The sergeant turned to her with a wink and asked :

" Now tell me, my beauty, have you a runaway boy from town here ? His mother is looking for him, and she's notified the police. If he's here with you, we've got to return him to town."

" Yes," said Zinaida. " A town boy did spend a week with us here. We sent him home only to-day. He's very likely with his mother now."

The sergeant smiled incredulously, and asked :

" You're not fibbing ? "

Zinaida shrugged her shoulders. She looked sternly at the man, and said in astonishment :

" What are you saying ? How is it possible

274

to tell an untruth? And why should I tell you an untruth?"

"How is one to tell?" growled the sergeant. "Once I begin to believe you there are lots of things you might say."

"I've told you the truth," asserted Zinaida once more.

"Well, just be careful," said the sergeant with dignity. "We'll find out all the same. You are sure you've returned him home?"

"Yes, home to his mother," replied Zinaida.

"Very well, I shall report that to the Captain of the police." He told a lie for dignity's sake. It was the Commissary of the police who sent him here, and not the Captain. But it was all the same to Zinaida. She had got quite accustomed to thinking mostly about the children and her work. The stern reference to the police authorities did not impress her very much.

The police sergeant left. He kept up his broad smile. He looked back several times at the instructress. He was gay and flustered all the way to town. His thoughts were coarse and detestable. Such are the thoughts of the savages who take shelter in the grey expanses of our towns—savages who hide under all sorts of masks, and who strut about in all sorts of clothes.

Zinaida looked sadly after the police sergeant. Coarse recollections of former days revived in her soul, now full of delicious soothings of a different, blessed existence created by Trirodov in the quiet coolness of the beloved wood. Then Zinaida sighed as if awakened from a midday nightmare. She went quietly her own way.

In the course of several days Trirodov's colony was visited by the Commissary of the police. He comprehended and considered the chaste world of the Prosianiya Meadows in the same way as the illiterate sergeant. Only this consideration expressed itself in a milder form.

The Commissary of the police tried to be very amiable. He paid awkward compliments to Trirodov and his instructresses. But when he looked at the instructresses the Commissary smiled as detestably as the sergeant. His small, narrow eyes, which resembled those of a Kalmyk, became oily with pleasure. His cheeks became covered with a brick-red ruddiness.

When the girls walked off to one side he gave a wink at Trirodov in their direction, and said in a *sotto voce* :

" A flower garden, eh ? "

Trirodov looked severely at the Commissary, who became flustered and rather angry. He said :

" I have come to you, I'm sorry to say, on unpleasant business."

Indeed, he came under the pretext of discussing the arrangements of Egorka's position. Incidentally, he hinted that the illegal opening of Egorka's grave might give cause to an official investigation. Trirodov gave the Commissary a bribe and treated him to lunch. The Commissary of the police left in high spirits.

At last Trirodov had a visit from the Captain of the police. He had a gloomy, inaccessible look. He began quite bluntly about the illegal digging up of Egorka's grave. Trirodov said :

"Surely it was impossible to leave a live boy to suffocate in a grave."

The Captain replied in a rather austere voice :

"You should have notified the Prior of the cemetery church of your suspicions. He would have done all there was to be done."

"But think how much time would have been lost in going after the priest," said Trirodov.

The Captain, without listening, replied :

"It's irregular. What would become of us if every one should take it into his head to open up graves ! A chap might do it to steal something, and when he's caught he might say that he's heard the corpse was alive and turning in its grave."

"You know very well," retorted Trirodov, "that we didn't go there with the object of robbery."

But the Captain reiterated harshly and sternly :

"It's irregular."

Trirodov invited the Captain to dinner. The Captain's bribe was, of course, considerably larger than the Commissary's. After a sumptuous dinner and drinks, and the bribe, the Captain suddenly became softer than wax. He began to dwell on the difficulties and annoyances of his position. Then Trirodov mentioned the search that had been made lately, and the beating the instructress Maria received at the police station. The Captain flushed with embarrassment and said with some warmth :

"Upon my honour, it didn't depend upon me. I must follow orders. Our new Vice-Governor— forgive the expression—is a regular butcher. That's how he's made his career."

"Is it possible to make one's career by such means?" asked Trirodov.

The Captain spoke animatedly—and it was evident that the career of the new Vice-Governor agitated his official heart considerably.

"The facts must be familiar to you," he said. "He killed his friend when he was drunk, was confined in a lunatic asylum, and how he ever got out is beyond comprehension. With the help of patronage he was given a position in the District Government and showed himself to be such an asp that every one marvelled. He quickly galloped into a councillorship. He subdued the peasants. Of course you must have heard about it?"

"Who hasn't heard about it?" asked Trirodov quietly.

"The newspapers have certainly published enough about him," the Captain continued. "Sometimes they added a trifle, but this was to his good. It turned every one's attention to him. He was made Vice-Governor, and now he has redoubled his efforts, and is trying to distinguish himself further. He has an eye on the governorship. He is sure to go a long way. Our own Governor is on his guard on his account. I need not tell you what a powerful arm our Governor has in Petersburg. Nevertheless he can't decide to thwart Ardalyon Borisovitch.*

"And yet in spite of that you . . ."

"Do please consider what a time we are living in," said the Captain. "There never was any-

* Readers of "The Little Demon" will have no trouble in recognizing in Ardalyon Borisovitch an old aquaintance—Peredonov.

278

thing like it. There is such an unrest among the peasants that may God have mercy on us. Only the other day they played the deuce on Khavriukin's farm. They carried away everything that could be carried away. The muzhiks even took away all the live stock. A pitiful case. Khavriukin is considered among the better masters in our government. He held the peasants in the palm of his hand. And now they've paid him back!"

"Howsoever it may have happened," said Trirodov, "still you did whip my instructress. That was rather shocking."

"Please!" exclaimed the Captain. "I will personally ask her pardon. Like an honest man."

Trirodov sent for Maria. Maria came. The Captain of the police poured out his apologies before her, and covered her sunburnt hands with kisses. Maria was silent. Her face was pale, and her eyes were aflame with anger.

The Captain thought cautiously:

"Such a woman would not stop at murder."

He made haste to take his leave.

CHAPTER XXIX

THE educational police also conferred its presence on Trirodov's school in the person of the Inspector of the National Schools.

The local Inspector of the National Schools, Leonty Andreyevitch Shabalov, had served all his life in remote, wooded places, and was for that reason quite an uncivilized being. Tall, robust, shaggy, unharmonious, he resembled even in external appearance a bear of Vologda or Olonetz. His face was overgrown with a thick beard. His thick hair crept down his low forehead towards his eyebrows. His back was broad and somewhat stooped, like a huge trough.

Shabalov frequently said to the instructors and instructresses in his district in a hoarse drawl :

" Batenka * (or " golubushka " † if it happened to be an instructress), brilliant instructors are not necessary. I don't like clever men and women, I'm no respecter of modern ladies and dandies. The chief thing, batenka, in life and in service, is not to put on airs. In my opinion, batenka, if you perform your State obligations and conduct yourself peacefully you will find yourself well off. The educational programme has been worked out by people not more stupid than you and me, so

* Diminutive for father, and used in the sense of " my good fellow," etc.

† "Golubushka" is "little dove." English equivalent as used here : " my dear."

280

that you and I needn't spend our time philoso-
phizing about programmes. That's what I think,
batenka ! "

But, notwithstanding all his respect for educational programmes, Shabalov knew the educational
business badly. It would be truer to say that
he did not know it at all. He was hardly interested
in it. He was not even very literate. He received
his inspector's position as a reward for his piety,
patriotism, and correct mode of thinking, rather
than for his labours in the interest of public
instruction. He had served in his youth as a
class assistant in the gymnasia. There, by a steady
attendance at the gymnasia chapel and the reading
of the apostles in a stentorian voice, he turned upon
himself the attention of an old bigot of a general's
wife. She procured him the inspector's position.

There was no way in which he could help the
young and little-experienced instructors. When
he visited the schools he limited himself to a superficial examination and gave the pupils several
stupid questions, mostly on matters of piety, of
" love towards the Fatherland and national pride." *

Above all, Shabalov loved to collect rumours
and gossip. He did this with great ability and
zeal. Every one knew this weakness of his.
Consequently there were many eager to gossip
and to inform against some one. There were
even a number of informers among the instructors
and instructresses who wished to gain favour and
promotion. Once it was reported to Shabalov
that teachers of both sexes in some of the neighbouring schools had gathered one holiday eve in

* Title of standard didactic work by Karamzin (1766–1826).

one of the schools and sang songs there. He immediately sent them all a notification composed as follows :

No. 2187

The School District of
Rouban.

Skorodozh,
16th of September, 1904.

Inspector of the National Schools of the first section of the Skorodozh Government. *To* Instructor of the Vikhliaevsky one-class rural school, Ksenofont Polupavlov :

" DEAR SIR, It has come to my knowledge that on the evening of the 7th of September you participated at a meeting of instructors and instructresses, which had been arranged without the necessary permit, and that you sang there with them songs of a worldly and reprehensible character. Therefore, dear sir, I beg you in the future not to permit yourself similar actions unbecoming to your schoolmaster's vocation, and I herewith warn you that at a repetition of such behaviour you will be immediately discharged from the service.

" INSPECTOR SHABALOV."

On another occasion he wrote to the same instructor :

" On the occasion of an inspection of the schools of the section intrusted to me, a number of instructors and instructresses, and you, dear sir, among that number, have transgressed the limits of the programme ratified for Primary Schools by the authorities, in imparting to your pupils facts from history and geography unnecessary to the people ; and therefore, in confirmation of

282

certain verbal instructions I have already made to you in person, I beg you in the future to maintain strictly the established programmes ; and I warn you that if you fail to comply you will be discharged from the service."

Shabalov was particularly displeased with the participation of certain instructors and instructresses in the local pedagogical circle. This circle was initiated in the town of Skorodozh some three years before by the gymnasia instructor Bodeyev and the town school instructor Voronok. The circle discussed various questions of upbringing, instruction, and school affairs generally which interested in those years many teachers and parents. Some of the members read their reports here. It was particularly provoking to Shabalov that these reports occasionally recounted certain episodes in school life and eccentricities of the educational authorities. Shabalov wanted to discharge the audacious ones. The District School Council did not agree with him. Then followed a long and unpleasant discussion, out of which Shabalov did not issue as conqueror.

Trirodov found it painful and difficult to talk with Shabalov.

Shabalov said in a slow, creaking voice :

" Giorgiy Sergeyevitch, you will have to send your wards to town for examination."

" Why is it necessary ? " asked Trirodov.

Shabalov laughed his creaking " he-he " laugh and said :

" Well, it's necessary. We'll give them certificates."

" What's the use of your certificates to them ? " asked Trirodov. " They need knowledge and not certificates. Your certificates won't feed their hunger."

" The certificates are necessary for military service," explained Shabalov.

" They will remain pupils here," said Trirodov, " until they are ready for practical work or for scientific and artistic occupations. Then some of them will go to technical schools, others to universities. Why, then, should they have certificates for a course in a Primary School ? "

Shabalov repeated dully and stubbornly :

" Things are not done that way. Your school is counted among the Primary Schools. Those who have completed the course should receive certificates. How else can it be ?—judge for yourself ! And if you wish to go beyond the primary course, then you'll have to procure for yourself a private gymnasia or a professional school, or, if you like, a commercial one. But what you want is impossible. And, of course, you'd have to engage real teachers in place of your cheap barefoots."

" My barefoots," retorted Trirodov, " have the same diplomas and learning as the real teachers, to use your expression. It is strange that you do not know or realize that fact. And they receive such ample pay from me that I should hesitate to call them cheap. Generally speaking, it seems to me that in its relation to private schools the so-called educational council would do well to limit itself to an external police surveillance of a purely negative character. They should merely see whether we commit anything of a criminal nature. But what business have you with the direction of schools? You have so few schools of your own, and yet they are so poor that you have quite a time to attend to them."

Shabalov, somewhat subdued, replied:

" Still, the examination will have to be held. Surely you understand that? And the Headmaster of the National Schools is anxious to be present at the examination. We have our instructions from the Ministry, and it is impossible to discuss the matter. Our business is to execute orders."

" Come here yourselves if it is absolutely necessary to hold an examination," said Trirodov coldly.

" Very well," said Shabalov upon reflection. " I will report your wish to the Headmaster of the National Schools. I don't know how he will look upon the matter, but I will make my report."

Then he reflected again briefly. He rubbed his back, covered by its blue official frock, against the back of his chair—the greasy, faded cloth against the handsome dark-green leather—and said:

" If the Headmaster agrees to it, we will appoint the day and send you the notification, that you may expect us."

In the course of a few days Shabalov sent the announcement that the examination in Trirodov's school was appointed to be held on May 30, at ten o'clock in the morning, on the premises.

This meddling on the part of the educational police annoyed Trirodov, but he had to submit to it.

CHAPTER XXX

KIRSHA was acquainted with many boys in town.
Some of them were pupils of the gymnasia, some
of the town school. Kirsha was also acquainted
with some of the students who attended the girls'
gymnasia. He told his father a great deal about
the affairs and ways of these institutions. His
information contained much that was singular and
unexpected.

The personality of the Headmaster of the
National Schools, Doulebov, particularly interested
Trirodov of late. The schools under his guidance
included the school established by Trirodov,
though Doulebov contributed nothing to the school.
He conducted himself with complete indifference
to the aspersions cast at Priest Zakrasin and did
not defend him before the Diocesan Bishop. He
and his subordinate, the Inspector, showered
official papers upon Trirodov and demanded
various reports in the established form, so that
Trirodov had to prevail upon a small official of
the Exchequer to come evenings and copy out all
this absurd nonsense. But neither Doulebov nor
Shabalov looked in even once into Trirodov's
school. When Trirodov happened to be in the
Headmaster's office the conversation usually
turned on documents concerning the instructresses
and various petty formalities.

The calumnies of Ostrov and of his friends in
the Black Hundred disturbed Doulebov. To avoid

unpleasantness Doulebov decided to take advantage of the first opportunity to close Trirodov's school.

The Headmaster of the National Schools, Actual State Councillor, Grigory Vladimirovitch Doulebov, had his eye on a higher position in the educational department. That was why he tried to gain favour by showing a meticulous attentiveness to his duties. His perseverance was astonishing. He never gave an impression of haste. His reception of subordinates and petitioners, announced on a placard on his door to take place on Thursdays between one and three, actually began at eleven in the morning, and continued until late in the evening. Doulebov spoke with each visitor slowly and showed his interest in the slightest detail.

But Doulebov, of course, knew very well that however great was his attentiveness to his duties, that in itself would not take him very far. It was indispensable to cultivate the proper personages. Doulebov had no influential aunts and grandmothers, and he had to make efforts on his own behalf. And in the whole course of his twenty-five years' service, beginning as a gymnasia instructor, Doulebov uninterruptedly and skilfully concerned himself with establishing improved relations with all who were higher in rank than he or equal with him. He even made an effort to keep on good terms with the younger set—that was for an emergency ; for—who can tell ?—the younger sometimes go ahead of the old, and, being young, they might do one an injury—or a good service—when the opportunity offered.

Never to commit an untactful action—in that

consisted the chief precept of Doubelov's life. He knew very well that this or that action was not good in itself, and that the chief thing was " how they would look upon it "—they, that is, the authorities. The authorities were favourably inclined towards Doulebov. He had already been almost promised an assistantship to the head of the Educational District.

Doulebov adopted an attitude towards his subordinates consistent with this personal attitude. To those who acted respectfully towards him and his wife he gave his patronage and made efforts to improve their position. He defended them in unpleasant situations, though very cautiously, in order not to hurt his own position. He was not very fond of those who were disrespectful and independent, and he hindered them all he could.

Recognizing a rising luminary in the newly appointed Vice-Governor, who lately had been a Councillor in the District Government, Doulebov tried to come into agreeable relations with him also. But he conducted himself towards him very cautiously, so that he might not be suspected of too intimate relations with this evil, morose, badly trained man and his vulgar wife.

Doulebov had pleasant manners, a youngish face, and a slender voice which resembled the squeal of a young pig. He was light and agile in his movements. No one had ever seen him drunk, and as a visitor he either did not drink at all or limited himself to a glass of Madeira. He was always accompanied by his wife. It was said that she managed all his affairs, and that Doulebov obeyed her implicitly in everything.

The wife of the Headmaster, Zinaida Grigorievna, was a plump, energetic, and shrewish woman. Her short hair was beginning to get grey. She was very jealous of her influence and maintained it with great energy.

At Doulebov's invitation the Vice-Governor visited the town school. In inviting the Vice-Governor Doulebov had especially in view the idea of taking him to the Trirodov school. In the event of the school being closed, he wanted to say that it was done at the instigation of the governmental authorities. But Doulebov did not wish to invite the Vice-Governor direct to Trirodov's school, so as to give no one any reason for saying that he did it on purpose. That was why he persuaded the Vice-Governor to come to the examination at the town school on the eve of the day appointed for the examinations at the Trirodov school.

The town school was situated in one of the dirty side streets. Its exterior was highly unattractive. The dirty, dilapidated wooden structure seemed as if it were built for a tavern rather than for a school. This did not prevent Doulebov from saying to the inspector of the school :

" The new Vice-Governor will visit you to-day. I invited him to you because you have such a fine school."

Inspector Poterin, fawning before Doulebov and his wife, said in a flustered way :

" Our building is anything but showy."

Doulebov smiled amiably and replied encouragingly :

" The building is not the important thing. The

289

school itself is good. The instruction is to be valued and not the walls."

The Vice-Governor arrived rather late, at eleven, together with Zherbenev, who was an honorary overseer of the school.

There was a very tense feeling in the school. The instructors and the students alike trembled before the authorities. Stupid and vulgar scenes with the Headmaster in the town school were common with Doulebov and did not embarrass him. As for Doulebov and his wife, they were fully alive to their importance. They had received only two or three days before definite news of the appointment of Doulebov as assistant to the head of the Educational Department.

Inspector Shabalov arrived at the school very early that day. He occupied himself with attentions to Zinaida Grigorievna Doulebova, to whom he showed various services with an unexpected and rather vulgar amiableness.

The instructor-inspector, Mikhail Prokopievitch Poterin, conducted himself like a lackey. It was even evident at times that he trembled before the Doulebovs. What reason had he to be afraid? He was a great patriot—a member of the Black Hundred. He accepted bribes, beat his pupils, drank considerably—and he always got off easily.

Zinaida Grigorievna Doulebova examined the graduating classes in French and English. These studies were optional. Inspector Poterin's wife gave instruction in French. She had not yet fully mastered the Berlitz method, and looked at the Doulebovs cringingly. But at heart she was bitter—at her poverty, abjectness, and dependence.
290

Poterin knew no languages; but he was also present here, and hissed malignantly at those who answered awkwardly or did not answer at all:

" Blockhead ! Numskull ! "

Doulebova sat motionless and made no sign that she heard this zealous hissing and these coarse words. She would give freedom to her tongue later, at luncheon.

A luncheon had been prepared for the visitors and the instructors. It cost Poterin's wife much trouble and anxiety. The table was set in the large room, where on ordinary days the small boys made lively and wrangled in recess-time. They were excluded on this day, and raised a racket outside.

Doulebova sat at the head of the table, between the Vice-Governor and Zherbenev; Doulebov sat next to the Vice-Governor. A pie was brought in; then tea. Zinaida Grigorievna abused the instructors' wives and the instructresses. She loved gossip—indeed, who does not? The instructors' wives gossiped to her.

During the luncheon the small boys, having resumed their places in the neighbouring class, sang:

> *What songs, what songs,*
> *Our Russia does sing.*
> *Do what you like—though you burst,*
> *Frenchman, you'll never sing like that.*

And other songs in the same spirit.

Doulebov wiped his face with his right hand—like a cat licking its paw—and piped out:

" I hear that the Marquis Teliatnikov is to pay us a visit soon."

"We are not within his jurisdiction," said Poterin.

But his whole face became distorted with apprehension.

"All the same," said Doulebov in his thin voice, "he possesses great powers. He can do what he likes."

The Vice-Governor looked gloomily at Poterin and said morosely:

"He's going to pull you all up."

Poterin grew deathly pale and broke out into perspiration. The conversation about the Marquis Teliatnikov continued, and the local revolutionary ferment was mentioned in the course of it.

Revolutionary proclamations had appeared in all the woods of the neighbourhood. Large pieces of bark were cut off the trees and proclamations pasted on. It was impossible to remove these bills, which were overrun by a thin, transparent coating of resin. The zealous preservers of order had either to chop out or to scrape off the obnoxious places with a knife.

"I think," said Doulebova, "that it must be an idea of our chemist, Mr. Trirodov."

"Of course." She was confirmed in her suggestion by the cringing, dry-looking instructress of German.

Zinaida Grigorievna turned towards Poterina in order to show favour to her hostess by her conversation, and asked her with an amused smile:

"How do you like our celebrated Decadent?"

The instructress tried to understand. An expression of fear showed on her flat, dull face. She asked timidly:

292

"Whom do you mean, Zinaida Grigorievna?"

"Whom else could I mean but Mr. Trirodov," replied Doulebova malignantly.

The malice was all on Trirodov's account, but nevertheless Poterina trembled with fear.

"Ah, yes, Trirodov; how then, how then . . ." she repeated in a worried, flustered way, and was at a loss what to say.

Doulebova said bitingly:

"Well, I don't think he laughs very often. He ought to be to your taste."

"To my taste!" exclaimed Poterina with a flushed face. "What are you saying, Zinaida Grigorievna! As the old saying goes: 'The Tsar's servant has been bent into a harness arch!'"

"Yes, he always looks askance at you and talks to no one," said the wife of the instructor Krolikov; "but he is a very kind man."

Doulebova turned her malignant glance upon her. Krolikova grew pale with fear, and guessed that she had not said the right thing. She corrected herself:

"He is a kind man in his words."

Doulebova smiled at her benevolently.

"Do you know what I think?" said Zherbenev, addressing himself to Doulebova. "I have seen many men in my time, I may say without boasting; and in my opinion, it is a very bad sign that he looks askance at you."

"Of course!" agreed Poterina. "That is the honest truth!"

"Let a man look me straight in my face," went on Zherbenev. "But the quiet ones . . ."

Zherbenev did not finish his sentence. Doule-bova said :

" Frankly, I don't like your poet. I can't understand him. There is something strange about him—something disagreeable."

" He's altogether suspicious," said Zherbenev with the look of a person who knew a great deal.

It was asserted that Trirodov and others were collecting money for an armed revolt. At this they looked significantly at Voronok. Voronok retorted, but he was not heard. There was an outburst of malignant remarks against Trirodov. It was said that there was a secret underground printing establishment in Trirodov's house, and that not only the instructresses worked there but also Trirodov's young wards. The women exclaimed in horror :

" They are mere tots ! "

" What do you think of your tots now ? "

" There are no children nowadays."

" I've just heard," said Voronok, " that a nine-year-old boy is kept in confinement by the police."

" The young rebel ! " said the Vice-Governor savagely.

" Yes, and I've also heard," said Poterin, " that a thirteen-year-old boy has been arrested. Such a little beggar, and already in revolt."

The Vice-Governor said morosely :

" He's going with his grandfather to Siberia."

" Why ? " asked Voronok with a flushed face.

" He laughed," growled the Vice-Governor morosely.

Doulebov turned to Poterin and asked in a loud voice :

"And I hope you have no rebels in your school."

"No, thank God, I have nothing of that kind," replied Poterin. "But, to tell the truth, the children are very loose nowadays."

Doulebov, with a patronizing amiableness, said again to him:

"You have a good school. Everything is in exemplary order."

Poterin grew radiant and boasted:

"Yes, I know how to pull them up. I treat them sternly."

"A salutary sternness," said Doulebov.

Encouraged by these words, the instructor-inspector asked:

"Do you think one might also beat them?"

Doulebov avoided a direct answer. He wiped his face with his hand—like a cat using its paw —and changed the subject.

They began touching recollections about the good old times. They began to relate how, where, and whom they birched.

"They birch even now," said Shabalov with a quiet joy.

CHAPTER XXXI

AFTER luncheon they went into the assembly room. Some of them began to smoke. Instructor Mouralov's wife took advantage of an opportune moment to speak to Doulebova. She cautiously stole up to her when she saw her standing aside and told her that Poterin took bribes. Separate phrases and words were distinguished from the rest of the conversation.

" Have you noticed, Zinaida Grigorievna ? "

" What's that ? "

" Our inspector is parading in gloves."

" Yes ? "

" Gloves ! Yellow ones ! "

" What of that ? "

" Out of bribes."

Zinaida Grigorievna was overjoyed, and grew animated. For a long time the whispers of the malicious women were audible, and between their whispers their hissing, snake-like laughter.

Then the women, together with Shabalov and Voronok, went off to finish the examination. Doulebov and the Vice-Governor went in to look at the library. Poterin accompanied them. Everything was in order. The thick volumes of Katkov * quietly slumbered ; the dust had been wiped from them on the eve of the Vice-Governor's visit.

Poterin made use of an opportunity to make

* Mikhail Katkov (1820–1887), a celebrated reactionary and Slavophil.

insinuations against the instructors. He reported that Voronok did not go to church, and that he collected schoolboys at his own house in order to read something or other to them.

"I shall have to have a talk with him," said Doulebov. "Ask him into your study and I will talk to him. In the meantime, show Ardalyon Borisovitch the laboratory."

Doulebov and Voronok spoke for a long time in Poterin's study.

"I don't question your convictions," said the Headmaster, "but I must make it clear to you that it is impossible to introduce politics into schools. Children cannot discuss such questions; it does them harm."

"Agents' reports are not always to be believed," said Voronok restrainedly.

Doulebov flushed slightly and said in an annoyed manner.

"We don't maintain agents, but we have many acquaintances. We have lived here a long time. It is impossible not to hear what is told us."

The honorary overseer, Zherbenev, invited all who attended the examination to his house to dinner. Only Voronok refused the invitation. But Zherbenev invited others to the dinner—the general's widow, Glafira Pavlovna, and Kerbakh among them. It was a long and lavish dinner. The guests drank much during and after the meal. Every one got tipsy. Doulebov alone remained sober. The liqueurs only made him look slightly ruddier—he was very fond of them.

The members of the Black Hundred took advantage of the occasion to say something malicious about Trirodov to Doulebov and the Vice-Governor. The Trirodov school began to be discussed rather vulgarly.

" He's taken up photography; quite keen on it."

" He calls in children, makes them take everything off, and photographs them."

" Yes, and he's got naked children running about in the woods."

" Children ? The instructresses too ! "

" They may not be exactly naked, but they are always running about barefoot."

" Just like peasant women," said Zherbenev.

" Yes," said the Vice-Governor. " It is very immoral for women to go about barefoot. It must be stopped."

" They are poor people," said some one.

" It is pornography ! " said the Vice-Governor savagely.

And every one suddenly believed him. The Vice-Governor said morosely :

" He's lodged a complaint against us for whipping his instructress. But he is lying; he's whipped her himself. We have no need of whipping girls—but he does it because he's a corrupt man."

Some one made the observation that Trirodov was friends with dangerous sects, at which Kerbakh remarked :

" He now has horses and carriages, but I know a man who knew him when he had only his shirt. It is rather suspicious as to where he got his money."

298

Glafira Pavlovna looked at Shabalov and whispered to Doulebov :

" I know he is a patriot, but he has terrible manners."

Doulebov said :

" I know he is very stupid and undeveloped, but zealous. If directed properly he can be very useful."

Next morning the Headmaster of the National Schools, accompanied by the Vice-Governor and Shabalov, started in their carriages from the Headmaster's offices and drove off to Trirodov's school in the Prosianiya Meadows. They had not yet fully recovered from the previous day's carouse. They carried on their indecent, half-tipsy conversations in the midst of nature's loveliness. They looked like a lot of picnickers.

Zinaida Grigorievna and Kerbakh, who were in one carriage, were engaged in a malicious conversation. They tore their acquaintances to shreds. She began with Poterin's gloves. Then she related about the suicide of another inspector's mistress ; she drowned herself because she was about to have a child. Then she told about a third inspector who got drunk in a bath-house and got into a tussle there with the mayor of the town.

Shabalov was riding in a trap with Zherbenev.

" It would be good to have a tasty snack," he said.

" We are sure to get something there," replied Zherbenev confidently.

The visitors were all confident that they were being awaited. Zinaida Grigorievna said :

" The most interesting part of it will be hidden of course."

" Yes, but we'll investigate."

It was a fresh, early morning. The road went through the wood. They had now driven for a long time. It seemed as if the same meadows and woods, copses, streams, and bridges repeated themselves again and again. They began to ask the drivers :

" Are you sure you're going the right way ? "

" Perhaps you've lost your way."

" I think it's in that direction."

The two towers of Trirodov's house soon became visible. They appeared to the right, and yet it was impossible to find the way to them. For a long time they blundered. The roads spread and branched out at this point. At last the driver of the first carriage stopped his horses, and behind it the other carriages came to a standstill.

" I'll have to ask some one," said the driver. " There's some sort of a boy coming this way."

A ten-year-old, barefoot boy could be seen coming down the road from the wood. Shabalov shouted savagely at him :

" Stop ! "

The boy glanced at the carriages and calmly walked on. Shabalov cried more furiously this time :

" Stop, you young brat ! Off with your cap ! Don't you see that gentlemen are coming—why don't you bow to them ? "

The boy paused. He looked in astonishment at the variety of carriages and did not take his cap off. Doulebova decided :

" He's simply an idiot ! "

300

" Well, we shall make him talk," said Kerbakh.

He left his carriage and, going up to the boy, asked him :

" Do you know where Trirodov's school is ? "

The boy silently pointed to one of the roads with his hand. Then he ran off quickly, and disappeared somewhere among the bushes.

At last the road went along a fence. Everything all around seemed deserted and quiet. Evidently no one awaited the visitors or had arranged to meet them.

Finally they reached the gates of the enclosure. They looked around. It was very quiet. No one was visible anywhere. Shabalov jumped out of his trap and began to look for the bell. Madame Doulebova said in great irritation :

" What do you think of that ? "

They tried to open the small gate by themselves but were unable. Shabalov cried out :

" Open the gate ! You devils, demons, sinners ! "

Madame Doulebova tried to soothe Shabalov, who justified himself :

" Forgive me, Zinaida Grigorievna. It is most annoying. If I had come myself I shouldn't have minded waiting, though even then it would have been discourteous—being, after all, an official. And here the higher authorities have announced their coming, and these people pay absolutely no attention to it."

At last the small gate opened, suddenly and noiselessly. A boy, sunburnt and barefoot, in a white shirt and short white breeches, stood on the threshold. The angry Doulebov said in his thin, shrill voice :

" Is this Trirodov's school ? "

" Yes," said the boy.

The visitors entered and found themselves in a small glade. Three barefoot girls slowly came to meet them. These were instructresses. Nadezhda Vestchezerova looked with her large dark eyes at Madame Doulebova, who whispered to the Vice-Governor :

" Have a look at her. This girl had a scandal in her life, but he's taken her on."

Doulebova knew every one in town, and she knew especially well those who have had an unpleasant experience of some sort.

Presently Trirodov appeared in a white summer suit. He looked with an ironic smile at the gaily dressed party of visitors.

The visitors were met with courtesy ; but the Headmaster was displeased because no honour was shown them and no special preparations were evident. The instructresses were dressed as simply as always. Doulebov was especially displeased because both the instructresses and their pupils walked about barefoot. The naïveté of the children irritated the visitors. The children looked at the party indifferently. Some of them nodded a greeting, others did not.

" Take off your cap ! " shouted Shabalov.

The boy pulled his cap off and reached it out to Shabalov with the remark :

" Here ! "

Shabalov growled savagely :

" Idiot ! "

Then he turned away. The boy looked at him in astonishment.

302

Doulebov, and even more his wife, were terribly annoyed because they had not put on more clothes for their visitors, not even shoes. The Vice-Governor looked dully and savagely. Everything displeased him at once. Doulebov asked with a frown :

" Surely they are not always like that ? "

" Always, Vladimir Grigorievitch," replied Trirodov. " They have got used to it."

" But it is indecent ! " said Madame Doulebova.

" It is the one thing that is decent," retorted Trirodov.

CHAPTER XXXII

THE windows of the house in the small glade were wide open. The twitter of birds was audible and the fresh, delicious aroma of flowers entered in. It was here the children gathered, and the miserable farce of the examination began. Doulebov stood up before an ikon on one side of the room, assumed a stately air, and exclaimed :

" Children, rise to prayer."

The children rose. Doulebov thrust a finger forward towards a dark-eyed boy's breast and shouted :

" Read, boy ! "

The thin, shrill outcry and the movement of the finger towards the child's breast were so unexpected by the boy that he trembled and gave a choking sound. Some one behind him laughed, another gave an amused chuckle. Doulebova exchanged glances with Kerbakh and shrugged her shoulders ; her face expressed horror.

The boy quickly recovered himself and read the prayer.

" Sit down, children," ordered Doulebov.

The children resumed their places, while the elders seated themselves at a table in the order of their rank—the Vice-Governor and Doulebov in the middle, with the others to their right and left. Doulebova looked round with an anxious, angry expression. At last she said in a bass voice, extraordinarily coarse for a woman :

" Shut the windows. The birds are making a
304

noise, and the wind too; it is impossible to do anything."

Trirodov looked at her in astonishment. He said quietly to Nadezhda:

"Close the windows. Our guests can't stand fresh air."

The windows were shut. The children looked with melancholy tedium at the depressing window-panes.

Writing exercises were given. A little tale was read aloud from a reader brought by Shabalov. Doulebov asked the class to compose it in their own words.

The boys and girls were about to pick up their pens, but Doulebov stopped them and delivered a long and tedious dissertation on how to write the given composition. Then he said:

"Now you can write it."

The children wrote. It was quiet. The writers handed in their papers to their instructresses. Doulebov and Shabalov looked them over there and then. They tried to find mistakes, but there were few. Then dictation was given.

Doulebova looked morosely the whole while and blinked often. Trirodov tried to enter into conversation with her, but the angry dame answered so haughtily that it was with great difficulty he refrained from smiling, and finally he left the malicious woman to herself.

After the written exercises Trirodov asked the uninvited guests to luncheon.

"It was such a long journey here," said Doulebov as if he were explaining why he did not refuse the invitation to eat.

The children scattered a short way into the wood, while the elders went into a neighbouring house, where the luncheon was ready. The conversation during luncheon was constrained and captious. The Doulebovs tried all sorts of pinpricks and coarse insinuations ; their companions followed suit. Every one tried to outdo the other in saying caustic, spiteful things.

Doulebov looked with simulated horror at Trirodov's instructresses who happened to be present, and whispered to Kerbakh :

" Their feet are soiled with earth."

After luncheon they returned to the school. All resumed their former places. Then the oral examination began. Doulebov bent over the roll-call and called out three boys at once. Each of them was questioned first about the Holy Scriptures, and immediately afterwards about the Russian language and arithmetic.

The examiners cavilled at everything. Nothing satisfied Doulebov. He gave questions the answers to which were bound to make evident whether higher feelings were being instilled in the children— of love for the Fatherland, of allegiance to the Tsar, and of devotion to the Orthodox Church. He asked one boy :

" Which country is better, Russia or France ? "

The boy thought a while and said :

" I don't know. It depends upon which place a man is used to—there he is better off."

Doulebova laughed viperously. Shabalov said in a preceptorial manner :

" The orthodox *matushka* * Russia ! Is it pos-

* Little Mother.

sible to compare any kingdom with ours ? Have you heard how our native land is called ? Holy Russia, Mother Russia, the holy Russian soil. And you are an idiot, blockhead, a little swine. If you don't like your Fatherland what are you good for ? "

The boy flushed. Tiny tears gleamed in his eyes. Doulebov asked :

" Now tell me what is the very best faith in this world."

The boy fell into thought. Shabalov asked malignantly :

" Can't you answer even that ? "

The boy said :

" When one believes sincerely, then it is the very best faith for him."

" What a blockhead ! " said Shabalov with conviction.

Trirodov looked at him in astonishment. He said quietly :

" The sincerity of religious mood is surely the best indication of a saving faith."

" We'll discuss that later," piped out Doulebov sternly. " This is not a convenient moment."

" As you like," said Trirodov with a smile. " It is all the same to me when you discuss it."

Doulebov, red with agitation, rose from his chair and, going up to Trirodov, said to him :

" It is absolutely necessary that I should have a talk with you."

" At your service," said Trirodov, not without some astonishment.

" Please continue," said Doulebov to Shabalov.

Doulebov and Trirodov went into the next room. Their conversation soon assumed a very sharp character. Doulebov made some savage accusations and said rather vehemently :

" I have heard improper things about your school, but, indeed, the reality exceeds all expectations."

" What is there precisely improper ? " asked Trirodov. " In what way has reality surpassed gossip ? "

" I don't collect gossip," squealed Doulebov excitedly. " I see with my own eyes. This is not a school but a pornography ! "

His voice had already passed into piggish tones. He struck the table with his palm. There was the hard sound of the wedding-ring against the wood. Trirodov said :

" I too have heard that you were a man with self-control. But this is not the first time to-day that I've noticed your violent movements."

Doulebov made an effort to recover himself. He said more quietly :

" It is a revolting pornography ! "

" And what do you call pornography ? " asked Trirodov.

" Don't you know ? " said Doulebov with a sarcastic smile.

" Yes, I know," said Trirodov. " In my conception every written lechery and disfigurement of beautiful truth to gratify the low instincts of the man-beast—that is pornography. Your thrice-assured State school—that is the true example of pornography."

" They walk about naked here ! " squealed Doulebov.

Trirodov retorted :

" They will be healthier and cleaner than those children who leave your school."

Doulebov shouted :

" Even your instructresses walk about naked. You've taken on depraved girls as instructresses."

Trirodov replied calmly :

" That's a lie ! "

The Headmaster said sharply and excitedly :

" Your school—if this awful, impossible establishment can be called a school—will be closed at once. I will make the application to the District to-day."

Trirodov replied sharply :

" That you can do."

Soon the visitors left in an ugly frame of mind. Doulebova hissed and waxed indignant the whole way back.

" He's clearly a dangerous man," observed Kerbakh.

CHAPTER XXXIII

Piotr and Rameyev arrived at Trirodov's together.
Rameyev more than once said to Piotr that he had
been very rude to Trirodov, and that he ought to
smooth out matters somehow. Piotr agreed very
unwillingly.

Once more they talked about the war.* Trirodov
asked Rameyev :

"I think you see only a political significance in
this war."

"And do you disagree with me?" asked
Rameyev.

"No," said Trirodov, "I admit that. But, in
my opinion, aside from the stupid and criminal
actions of these or other individuals, there are
more general causes. History has its own dialectic.
Whether or not a war had taken place is all the
same : there would have been a fated collision in
any case, in one or another form ; there would
have begun the decisive struggle between two
worlds, two comprehensions of the world, two
moralities, Buddha and Christ."

"The teachings of Buddhism resemble those of
Christianity considerably," said Piotr. "That is
its only value."

"Yes," said Trirodov. "There appears to be a
great resemblance at the first glance ; but actually
these two systems are as opposite as the poles.
They are the affirmation and the denial of life, its

* The Russo-Japanese War.

310

Yes and its No, its irony and its lyricism. The affirmation, Yes, is Christianity ; the denial, No, is Buddhism."

" That seems to me to be too much of a generalization," said Rameyev.

Trirodov continued :

" I generalize for the sake of clearness. The present moment in history is especially convenient. It is history's zenith hour. Now that Christianity has revealed the eternal contradiction of the world, we are passing through the poignant struggle of those two world conceptions."

" And not the struggle of the classes ? " asked Rameyev.

" Yes," said Trirodov, " there is also the struggle of the classes, to whatever degree two inimical factors enter into the struggle—social justice and the real relation of forces—a common morality, which is always static, and a common dynamism. The Christian element is in morality, the Buddhistic in dynamism. Indeed, the weakness of Europe consists in that its life has already for a long time nourished itself on a substance Buddhistic in origin."

Piotr said confidently, in the voice of a young prophet :

" In this duel Christianity will triumph—not the historic Christianity, of course, and not the present, but the Christianity of St. John and the Apocalypse. And it will triumph only then when everything will appear lost, and the world will be in the power of the yellow Antichrist."

" I don't think that will happen," said Trirodov quietly.

" I suppose you think Buddha will triumph," said Piotr in vexation.

" No," replied Trirodov calmly.

" The devil, perhaps ! " exclaimed Piotr.

" Petya ! " exclaimed Rameyev reproachfully.

Trirodov lowered his head slightly, as if he were confused, and said tranquilly :

" We see two currents, equally powerful. It would be strange that either one of them should conquer. That is impossible. It is impossible to destroy half of the whole historical energy."

" However," said Piotr, " if neither Christ nor Buddha conquers, what awaits us ? Or is that fool Guyau right when he speaks of the irreligiousness of future generations ? " *

" There will be a synthesis," replied Trirodov. " You will accept it for the devil."

" This contradictory mixture is worse than forty devils ! " exclaimed Piotr.

The visitors soon left.

Kirsha came without being called—confused and agitated by an indefinable something. He was silent, and his dark eyes flamed with sadness and fear. He walked up to the window, looked out in an attitude of expectancy. He seemed to see something in the distance. There was a look of apprehension in his dark, wide-open eyes, as if they were fixed on a strange distant vision. Thus people look during a hallucination.

Kirsha turned to his father and, growing pale, said quietly :

* A reference to J. M. Guyau's book, " Non-Religion of the Future."

312

"Father, a visitor has come to you from quite afar. How strange that he has come in a simple carriage and in ordinary clothes! I wonder why he has come?"

They could hear the crunching sound of the sand under the iron hoops of the wheels of the calash which had just entered the gates. Kirsha's face wore a gloomy expression. It was difficult to comprehend what was in his soul—was it a reproach?—astonishment?—fear?

Trirodov went to the window. A man of about forty, impressive for his appearance of calm and self-assurance, stepped out of the calash. Trirodov recognized his visitor at the first glance, though he had never met him before in society. He knew him well, but only from portraits he had seen of him, from his literary works, and from the stories of his admirers and articles about him. In his youth Trirodov had had some slight relations with him through friends, but this was interrupted. He had not even met him.

Trirodov suddenly felt both cheerful and sad. He reflected:

"Why has he come to me? What does he want of me? And why should he suddenly think of me? Our roads have diverged so much, we have become such strangers to one another."

There was his disturbing curiosity:

"I'll see and hear him for the first time."

And the mutinous protest:

"His words are a lie! His preachings the ravings of despair. There was no miracle, there is none, and there will not be!"

Kirsha, very agitated, ran out of the room.

313

The sensitive and painful feeling of aloneness seized Trirodov as in a sticky net, entangled his legs, and obstructed his glances with grey.

A quiet boy entered, smiling, and handed him a card, on which, under a princely crown, was the lithographed inscription :

*Immanuel Osipovitch Davidov.**

In a voice dark and deep with suppressed excitement Trirodov said to the boy :

" Ask him to come in."

The provoking and unanswerable question persisted in his mind :

" Why, why has he come ? What does he want of me ? "

With an avidly curious glance he looked at the door, and did not take his eyes away. He heard the measured, unhastening footsteps, nearer and nearer—as if his fate were approaching.

The door opened, admitting the visitor—Prince Immanuel Osipovitch Davidov, celebrated as author and preacher, a man of a distinguished family and democratic views, a man beloved of many and possessed of the mystery of extraordinary fascination, attracting to him many hearts.

His face was very smooth, quite un-Russian in type. His lips, slightly descending at the corners, were marked with sorrow. His beard was reddish, short, and cut to a point. His red-gold, slightly wavy hair was cut quite short. This astonished

* There is an evident effort here to identify "Immanuel Osipovitch Davidov" as a modern symbol of Christ, or more properly of Christ's teachings, "Osipovitch" means the "son of Joseph " ; "Davidov," " of David."—TRANSLATOR.

Trirodov, who had always seen the Prince in portraits wearing his hair rather long, like the poet Nadson. His eyes were black, flaming and deep. Deeply hidden in his eyes was an expression of great weariness and suffering, which the inattentive observer might have interpreted as an expression of fatigued tranquillity and indifference. Everything about the visitor—his face and his ways—betrayed his habit of speaking in a large company, even in a crowd.

He walked up tranquilly to Trirodov and said, as he stretched out his hand :

" I wanted to see you. I have observed you for some time, and at last have come to you."

Trirodov, making an effort to control his agitation and his deep irritation, said with an affectedly amiable voice :

" I'm very pleased to greet you in my house. I've heard much about you from the Pirozhkovskys. Of course you know that they have a great admiration and affection for you."

Prince Davidov looked at him piercingly but calmly, perhaps too calmly. It seemed strange that he answered nothing to the remark about the Pirozhkovskys—as if Trirodov's words passed by him like momentary shadows, without so much as touching anything in his soul. On the other hand, the Pirozhkovskys have always talked about Prince Davidov as of an intimate acquaintance. " Yesterday we dined at the Prince's " ; " The Prince is finishing a new poem "—by simply " the Prince " they gave one to understand that their remark concerned their friend, Prince Davidov. Trirodov recalled that the Prince had many

315

acquaintances, and that there were always large gatherings in his house.

"Permit me to offer you some refreshment," said Trirodov. "Will you have wine?"

"I'd rather have tea, if you don't mind," said Prince Davidov.

Trirodov pressed the button of the electric bell. Prince Davidov continued in his tranquil, too tranquil, voice:

"My fiancée lives in this town. I've come to see her, and have taken advantage of this opportunity to have a chat with you. There are many things I should like to discuss with you but I shall not have the time. We must limit ourselves to the more important matters."

And he began to talk, and did not wait for answers or refutations. His flaming speech poured itself out—about faith, miracles, about the likely and inevitable transfiguration of the world by means of a miracle, about our triumph over the fetters of time and over death itself.

The quiet boy Grisha brought tea and cakes, and with measured movements put them on the table, pausing now and then to look at the visitor with his blue, quiet eyes.

Prince Davidov looked reproachfully at Trirodov. A repressed smile trembled on Trirodov's lips and an obstinate challenge gleamed in his eyes. The visitor affectionately drew Grisha to him and stroked him gently. The quiet boy stood calmly there—and Trirodov was gloomy. He said to his visitor:

"You love children. I can understand that. They are angelic beings, though unbearable sometimes. It is only a pity that they die too often
316

upon this accursed earth. They are born in order to die."

Prince Davidov, with a tranquil movement, pushed Grisha away from him. He put his hand on the boy's head as if in blessing, then suddenly became grave and stern, and asked quietly :

" Why do you do this ? "

He asked the question with a great exertion of the will, like one who wished to exercise power. Trirodov smiled :

" You do not like it ? " he asked. " Well, what of it—you with your extensive connexions could easily hinder me."

The tone in which he uttered his words expressed proud irony. Thus Satan would have spoken, tempting a famished one in the desert.

Prince Davidov frowned. His black eyes flared up. He asked again :

" Why have you done all this ? The body of the malefactor and the soul of an innocent—why should you have it all ? "

Trirodov, looking angrily at his visitor, said resolutely :

" My design has been daring and difficult—but have I alone suffered from despondency, suffered until I perspired with blood ? Do I alone bear within me a dual soul, and unite in me two worlds ? Am I alone worn out by nightmares as heavy as the burdens of the world ? Have I alone in a tragic moment felt myself lonely and forsaken ? "

The visitor smiled a strange, sad, tranquil smile. Trirodov continued :

" You had better know that I will never be with

317

you, that I will not accept your comforting theories. All your literary and preaching activity is a complete mistake. I don't believe anything of what you say so eloquently, enticing the weak. I simply don't believe it."

The visitor was silent.

"Leave me alone!" said Trirodov decisively. "There is no miracle. There was no resurrection. No one has conquered death. The establishment of a single will over the inert, amorphous world is a deed not yet accomplished."

Prince Davidov rose and said sorrowfully:

"I will leave you alone, if you wish it. But you will regret that you have rejected the path I have shown you—the only path."

Trirodov said proudly:

"I know the true path—my path."

"Good-bye," said Prince Davidov simply and calmly.

He left—and in a little while it seemed that he had not been there. Lost in painful reflections, Trirodov did not hear the noise of the departing carriage; the unexpected call of the dark-faced, fascinating visitor, with his flaming speech and his fiery eyes, stirred his memory like a midday dream, like an abrupt hallucination.

"Who is his fiancée, and why is she here?" Trirodov asked himself.

A strange, impossible idea came into his head. Did not Elisaveta once speak about him with rapture? Perhaps the unexpected visitor would take Elisaveta away from him, as he had taken her from Piotr.

This misgiving tormented him. But Trirodov
318

looked into the clearness of her eyes on the portrait taken recently and at the grace and loveliness of her body and suddenly consoled himself. He thought :

" She is mine."

But Elisaveta, musing and burning, was experiencing passionate dreams ; and she felt the tediousness of the grey monotony of her dull life. The strange vision suddenly appearing to her in those terrible moments in the wood repeated itself persistently—and it seemed to her that it was not another but she herself who was experiencing a parallel life, that she was passing the exultantly bright, joyous, and sad way of Queen Ortruda.

THE END